**W9-BOB-843**

Tennessee. Brynn Callahan, a Marine veteran, and her cadaver dog Wilco, both severely wounded in action and suffering from PTSD, return to Brynn's insular Bone Gap home, with the hope of finding peace and healing. Instead, she finds murder, deception and prejudice. Furlong's beautiful prose combined with an engrossing mystery make this a terrific read. I hope there is a sequel."
—**Christine Carbo, Author of** *The Weight of Night*

"Readers will be drawn into the well-crafted world of a secretive clan living in the shadows of dense Appalachian forests. In *Splintered Silence* Susan Furlong creates a flawed heroine returning to a community despised by its 'settled' neighbors, to make peace with her family while trying to overcome her own inner demons. But old secrets and long-held grievances come to light as her ex-Marine cadaver dog keeps unearthing fresh bodies."
—**Sara Driscoll, Author of** *Lone Wolf* **and**
*Before It's Too Late*

"Susan Furlong has created Brynn Callahan—the ultimate outsider—to star in her new thriller series. Well-crafted and deeply moving, *Splintered Silence* delivers a powerful message about family. Furlong spins a mystery that will keep you on the edge of your seat until the adrenalized ending, and you'll fall in love with Wilco, one of the most compelling dogs to ever appear in fiction."
—**K.J. Howe, Author of** *The Freedom Broker*

"An auspicious series debut . . . Readers will want to see more of the intrepid Brynn, who must face her personal demons as she tries to find her place in a hostile community."
—*Publishers Weekly*

## Also by Susan Furlong

*Fractured Truth*
*Splintered Silence*
*Peaches and Scream*
*Rest in Peach*
*War and Peach*

## Written as Lucy Arlington

*Played by the Book*
*Off the Books*

# FRACTURED TRUTH

## SUSAN FURLONG

KENSINGTON BOOKS
www.kensingtonbooks.com

KENSINGTON BOOKS are published by

Kensington Publishing Corp.
119 West 40th Street
New York, NY 10018

All Kensington titles, imprints and distributed lines are available at special quantity discounts for bulk purchases for sales promotion, premiums, fund-raising, educational or institutional use. Special book excerpts or customized printings can also be created to fit specific needs. For details, write or phone the office of the Kensington Special Sales Manager: Kensington Publishing Corp., 119 West 40th Street, New York, NY, 10018. Attn. Special Sales Department. Phone: 1-800-221-2647.

Kensington and the K logo Reg. U.S. Pat. & TM Off.

ISBN-13: 978-1-4967-1170-0
ISBN-10: 1-4967-1170-X
First Kensington Hardcover Edition: January 2019
First Kensington Trade Edition: April 2019
First Kensington Mass Market Edition: December 2019

ISBN-13: 978-1-4967-1171-7 (e-book)
ISBN-10: 1-4967-1171-8 (e-book)

10 9 8 7 6 5 4 3 2 1

Printed in the United States of America

To our children:
Quinn, Regan, Fiona
and
Patrick, in Heaven and always in my heart

*Truth suffers, but never dies.*
    —St. Teresa of Avila

# CHAPTER 1

I blinked, shook my head, and blinked again. Either I'd had too much whiskey, or a headless chicken hung before me.

My eyes skimmed the skeletal tree branches bent with the weight of not just one, but several shriveled carcasses, their scrawny legs tethered together, claws curled under, white wings limp and splayed outward like the mangled helicopter blades I'd witnessed in Iraq combat zones. Underneath each, blood pitted the white snow, pooling in spots and seeping outward in spidery pink veins.

This sight would've sobered anyone.

"Sick bastards," I said, not that my dog could hear me. Both maimed and rendered deaf by an IED, Wilco relied solely on his eyes and nose. Right now, his nose flared and twitched, as he strained against his lead. Wilco was a *human*-remains-detection canine. He had no interest in dead chickens.

That meant one thing: He'd found the scent line to a dead body.

My insides rolled with dread as I took a deep breath and brought the radio to my mouth. "I think we've got the location. Take the north branch until you see the first fork. Go left and continue about a quarter of a mile. You should see my tracks leaving the trail. I'm on the ridge east of Higgins Falls."

As I spoke, the nylon cord of Wilco's lead pulled taut and bit into my other palm. I pocketed my radio and focused on my dog. He lifted his black snout to fill his lungs with tainted air as he tottered on three legs, no longer letting his injury hold him back. Wish I could say the same. I rotated my left shoulder, and the burn scars that marred half my body pulled the skin tight. But those scars I could hide. Others weren't so easy.

Wilco let loose a low, mournful whine.

"Hold on, boy." I leaned down and gave him a pat. He shook with excited anticipation of a successful find.

The 911 call had come in a couple of hours ago. A cross-country skier found a mutilated female body in a small cave off the trail. He was too repulsed to give much more information, not even the exact location, and hundreds of small caves dotted the rocky ridges along this branch of the Appalachian Trail. So Wilco and I were immediately dispatched for search and recovery.

Not many could stomach unearthing stiff and blood-ied cadavers. But, thanks to Uncle Sam, I'd been con-ditioned for this type of work. Back in the war, at the height of combat, there was a great need for a "cleanup crew" or "bone patrol" or whatever lingo they'd thought up at the time. And we took that need seriously, doing what we could to find our soldiers, no matter how ugly it got. And it was always ugly. Extreme desert heat quickly transformed dead bodies into swollen, stinking carrion. Now, in a true-glutton-for-punishment fashion, I'd signed up for doing that task again. This was my first homicide since taking the oath as one of Mc-Creary County's finest three months ago.

Backtracking a little, I secured Wilco's leash to a tree, double-checking a couple times to make sure he couldn't get loose. He immediately began working himself into a frenzy, turning around and around, his nose low to the ground at first, then raising upward, high into the air, as if he was scooping up the scent. It felt almost cruel to hold him back from his quarry, not to allow him to achieve his ultimate goal of locating and alerting me to the dead body. But in the military, we knew the cause of death: bombs, bullets, rockets, and shrapnel. And we knew the source: the enemy. Here we didn't know and I couldn't risk Wilco disturbing evidence.

"Sorry, boy." I ran my hand down the long side of his back, then stood and pulled up the collar of my parka, tucking my chin against the wind. The night before, a freak weather pattern blew in from the northwest, bringing several inches of fresh snow. It was still coming down in spurts and the elongated ski grooves left over from the cross-country trekker were already partially covered. I scanned the forest floor around me. No other tracks.

A couple minutes later, Sheriff Pusser plowed down the trail, in the lead of the rest of the team. At six feet plus, an extra twenty pounds or so around his midsection, and a booming voice to match, "stealthy" would never describe my boss.

He broke into the clearing with Officers Harris and

Parks, and a handful of crime scene techs and motioned for them to stay back while he approached me. He stopped about five yards away and raised his eyes. "What the hell? Are those . . . ?"

"Yup. Chickens."

His face grew ashen, making his pockmarks more pronounced. After a couple beats, I cleared my throat. "You okay, boss?"

He swiped his upper lip and slid his eyes my way. "I got a bad feeling about this one." He reached into his pocket for a small plastic cylinder of cinnamon toothpicks he always kept on hand. He fumbled a bit before getting one out, then placed it between his lips and bit down hard.

Harris joined us. "Looks like a butcher shop out here."

Pusser frowned. "Did I call you over here, Harris? Watch yourself. I don't need this scene contaminated."

Harris swallowed hard, his cold eyes piercing me, like it was my fault he'd puked all over our last homicide scene. No one moved, waiting for Pusser's command. But he just stood there, sucking on his toothpick and staring at the dead chickens.

I spoke up. "Hey, Sheriff. My dog's going nuts. The body can't be far. The skier said she was in a small cave. Probably below us."

"Okay then. Let's go check it out." He turned to Harris. "You stay here with the rest of these guys until we can figure out the best way to approach the scene."

Harris swore under his breath and shot me one last glare as he stepped back to the others.

Harris hated me—wussy-ass guys like him always

do—but like with death, I was no stranger to hate. As a female in the Marines, or even more so as an American soldier on foreign soil, I'd earned more than just my stripes as I faced down old-school chauvinists. But hatred had hounded me long before the military. It started at birth.

During the Great Famine, my nomadic Irish ancestors migrated here, looking for work and a place to preserve their itinerant culture, but somehow ended up settling in this backwoods area of Appalachia. We're known as Travellers, or Pavees as we call ourselves. Gypsies, knackers, or pikies, as others sometimes call us. I've been called them all. And worse. But prejudice poisons both ways. Most Pavees despised "settled" or non-Traveller folks. Sometimes it was difficult to discern "who hated who" the most. Which is another reason Sheriff Pusser hired me. I was to be a liaison of sorts.

I glanced back at Harris's icy stare. *Easier said than done.*

Pusser and I half climbed/half slid down the slope, stopping about a hundred yards down in front of a small cave. Sweaty from the descent, I loosened the collar of my jacket. Cold air hit the nape of my neck and sent shivers down my back. Something in me shifted, and fear rose from my gut, worming its way through my body.

Pusser must have felt it, too. His hand moved over his weapon, his fingers twitched. He lifted his chin toward the cave, where a symbol marked the entrance. "That's one of those satanic things, isn't it?"

"Yeah. A pentagram. It's used in witchcraft and other pagan religions, too." I pulled out my flashlight and stepped forward into the cave. A musty smell mixed with a coppery tang stung my nostrils. "Chicken blood." Pusser looked at me. I shrugged, hoping I was right. But I wasn't. As I bounced my beam around the rocky walls, I hit on something in the back of the cave, where the rocks formed a natural shelf.

The girl.

I moved forward, careful not to disturb too much of the cave floor, avoiding any previous tracks. Extinguished and half-burned candles surrounded the body and more symbols smeared the rocks above her, dark and dripping along the edges. Deep crimson. Her head was turned toward the wall, hair covering most of her features. Her shirt had been torn open exposing a now blackened wound in her chest cavity.

I stepped back. " '*Graaltcha Mary . . .*' " Part of a prayer I'd memorized as a young Pavee. Comfort from the past.

"What did you say?"

"Nothing." Shelta or Gammon, as some called it, the Traveller language of my childhood. It spewed unbidden from my lips at times.

I stepped forward again. Behind me, Pusser spoke into his radio. "We've got her. Tell the photographer to bring down the strobes. It's dark. And no one comes in until I give the okay." He disconnected and spoke to me. "I'm coming forward."

I glanced over my shoulder. He used his light to pick out my tracks and mimic my steps. "The dirt's soft. The forensic guys should be able to lift shoe prints."

I nodded and reluctantly turned back to the victim. She was fully dressed, long skirt tucked under her knees, heavy tights, and calf-hugging boots. I focused again on the wound. Blood had spewed from the gaping hole in her chest, oozed over the rock edge, and flowed into fractured etchings to form a pool of dried blood on the floor below. "I've never seen a stab wound like this."

"Looks like one single thrust. No hesitation, clean penetration." Pusser was right behind me now, looking over my shoulder. "And not much of an entry angle. The killer was standing over her."

I pointed to the edges of the wound. "This shape is odd."

"Because there's no fishtail, no dull side of the wound. I'm betting he used a double-edged knife." He shrugged. "The ME will be able to tell us more."

I pocketed my own light and pulled a ballpoint pen and a pair of gloves from my pocket. "Focus your beam on her face, will you?" I snapped on the gloves and leaned forward, using my free hand for balance, as I slid the pen under her hair, lifting it just enough to see her features.

I flinched and stepped back.

Pusser put his hand on my shoulder. "Callahan?" I heard the worry in his voice. He thought my PTS had kicked in again. "You okay?"

I nodded. It wasn't past horrors—red bits of bodies blown into the air, searing skin, burning flesh—that made my heart jackhammer now. It was the present . . . and future. "She's a neighbor of mine. Just a girl."

Pusser mercifully moved the light off her dead white skin, her glazed eyes, and scanned it over the improvised ritualistic altar, the burned-out candles, the blood-scrawled symbols. "A Traveller?"

"Yeah."

I bit my lip over the questions clawing at my thoughts: Was she chosen at random, or were we looking at a hate crime against Travellers?

And the bigger question: Was this just the beginning?

# CHAPTER 2

Maura Keene's mother opened the door before I knocked. She looked from Pusser to me, her eyes questioning ours for a brief second before they widened with pain. Her hand flew to her womb, clutched at her blouse, and twisted the fabric into a tight ball. No one had spoken a single word, yet she knew.

A mother always does.

Still, words needed to be spoken. Harsh truths delivered softly and with compassion, but blunt enough to leave no room for questioning or denial. I steeled myself and delivered the news no mother should ever hear. "I'm sorry, Ona. Maura is dead. Your daughter is dead."

She gasped and retreated backward into the small confines of their camper. I stepped up and followed, reaching out to provide comfort. She batted my hand away. "No!"

"Ona."

"No. No. No!"

Pusser stepped around me. "You should sit down, Mrs. Keene."

She allowed him to gently guide her into one of the benches flanking a small pop-out table. I slid into the bench next to her and placed my hand on her shoulder. This time, she didn't pull away, but leaned into me. Her shoulders heaved, once, twice . . . and the sobbing began.

After a while, Pusser pulled a pad and pen from his shirt pocket. He cleared his throat. "Where's your son, Mrs. Keene?"

She looked up, her face raw with pain. "I sent him out looking for Maura. I was worried when she didn't come home."

"When did you see her last?" he asked.

"Yesterday before school."

*Yesterday? That can't be right.* I leaned in closer. "Over a day ago? Are you sure, Ona?"

She stared at her palms, her expression blank.

"Ona?"

She looked my way. "What do you mean?"

I spoke firmly, trying to break through the shock. "Today is Saturday. Saturday evening. Didn't Maura come home after school yesterday?"

"No. She was going wedding-dress shopping with a friend after school, then staying overnight." She pointed through a partially drawn curtain to a work uniform, laid out neatly on a flowered bedspread. "She was supposed to work at the diner this morning. I was expecting her home to change."

"Who was the friend?"

"The Joyce girl. Winnie. Winnie Joyce." Her expression shifted. "When she didn't show, I called Carol. That's Winnie's mother." I nodded and she continued.

"Carol thought the girls were planning to sleep over here. There must have been some misunderstanding. But . . . I was sure she said . . ." Her hand flew to her mouth. "Did they . . . did they get in a car accident?"

I looked to Pusser for help. He offered nothing. I looked back at Ona and drew in my breath. "No. Maura's body was found in a cave up by Higgins Falls. She was murdered."

She recoiled and pressed a fist to her lips. *"Cher-pyra!"* Shelta for "You lie!" A guttural sound erupted from her lips. My muscles tightened at her fierce glare.

"Ma?" Eddie, the son, pushed through the door. "Ma? What is it?" He stood rigid in the doorway, his thin shoulders curved inward. He had the same dark hair as his sister. It fell forward, low on his forehead, partially concealing thick brows and dark, round eyes on his acned face. He was seventeen, Maura's twin, but seemed younger. Much younger.

Ona grew quiet. She straightened her shoulders and steadied her breath, summoning the strength to be strong for her living child.

Eddie looked from his mother to Pusser, his features hard and accusing. "Where's my sister? Where's Maura?"

Ona pushed against my arm. I stood to let her by, and she went to her son, grabbing him by the shoulders. She lowered her chin and looked him directly in the eyes. "Our Maura's dead. She's been murdered."

Eddie pushed back, his features wrenching with pain. "Murdered? But who?"

"We're trying to figure that out," Pusser said. He looked at Ona, prodding. "You said she was wedding-dress shopping. So Maura was engaged?"

Ona slumped to the side of the doorway, her face

ashen. Eddie stiffened. "Yeah. To Nevan. But what's that have to do with anything?"

Pusser jotted the name down. "Nevan?"

"Nevan Meath." Eddie's mouth tightened as he spoke. He was sucking it up, trying to be tough, strong, but the tremble in his hands gave him away. "Nevan is our friend. He would never hurt my sister."

I stepped between him and Pusser, trying to soothe Eddie's emotions. "That's not what we're saying. We've just got to check out all the angles."

*"Angles?"* He picked at his lip as he spoke. "You mean 'suspects'? Nevan's a suspect." *Pick . . . pick . . .* a spot of blood burst forth. He swiped at it, then stared down at the red smear on his fingertip.

"Something you want to tell us, boy?"

Eddie's head snapped toward Pusser. "No. Why?"

Pusser stared at him.

Eddie shifted, crossed and uncrossed his arms, then wheeled and bolted out the door.

I followed. "Eddie. Stop!" But he was already halfway across the yard. As he ran past Pusser's Tahoe, Wilco erupted in snarls from his cage in the back of the cruiser. Eddie, startled, scrambled to keep his feet under him, disappearing between the neighbors' trailers.

"Let him go." Pusser came up behind me. "We need to find the Meath kid, while things are still fresh. See what the Joyce family says, too."

He was right. We could catch up to Eddie later.

I rolled the tension from my shoulders, inhaled the cold mountain air, and took in my surroundings. The sun was slipping below the late-winter horizon. Low hues of diffused gray gave way to slivers of brilliant orange and yellow that cast a warm glow over the snow-blanketed ground. A pretty sky and clean snow didn't change things, though. Bone Gap was nothing more than a glorified parking lot: a conglomerate of trailers, mobile homes, motorcycles, souped-up muscle cars, and jacked-up trucks, all haphazardly arranged and crammed into a rural backwoods holler. Hicksville to most outsiders. Home to us Pavees. I looked back at Ona's place, a sky-blue, yellow-trimmed tag-along camper, barely big enough for a weekend getaway, let alone a permanent residence for a widow and her two children. One child now.

The sound of Ona's sobbing leaked through the camper's thin walls and filled the night air. "I should go back in there. She needs someone to sit with her."

"Call someone. Your grandmother, maybe. Or the priest. You've got work to do. Finding justice for Maura."

*Justice.* Pusser had no idea how strong our clan's sense of justice could be.

I pulled my collar tight against a sudden breeze. There was movement in the trailer next door. And the one next to it, too. Curtains shuffled and blinds parted as neighbors peeked through backlit windows. Pusser was looking at me, frowning. "What is it?"

"You remember that fatal car accident a few years back?"

"Head-on out on Highway 2? Two men died."

"Yeah. Rory Keene and Cormac Meath. Eddie and Nevan's fathers. Two women widowed, two families without fathers. That's when the families became close."

Pusser frowned. "Bound by a common loss. And now, more loss, but even worse this time. A kid, child really."

"Word will be out soon about Maura's death. When

people hear the way she was killed, the wicked brutality . . ." I glanced at Pusser's pockmarked face, stoic and void of any real emotion. No way was he going to understand this. "Maura was young, pretty, about to be married. She comes from a good family who's already experienced a horrific tragedy. . . . What happened to her wasn't right."

"Nothing we deal with is ever right. You know that, Callahan."

I rotated my neck, rubbed at my marred, war-burned skin. *Yeah. I know that better than most.* "You don't understand."

"Then explain to me what you mean. And do it fast. We need to talk to the fiancé."

"Eddie's right. Nevan didn't do this. This wasn't one of us. No Pavee could do what was done to that girl."

"How can you be so sure?"

The *yonks* (or "wayward") among us—scammers and thieves—had earned a certain reputation for all Travellers. And rightly so. Our society had its share of issues. But this type of evil? I couldn't accept that. I looked back at the Keenes' front yard and the statue of the Virgin Mary placed front and center, in a place of great reverence, and surrounded by colorful plastic flowers, even in the winter months. The same could be seen in front of almost every trailer, mobile home, and camper in Bone Gap. A homage to our faith. A fervent, deeply felt faith that dictated the very moral fabric of our culture. And the threads that bound that fabric were the family and clan code. Murder rarely happened among Travellers. When it did, it was dealt with inside the clan, swiftly and mercilessly.

"I just am. No Pavee did this. I'm sure of it."

Pusser rocked back on his heels, snow crunching under his boots. "We'll see."

"Nevan's not here." Mrs. Meath spoke to me through the barely cracked door of her double-wide mobile home. Her drawn face looked washed out in the glow of the porch light. We'd come straight to their trailer, while Pusser sent one of the other deputies to the Joyce residence to question Winnie.

Barking erupted from several large dog kennels positioned along the tree line on the edge of their lot. The Meaths earned extra money breeding dogs. Lurchers mostly. A fast, intelligent mix, usually between a greyhound and some sort of herder, and the best hare-coursing breed around.

"Do you know where we can find him?"

"No. 'Fraid not. He's a grown boy. He doesn't always tell me where he's going."

I looked toward the side of the mobile home. A security light bounced off the chrome accents of Nevan's jacked-up Silverado. I shifted and wedged my foot between the frame and the door. "When are you expecting him back?"

She wouldn't meet my gaze. "Can't be sure."

Something wasn't right. I'd known Kitty Meath most of my childhood. Her oldest daughter, Riana, and I were the same age. When we were younger, a group of us girls used to come over and play with Barbies in the back room of this very trailer. Riana was always the boss of Barbie world and of our group. Her doll was the most beautiful, married the prince and lived happily ever after, while my doll became the ugly under-ling—a precedence I could never shake.

"Mrs. Meath. Kitty. Don't you remember me? Brynn Callahan."

"I remember you."

I glanced over my shoulder to where Pusser stood, then looked down at my dog, tethered at my side. Both watched intently.

I pressed her. "Can we come in?"

"I'm 'fraid now's not a good time. Sorry." She backed up, preparing to shut me out.

Pusser's hand shot out and clanged against the metal door. "Maura Keene is dead, Mrs. Meath. And we need to talk to your son."

Anger sparked in her eyes. Not surprise, not shock, not sadness, but anger. She'd already known Maura was dead. But how?

"I told you he ain't here."

Pusser stepped forward. I ducked out of his way. "Where is he?"

"Like I said. He's out. I don't know where."

A door slammed at the back of the trailer and dogs erupted into a barking frenzy. Pusser stiffened. "He's making a run for it."

I reacted first, bolting from the porch with my flash-light in hand, Wilco's leash in the other. I reached the backyard with Pusser on my heels. He yelled over the Lurchers' barking, "Do you see him?"

I bounced my beam over the backyard: an old picnic bench, a birdfeeder, a lopsided swing set . . . "No. Noth-ing."

Behind us, an engine roared to life. I turned, ready to run back, when a popping sound came from up ahead. I panned my light, caught a flash of movement. "There! Heading into the trees." I unleashed Wilco and took off in pursuit, whipping branches clawing at my face, tearing my hair, my boot-clad feet sliding on the snow. I stumbled, fell, got up again. I spied Wilco running like an arrow, darting between nearby tree trunks. He's not trained for pursuit, attack, or anything other than sniffing out dead bodies, but he loved fun and games. Like a late-night romp through the woods.

I stopped. Panned my light again. Nothing. I'd lost him.

Pusser caught up to me, leaning forward and panting into his radio as he relayed Meath's address.

The dispatcher responded, "Roger that. Backup in progress."

Pusser disconnected and sucked at the air like his life depended on it. "Damn kid. If I catch him, I'll—"

"Shh!" I held up my hand. A faint whimpering noise came from our left.

It grew louder. Footsteps crunched over the forest floor, approaching quickly.

Pusser relieved his holster strap and rested his palm on his weapon. Wilco trotted back to my side and stood by, alert and on watch, with both his ears and nose twitching. I grabbed ahold of his collar and aimed my flashlight in the direction of the sound.

A figure approached. Pusser's stance stiffened. He drew his weapon. "Get your hands up, Nevan. Now!"

"Don't shoot. Don't shoot. I'm hurt." It wasn't Nevan's voice we heard, but Eddie's.

Pusser lowered his gun. "What the hell? Where's the Meath kid?"

I thought back to the engine I'd heard roar to life.

Eddie bounded from the shadows, holding his eye. He hunkered down and whimpered like an injured pup. Blood trickled between his fingers. "My eye . . ."

"Let me see." I raised the flashlight. "Move your hand." He did. I recoiled and gagged. A piece of a twig, about half an inch long, protruded from Eddie's eye. It'd impaled the iris.

"Son of a—" Pusser was back on the radio, calling for an ambulance.

I took Eddie's elbow. "Do not touch your eye. Do you hear me?" He cried out, pushed me away, and sank to his knees. "No, you don't, Eddie. Get up." I yanked him back to his feet and pulled him through the woods.

He stumbled on, half crying and half babbling. "It hurts. . . . I can't see. . . ."

"Shut up, boy." Pusser was losing it. The only thing he hated more than the woods was exerting himself. Not to mention being duped. "You did this to yourself. Didn't no one ever tell you you're not supposed to run from the cops?"

Somehow we made it to the back, to the trailer, where Eddie collapsed on the snow and balled up in pain. The Lurchers broke into wild barking. I flashed my light their way and saw Wilco prancing along the perimeter of their cages, tormenting them with his freedom.

Then I turned my beam to where Nevan's truck was parked earlier. Gone. That was the engine I'd heard.

Pusser swore, looking at the same empty parking spot. "You were the decoy." He stood over Eddie.

Eddie balled up tighter. "No. No."

"Like hell you weren't." Pusser squatted and got right up in his face. "You know what I think? I think you and Nevan were in on this. You helped him kill your sister."

"No. I would never hurt—"

"Was it your idea or his?"

"No. You've got it all wrong."

Pusser leaned closer yet, shouted, "Someone plunged a knife into your sister's heart, Eddie. Your buddy, Nevan? And now you're covering for him?"

Eddie clenched in tighter. His chin was buried against his chest, arms over his head.

"Look at me, boy." Pusser grabbed him by the wrists and ripped his arms down. I moved in closer and trained my light directly on them. The twig in Eddie's eye twitched as the boy shook, crying out in pain. Pusser was out of line. Too aggressive. Where was that ambulance? Pusser gripped his shoulders. "Why'd you kill her? Were you strung out on drugs? Or something else? What type of sick stuff are you into?"

"Hey. Easy, boss. He's injured."

Eddie went limp in Pusser's grip, his mouth slack and dripping drool mixed with streams of tears and blood that traced lines down his face. His left eye was almost swollen shut around the wooden projectile; his right eye round and glazed with fear. "You're wrong. You're wrong."

"Then why'd you come warn Meath?"

Eddie blubbered. "Because no one would believe . . . Nevan didn't kill my . . ."

A siren sounded in the distance.

Pusser shook him. "You're a liar, Eddie."

With each shake, Eddie's head snapped back like a broken bobblehead. He screamed out in raw pain; then he went quiet and limp.

I grabbed Pusser's shoulder. "That's enough. Let him be."

Pusser stood and wheeled on me, his eyes flashing. "He knows something."

I leaned in and lowered my voice. "You're crossing the line. The kid's in pain."

"Oh yeah? And what about Maura Keene? You think that girl didn't suffer? There may be even more girls we don't know about. Have you already forgotten what we saw out there today?"

I swallowed hard and squeezed my eyes shut against the image of Maura's young body—raw edges of flesh, blackened blood splattered on pale white skin—all of it burned into my memory along with the war-torn bodies of countless dead soldiers, all too young, all gone before their time. . . . "No. I haven't forgotten. I never forget."

# CHAPTER 3

After Eddie was transported to the hospital, Pusser went to the office to find out what his other deputies had discovered from Maura's friend Winnie Joyce. I went back to Ona's place to check on her.

People had already gathered, spilling out of the small camper and into the front yard, clustering together in groups: young and old, tearful and pissed off. Wilco and I lurked behind a blue Chevy truck, engine running, doors open, stereo emitting some angst-filled teen song while a pack of boys stood on the other side with fisted hands, fleece zipped over puffed-up chests, and mouths spurting curse-laced bravado. A square-jawed kid took the lead. "I'm going to find the bastard who did this and beat the shit out of him." He had a camo hat pulled low over his forehead. I'd seen him around, but couldn't remember who he was.

A runty kid got in on the action. "No shit, man. You know he's out there in the woods somewhere. Bring your daddy's shotgun and we'll flush him out tomorrow."

They all liked that idea, except one dissenter. "I don't know, man. Ya hear what the coppers did to Eddie? Messed him up. Shot out his eyeball."

"Frickin' pigs. They ain't going to do nothin' for us."

I moved on, threading my way toward the front door. Colm popped out before I got there. His face was drawn tight, not the saintly expression of comfort he might offer from his pulpit, but the fatigue of dealing with the realities of his flock. A beautiful woman clung to his arm, all tears and teased hair, soft leather calf-high boots, her slim hips swaying next to the priest. She looked up and a thousand memories flooded my mind: jump ropes and Barbie dolls, bras and makeup, talk of boys and first kisses. Riana Meath, Nevan's oldest sister. She was always pretty, popular, and my best friend, or at least she was until I refused to marry Dub Costello. Then she turned on me, slamming the door to our friendship, as if sealing off an enemy at the front door of the clan, and ensuring my alienation with a final vicious act.

I'd managed to avoid her since I'd returned to Bone Gap. Not hard to do. She ran in a whole different crowd than me. Yes, Pavees have cliques. And I was no longer in hers. The few times we'd accidentally run into each other, we both pretended the other was invisible. Hard to do now that we were standing five feet from each other.

Unlike me, Riana Meath hadn't changed since high school, still the center of attention, still smoldering hot (as opposed to burned up, like me), and every man's wet dream. She'd known it then; she knew it now.

Colm whispered something in her ear, comforting words, or a prayer, or whatever a priest would say. She pressed closer and nodded, all doe-eyed and mournful like. Hot jealousy shot through me, then chilling guilt. I still wasn't over him.

He noticed me. "Brynn."

She noticed me. "Brynn!" A little squeal, a smoky hug. Guess her pack-a-day habit hadn't changed over the years, either. "Brynn, sweetie. God, isn't this horrible? That poor girl." She stepped back, gave me a once-over, and grabbed both my hands. "And I heard you saw her . . . her body. You poor thing! You must be traumatized."

I muttered something appropriate, because I should be traumatized, but I wasn't. Dead bodies had become commonplace for me and Wilco. *Wilco? Where is . . .* I tracked him across the yard, caught up in a circle of young girls, his tail tucked and head bowed, submissive as they took comfort in his soft fur and brown puppy eyes. And people say dogs don't feel empathy. My dog was more empathetic than me. I'd grown calloused and jaded and felt absolutely nothing for Riana, who was apparently torn apart by Maura's death. Her penchant for drama made real and feigned emotions hard to discern. My indifference and skepticism probably had something to do with past run-ins with Riana— I could carry a grudge forever—or the fact that her nails were once again clenched around Colm's arm. She was going on about how her brother would be devastated over his fiancée's death. Maura was the love of his life. They all loved Maura. She was family . . . family!

More sympathetic words from Colm, followed by a

soft pat on her arm. My belly turned greasy and bitter from the green acid churning in my gut.

Riana moved from bereft to angry as she tried to make sense of the way Maura was murdered. "Evil," she said. And she blamed heavy-metal music, graphic video games, social media, and every other thing teens are into. She blathered on and on, Colm comforting her, until a loud metallic *whoosh* and a fiery explosion pierced the air.

I ducked and covered my head, my mind instantly propelled into one of my parallel worlds. This time it's a recovery mission on the outskirts of Baghdad. *It's sunset. I hear the distant Muslim call to prayer, that haunting echo over the city. My recovery unit is following the ground invasion after a massive air strike campaign. It's exhausting. So many bodies: soldiers, civilians, innocents, children. Yet, war sounds still pierce the sky: the* whomp, whomp *of copter blades, the revving of Humvee engines, the whir of diesel generators, explosions and machine-gun barrage, mortar, and . . . It goes on and on. Everything happens at night. And like the distant clamor of an approaching train, the sounds consume the dark stillness, growing and increasing, merging and blending, until it becomes a single obliterating roar. . . .*

"Brynn." Colm's voice.

I snapped back from the past. Crackling and popping noises, and red-hot embers erupted from a metal garbage can into the night sky. People gathered around for warmth, rubbing their hands over the heat. Just a campfire. A stupid campfire. Once again, I'd slid down that dark hole and into the abyss of post-trauma anxieties. For how long? I didn't know. I looked around, taking cues from my surroundings. Riana had moved on, now standing with a group of ladies not too far away, engaging in a lot of hugging and eye wiping. Wilco was still hanging with the girls.

Colm was the only one who seemed to notice my mental absence. "You okay?"

"I'm fine." Colm and I had a history, buried in our teen years. Since then, we'd gone very separate ways. Right now, I needed his expertise. I extracted my phone, shaky fingers bringing the screen to life. "I have a few questions."

I pulled up a photo of a handwritten note the crime scene unit had found lodged under Maura's body. Pusser had sent the original to the state lab for analysis, but we'd hoped Colm could give us a quicker opinion.

He squinted at the note. "This writing is in Latin."

"That's why I thought maybe you could translate."

"Looks to be a Bible verse about Queen Jezebel." He looked up. "Her name is usually associated with promiscuity or fallen women. But it could mean something like a false prophet. Or a manipulator."

"I don't know that Bible story."

"Jezebel was married to King Ahab. She was a pagan worshiper. She basically used sex to lure the king into slaughtering thousands of Jews."

"What would a woman like that have to do with Maura Keene?"

He handed my phone back to me. "I can't imagine."

*Me either. Maura was nothing like this Jezebel.*

"Another thing. I don't think whoever wrote this actually knew Latin."

"Why's that?"

"Too many mistakes. Things that someone trained

in Latin wouldn't make. Words are misspelled, out of order, stuff like that."

"So . . . ?"

"My guess is that they were copying it from something and were rushed, or whatever, and messed up the sentences."

"There's something else." I scrolled through a few more photos. After the shock had worn off from realizing the dead body belonged to Maura, I snapped a few pictures. I showed them to Colm now. "Do you recognize any of these symbols?"

"Other than the pentagram, no. Looks like they're"— he glanced up, kept his voice low, turned his back to the others still milling in the yard—"painted in blood?"

"We don't know for sure yet. But I think so."

"Maura's blood?"

"Maybe. It was pretty gruesome."

"How was she killed? Can you tell me?" His eyes met mine. Dark eyes, intense and piercing. My stomach lurched.

"It's confidential."

A small nod. "I'm good at confidential. I'm a priest."

*Yeah. No need to keep reminding me.* I hesitated, then decided the information was worth the risk. "She was stabbed. Something double-bladed, judging by the wound."

"A satanic ritual killing."

"We're not sure what we're looking at yet."

"Isn't it obvious? The pentagram. All the other pictures drawn at the scene . . ."

"The killers could have set it up to look that way. I'm not sure how much I buy into all that demonic stuff, anyway."

"Then you're already at a disadvantage."

"How's that?"

"You can't fight what you don't believe exists, Brynn. Evil is real."

*Like I don't know that evil is real.* Maybe I wasn't schooled on his devil, but for ten years I'd walked through hell on earth and faced down real demons—Al-Qaeda, Hamas, Hezbollah, ISIS—been baptized by the blood they'd left in their wake, mopped up the carnage, and inhaled the incense of the mordant corpses of the soldiers and innocents they'd annihilated. Colm knew nothing of real demons. I'd stared evil in the face, fought valiantly, and survived. *Or at least most of me has.* I jammed my fingers into my coat pocket and felt the pills I kept hidden in its recesses. I'd always fought demons of one sort or another.

And I could do it again.

# CHAPTER 4

I was fifteen minutes late to roll call the next morning, sucking down my second coffee, hoping to burn off the hazy after-fog of too much whiskey and Vicodin. Sleep never came easy for me.

A three-shift department, the Investigative Unit, which was basically me and a couple other officers and whoever else Pusser assigned to each case, reported at 8:00 A.M. with the other day shifters: patrol officers, clerks, parking enforcement, and dispatchers. Pusser pointed me out. "Glad you could join us, Callahan."

"My pleasure, boss." Smart-ass remark, but Pusser would let me slide. He always did. I had no idea why. I slinked past the others, Wilco at my heel, and slid into the only open chair, which, lucky me, was front and center. Wilco sauntered past me, looked up at Pusser, and circled a few times before plunking down at his feet. Pusser cracked a smile. Probably his first of the day. Harris occupied the seat next to me. He eyed me with a smug smirk and leaned in close, cupping his hand over his mouth as he spoke. "You smell like a distillery."

I smiled, did my own hand cupping, and whispered back, "You smell like a sweaty butt. Oh"—I touched my neck and smiled sweetly—"I'm sorry. Guess you can't help it, since you're . . . well, you know . . . an asshole."

The old guy in the chair next to him chuckled. I craned my neck and returned the chuckle. *Back at ya, buddy, whoever you are.* Must've been a new guy—it was Sunday, not my usual workday. At least he had a sense of humor. More than I could say for Harris. He'd flushed a deep purple. I'm not sure why. He'd started it and should've expected I'd fight back. We exchanged insults on a daily, sometimes hourly, basis.

I turned back to the front of the room, tuning into Pusser's shift update: a briefing on current cases, a couple alerts, a new department procedure . . . *blah, blah, blah.* My brain was blurry. Not enough caffeine yet, or too much booze still circulating in my system. *Not good, Brynn.* Likely, Harris had a point—I knew all too well that pores can keep gassing off fumes even after a morning shower. I'd brought it on myself. As soon as my head hit the pillow the night before, the day's events flooded back on me: dead chickens, Maura's body, Ona's anguish, Eddie's impaled eyeball. It all meshed together and raced through my mind like an R-rated horror film, tormenting me until I gave up and sought comfort with my two favorite boys: Wilco and Johnnie Walker.

Good, faithful friends.

Pusser stopped talking and motioned to the guy on

the other side of Harris. The guy stood and made his way up front, cowboy boots clicking. He was tall, thin, and hairless, with pasty skin and beetle-like eyes that glinted with confidence. Or fierceness. Both, I thought.

I was alert now. I gave him my full attention. So did the rest of the room.

Joe Grabowski was his name, an FBI criminal profiler, Pusser explained. "He'll be in-house for a while, assisting on Maura Keene's case, and will receive our full cooperation on all matters." Pusser then concluded roll call and dismissed everyone except Harris, Parks, and me.

Parks moved from the back of the room and settled in the seat next to me. "I read the case report late last night," she said. "I hardly slept. Scary stuff, huh?" Deputy Nan Parks, middle-aged mother of two teens, straightforward and hardworking, had earned my respect over the last year.

"Yeah. Not exactly bedtime reading." My eyes caught on a gold glint at the top of her uniform. "New necklace?"

She fingered the gold cross. "No. Old. I just dug it out last night."

"Didn't know you were religious."

"I'm not."

Pusser cleared his throat. "We have an update on Maura Keene's case. Patrol located Maura's vehicle late last night parked on a road off Old Highway 2." Pusser pinned up a photograph of the car, a late-model green Ford Explorer, on the front board. "Looks like she pulled off the main road and parked on a forestry service road, partially hidden from view." He pointed to the front of the car. "Notice the damage to the front. Markings are consistent with a baseball bat."

"Someone smashed her headlights?" Harris asked.

"Looks that way. The vehicle's being processed now. I'm also waiting for the crime scene report." Pusser leafed through some papers strewn over the table in front of him. "We called the mother first thing this morning. She wasn't aware of any previous damage to the vehicle."

I pulled out my notebook to jot down notes, dropped my pen, and watched it roll under Harris's desk. I bent over and started to reach for it, but my head shrieked in protest. I shrank back, squeezed my eyes shut against the throbbing. *Damn.* More questions fired back and forth. I glanced over. Parks was getting everything down. I'd copy her notes later. The pen could wait. For now, it was more important to keep my head from splitting wide open.

I waited for an opening in the discussion and inserted my own information. "My cousin Meg Callahan worked with Maura at the McCreary Diner. I talked to her last night. She had something interesting to say." Another reason I was late this morning. I'd stopped by the diner right before closing last night to inform Meg of Maura's death. She'd taken it hard.

"Enlighten us, please," Harris said.

"A while ago, cash went missing from the register. Only a few of the waitresses handle the money, Maura was one of them."

"When? And how much?" Parks asked.

"About a month ago. Twenties, here and there, then one night a hundred bucks went missing."

Pusser's toothpick moved to the other side of his mouth. "Interesting. Let's figure out where the money's gone. Parks. Check with the mother, see if any new things have 'shown up' at home—clothes, jewelry, whatever."

Parks made a note. The conversation lulled. I looked up to see Grabowski studying me. "You're Deputy Callahan?"

"Uh-huh."

"I need your help building a victim profile of Maura Keene."

I looked to Pusser. "Grabowski and I have already discussed it," he said.

Grabowski went on. "Maura was a Traveller. You're a Traveller. I need your insight."

Traveller, not gypsy, or *one of them.* He'd done his research. I respected that. "I'll help with what I can."

"We'll start with the autopsy." He looked at his watch. "She's on the table now. Let's go to the morgue."

The morgue was located in the basement of the Mc-Creary County Hospital, about a five-minute drive from the sheriff's department. We rode there in Grabowski's newer-model Crown Vic, Wilco sprawled over the back seat, the car vibrating with banjo-heavy hillbilly music. Real upbeat stuff.

A stark contrast to the morbid task ahead of us.

Anxiety coursed through me on the way down the hospital elevator. I should've been used to this type of thing, right? Morbidity was nothing new to me. I'd spent years retrieving bodies of fallen soldiers. Still, the idea of seeing Maura's body on a metal table . . . I ran my fingers under the wool scarf tied around my neck, my fingertips brushing up against puckered skin, and tried to loosen the tension in my neck. I'd only worn the scarf because it was cold today, but I used to wear a scarf full-time, winter and summer, to cover my war scars. I'd worked through that now. A small victory that I refused to relinquish.

Grabowski eyed me. "You okay?"

"Yeah. Fine."

"Frank speaks highly of you. You're a vet."

Frank, not Sheriff Pusser or even Pusser. Grabowski knew my boss on a personal level. "Yeah. Marine."

"And Wilco is a human-remains-detection dog."

"That's right." My fingers itched for Wilco's leash, but Doc Patterson didn't allow animals in his morgue. I'd had to leave him in the car.

"Tough line of work."

I punched the elevator button and watched the numbers flash above the door.

The door opened. We descended with a young black man in blue scrubs and a woman with thick-soled shoes. They were both busy looking at their phones.

The elevator opened onto a long linoleum-tiled, white-walled hallway, reminiscent of my months in a veterans hospital, and my anxiety kicked up another notch. I reached into the pocket of my parka and fingered one of my pills. Slowing my pace, I let Grabowski get a few steps ahead before popping it into my mouth.

He glanced over his shoulder. "You know the vic well?"

I swallowed. "Well enough."

He raised his chin as if he'd come to an important conclusion about something in his mind. I could only imagine about what. I tried not to think too hard about it, and continued to the clerk's desk, where we signed in before making our way through a second set of doors, down a short hallway, and to an office door marked MCCREARY COUNTY OME. Doc looked up as I entered. He was hunched over his desk, wearing light blue scrubs and a surgical cap over close-shaven black hair. On his desk-top sat a half-eaten bagel and an open travel magazine. He'd been reading an article on the Bahamas. A mid-winter trip, I wondered, or retirement plans?

His big paw engulfed mine. "Brynn!" The deep marionette lines along either side of his mouth turned upward and the wrinkles around his eyes deepened against his black skin. Doc's old. And wise.

He sized up my partner. I made introductions and we progressed to the prep room, where we shimmied into biohazard protection. Inside the lab, the smell of formalin and death climbed up my nose and settled in my nostrils. I let out a small cough and rubbed down goosebumps on my arms. The room was purposely kept cold, but my shiver had nothing to do with exter-nal temperatures.

My eyes were immediately drawn to a metal table and a body covered in a light blue sheet. We gathered around the gurney, Grabowski to my right, Doc Patter-son on the other side. He flipped on a stark overhead fluorescent light and adjusted the swinging head lower. Behind him a large computer monitor was mounted on the wall. He flipped it on, too.

Then he lowered the sheet.

My jaw tightened. I inhaled sharply and blew out my breath, stealing a moment to try to reconcile the contrast between the beautiful, dark-haired Maura I knew and the body on the table. I forced myself to survey the length of her: grayish-blue flesh; a massive Y-incision that dissected her chest and ran between two smallish breasts, which were upright and perky despite the supine position of her body; an elongated navel pierced with a smallish metal arrow; sharp hip bones jutting out over long legs, ending with brightly painted toenails . . . *Oh, Maura*. Tears threatened my eyes. I crossed my arms and stepped back from the table.

Grabowski eyeballed me.

Doc cleared his throat and traced his gloved finger along the outer edge of the wound. "This was made by a double-bladed knife, recently sharpened. I could tell by the formation of the wound. A six-inch blade, or pretty close to it. A sticking knife probably."

I looked up, forced myself to discuss this body as a victim, not as my young neighbor. "Sticking knife?"

Doc turned to a small laptop on the nearby counter and hit a couple keys. Several pictures of knives appeared on the wall-mounted monitor. "Like these," he said. "They're usually dagger-shaped, with a simple wood handle. They were mostly used in slaughtering farm animals. The farmer rams the blade behind the ear of the animal for the initial kill. Or he might use it later in the process to bleed out the animal. You don't see them around much anymore."

"Why's that?" Grabowski asked.

"Too much room for error. Miss a vital artery and the animal suffers."

I swallowed. "Did Maura suffer?"

Doc's features tightened. "I believe she died shortly after the wound was inflicted. The blow was delivered from above the chest, and severed the left anterior descending coronary artery. The pericardial sac filled, the resulting pressure restricted normal heart functioning, referred to as pericardial tamponade, and led to cardiac arrest. Further evident, you can see here that the jugular vein is disten—"

"In other words, the killer hit the target," Grabowski said.

"That's right." Doc looked at me. "You asked if she suffered. I don't think she suffered after she was stabbed. But up to that point, I don't know." He lifted one of her arms. "Note the ligature marks. They're on her ankles, too. I found traces of jute cording embedded in her skin. At some point, she was bound."

I didn't remember seeing jute cord on the evidence recovery list. I'd have to call CSU and double-check. Doc turned and entered something into the laptop. I looked toward the screen again and flinched when a picture of Maura's body appeared. Her skin looked like moldy blue cheese.

"These were taken before we started working on her. He pointed at the screen, calling our attention to several dark areas. "You can see where blood pooled in the dependent areas, back of the legs and arms and"—he called up another picture taken of her backside—"along her shoulder blades and her buttocks. The body wasn't moved after she was killed. " He zoomed in on her arm. "Note the discoloring of her hands. The purplish tips of her fingers."

Grabowski shifted, squinting to take in the details. "Is that because her hand was lower than the rest of her body?"

Patterson's face lit up like a teacher who'd just gotten through to a slow student. "That's correct. But that doesn't dismiss bindings at the time of the stabbing. In fact, constraints might have increased the amount of pooling in areas distal to the binding."

Grabowski was an eager student, taking it all in, nodding enthusiastically.

I forced my next question. "Was she raped?"

"I didn't find any tearing or bruising of tissues, or sexual fluids. Although, I found something else." His eyes darted between Grabowski and me. "My examination of her reproductive organs showed that she was approximately eight weeks pregnant."

# CHAPTER 5

I learned a couple more things about Grabowski that morning. Besides his unique taste in music, he loved dogs and had a stomach of steel. After leaving the morgue behind with its mutilated victim, he drove straight to a nearby drive-through and ordered two sausage, egg, and biscuit sandwiches for himself, and a side order of bacon for my dog. He looked my way as he unwrapped one of his sandwiches. "Sure you don't want one?"

Cheese oozed over the edge of the biscuit like some viscous fluid as he bit into it. I looked away and stared out my window. A guy across the street was on standby with a Baggie in hand while his dog took a dump in the neighbor's yard. "Thanks. But I'm not hungry." Wilco sat up and whimpered, his nose twitching.

Grabowski tossed him a piece of bacon and swiped his fingers over a napkin. "Pregnant."

"Yeah. I can't believe it."

"Why? She was seventeen. Almost eighteen. Engaged."

"It's just not common in our culture."

"Teen pregnancy is common in every culture."

"Not ours." *Except there is me—the child of an unwed teen mother.*

He took another bite, chewed, and swallowed. "Explain that."

"There's very little mixing between Pavee girls and boys before marriage. People don't believe that. They think we're all . . ."

"All what?"

"Uh . . . people think that we live immorally. But that's not true. They just don't understand our ways. Especially how our young women dress."

"And how's that?"

"Heavy makeup, low-cut tops, tight jeans, high heels . . . provocatively, I guess. I don't know why. It's just for show. Fashion. It has nothing to do with sexuality." Except when others made it that way. Little Birdie Rourke came to mind, Brigid was her birth name, but we all called her Birdie, which fit her dainty features and her helium-high laugh, which floated above the jukebox music that night. Talk of boys and makeup and movies, bites of ice cream, gooey and sweet, just the girls out having fun. No one noticed the man peeling off looks at us, greasy and hairy with pit stains and brown teeth. He'd singled out Birdie, cornered her in the back hall and felt her up. "She and that short skirt of hers were beggin' for it," he told the cop later after Birdie rushed out from the hall, her arms wrapped around herself, crying. We called the police. The cop gave poor Birdie the once-over, mumbled something about gypsies, and let the guy off the hook.

My phone rang. It was Pusser. "You still with Grabowski?"

"Yeah."

"Good. A call came in on the Meath kid. Someone spotted his truck heading up Rich Mountain Road. I'm heading up there now with a couple units."

"I want to be there." I knew how the authorities could treat a Traveller as the victim—ask Birdie about that. A Traveller being hunted down by the settled law might not get a fair shake, either.

"Figured you would. But let's bring this one in with both eyeballs intact."


Sheriff Pusser tracked Nevan's truck to Jack's, a honky-tonk located off Rich Mountain Road. We caught up to the sheriff in the nearly full parking lot. He was standing at the back of his Tahoe, hands jammed in his trousers, head down and mouth working over a toothpick. Grabowski pulled up next to him and lowered his window.

Pusser leaned in. "'Bout time you got here. I was wondering if maybe this piece of crap you're driving couldn't make it up this road."

"Hey, FBI isn't as privileged as you county boys. We're just damn happy they give us something to drive."

"I feel for you, buddy."

"Yeah. I bet." Grabowski nodded toward Jack's, which was nothing more than a giant metal barn with a wood façade made to look like an old shanty. A seven-foot statue of an ax-wielding lumberjack, who looked, weirdly enough, like my uncle Paddy, guarded the front entrance. "What's the deal here? Why's this place so busy? It's the middle of the afternoon."

Pusser yanked the toothpick from his mouth and tossed it onto the ground. "Hard telling. Used to be a decent place when the lumber mill down the road was still up and runnin', but it shut down a couple years back. Now it's a dive. Attracts all sorts of trash. I make a couple runs a month out here."

I'd answered a few calls at Jack's, too. Never a pleasant experience. And one I wouldn't make without plenty of backup. The patrons weren't the cop-loving type. Not to mention being drunk, doped, or just mean by nature.

Pusser motioned to his back hatch. "I've got a couple extra vests in the back. Why don't you two park and get suited up."

As I strapped on body armor, Pusser explained his strategy. "Thought maybe we could do this quiet-like. We'll go in together, but you do the talking, since you know him." He was looking at me. "See if you can convince him to come outside and talk to us. I looked at my dog's face smashed against the Crown Vic's back window. Pusser and I had an understanding. Wilco was under my command; what he did, what he was subjected to, was my call. Not Pusser's. Not anyone else's. Illegal activities at Jack's ran the gamut: petty drug deals, prostitution, illegal gambling. *You name it, it happens at Jack's.* I'd prefer to have my dog with me, but taking in a dog with a two-hundred-pound bite force wasn't probably what Pusser had in mind when he'd said "quiet-like."

For now, Wilco would have to stay in the vehicle. I slipped him a couple treats, cracked a window, and filled a portable bowl with bottled water—two things I always carried for my dog.

Pusser communicated back and forth on his radio for a couple minutes, then turned back to Grabowski and me. "Patrol's in place down the road in case he makes a run for it. Y'all ready?"

I zipped my jacket over the vest and looked at Grabowski. He shot me a thumbs-up. "Yup. Let's go."

Inside, I blinked against the darkness and heavy, wafting smoke. Heads turned, patrons giving us a once-over before turning back to their drinks. Nevan wasn't around. But the number of customers came nowhere close to matching the number of vehicles parked in the lot. Whatever was going on here was happening in the back room.

The bartender had one eye on us and was talking rapidly into his cell phone. I grabbed Pusser's arm and nodded toward a small brown door in the back. Grabowski picked up on my signal and headed that way. I fell in step behind him. It took all of three seconds for us to cross through the room and reach the door, the bartender's eyes following our every move. I kicked myself. Nothing about this was going to go down quiet-like. I should've brought my dog.

The door was closed. Pusser tried the knob. It turned. I looked over my shoulder at the bartender, but he was already gone. Others were making a run for it, too.

"Something big is going down here," Grabowski said as he drew his weapon. I did the same.

Pusser drew his own gun and pounded on the door with the heel of that hand. "Sheriff's department. Open up!" He pushed the door. It banged open. We proceeded inside, weapons out. The sounds hit me instantly: shouting, roosters crowing, metal cages rattling, splitting wood. Sunlight streamed through a boarded window and illuminated the haze of cigarette and marijuana smoke drifting over a pit in the center of the room. A pile of bloody feathers lay heaped in middle.

Grabowski pushed around me. "Cockfight!"

A jumble of maybe two dozen men scattered like scared rabbits. A man to my right ran for the door, dollar bills falling from his shirt. Pusser reached out and clotheslined him across the neck. He tumbled like a felled tree. Pusser straddled him and slapped on cuffs.

Grabowski nudged me. "You see Meath?"

I scanned the crowd. "No. He's not here. Maybe he's already run for it."

Several officers burst through the back door with their weapons drawn. The runners stopped and raised their hands, one of them dropping a black case. Several wicked-looking metal spurs spilled onto the dirt floor.

I looked from the cruel instruments to the corner of the room, where a pile of chicken carcasses lay, bloody bird on top of bloody bird, their mangled bodies twisted together like a heaping bowl of sauce-covered spaghetti noodles. I quickly looked away. "This is sick stuff."

Pusser let out a string of cusswords and started barking out orders. The runners were rounded up and plopped on the ground, their backs to the wall, hands drawn and cuffed behind them. Nevan wasn't one of them. Pusser addressed the group, all men, in boots and jeans, a few with dollars sticking out of their plaid shirt pockets like rural handkerchiefs. "We're looking for Nevan Meath."

No one moved. As far as I could tell, no one reacted at all.

Grabowski spoke up. "Come on, people. We know he was here. His truck's here. The black Silverado, the nice one with the chrome accents."

A head bobbed up, then quickly went down again.

I walked over to the guy, a scrawny young man with stringy hair hanging in his face. "You know something about the Silverado?"

No answer. Pusser and Grabowski joined me. Pusser snatched the guy by the arm and yanked him up. The guy glared at us, defiance and dirt creasing his brow. "We asked you a question. What's your name, boy?"

"Smith."

Pusser gritted his teeth. "Funny, wiseass."

Grabowski joined in. "Yeah. I'm laughing so hard I might just pee myself."

Pusser shook the guy. "The black Silverado. Where's the owner?"

The guy looked at Pusser and smirked. "You're looking at him. It's mine. I bought it last night." He rolled his eyes my way and gave me an up-and-down. "You like it, baby? I'd be happy to show it to you. We could go ridin' together."

Pusser shook him again. Harder. "Who'd you buy it from, Romeo?"

"Hey, man. Take it easy."

"Answer me."

"Some crazy kid offered me a straight trade for my 1997 Bonneville. Couldn't figure it out. Thought the kid was stupid to trade. Then I come to find out it's got an oil leak. Oil's practically pourin' out of that engine. Lucky it didn't blow on me. I'm going to have to pile a shitload of money into fixin' it." He gave me a dirty up-and-down. "Them leather seats it's got might be worth it, though. Don't ya think, baby?" He licked his cracked lips. *Gross.*

Pusser pushed the guy down and stepped back, rolling his neck a few times. "We've been looking for the wrong vehicle. Meath could be anywhere by now." He surveyed the makeshift arena. "This is a screwed-up mess. What a waste of time."

I looked around. "Maybe not. There may be something . . ."

Pusser followed my gaze to the pile of rooster carcasses. "Those chickens we saw hanging from the trees?"

I shrugged. "They had to come from somewhere."

Grabowski leaned over Smith, his lanky form shadowing the kid. "Who's the cock supplier?"

"I don't know nothing about that. I just come to bet."

We'd be hearing the same story all afternoon. Running a cockfight was a felony. Betting at one made you a spectator, a misdemeanor at best. Most of these guys would get slapped on the wrist and sent home.

Pusser waved over another officer. "Anyone searched you yet, Smith?"

The guy deflated as the officer pulled him back up, then pushed him into a prone position against the wall and rummaged a gloved hand through his jean pockets. He handed Pusser a wallet. Pusser opened it up and extracted the guy's driver's license. "Well, what do ya know? His name really is Smith." The officer also passed back a half-smoked joint and a small clear tube of whitish powder. Pusser squinted at it. "What's this? A little crank?" Marijuana was not that big a deal, but any form of meth could land this guy in big trouble.

"What? You ain't going to bust me over that, are you? It's just recreational."

Pusser narrowed his eyes. "Depends on whether or not you know who supplied these birds?"

Smith's gaze skittered and he bit his lip. "Man. I don't know his name. He's down in Jefferson County. Got a big spread down there. Raises gamecocks and other birds. Most of these birds come from down in those parts, one way or another."

Pusser looked at Grabowski. "Jefferson County's out of my jurisdiction."

"Not mine, though." Grabowski's long arm grabbed the guy by the sleeve. He towered over the kid, peered into his face, his eyes glistening, looking like a praying mantis about to eat its prey. "Seems like this is your lucky day, Smith. You're going to get to take a ride with one of us, after all."

# CHAPTER 6

We'd always had the same loopy pile shag carpet, brown with gold flecks woven throughout. When I was eight, I brought a stray kitten home, an orange fluffball with green eyes. Li'l Tom I called him and dressed him in doll clothes and tucked him next to me every night with a lullaby and kiss. But Li'l Tom took to peeing in the corner behind Gramps' chair. Then one day Li'l Tom was gone. "Damn male cats don't stick around," Gramps told me. But I'd secretly wakened early that morning to the soft sound of Gramps' footsteps by my bed, and a minute later, watched through my window as he trudged toward the darkened woods with Li'l Tom tucked under his arm. I wondered why he'd want to take Li'l Tom for a walk so early in the morning, but then, right before he disappeared into the trees, fingers of sunlight reached over the horizon and glistened off the cold steel of the hatchet tucked in his back waist-band.

I never brought another stray home after that. But I'd thought of my sweet kitten from time to time as I cared for Gramps in his final urine-sopped-sheets and poopy-butt-crack days. Lucky for Gramps, I gave him more compassion than he'd given Li'l Tom.

I shed my boots and parka at the door and wiped Wilco's paws with a rag I kept in the coat closet. No muddy paw prints tracking up this thirty-year-old shag. I'd learned my lesson.

Gran greeted me from the kitchen. "I've fixed roasted chicken," she said. "Your favorite."

My stomach soured. Yet one more chicken thrown in the mix. *I need a drink.* I pulled a bottle from the back of the cupboard. Gran turned from the sink and shot me a look. "Early for that, don't you think?"

"It's been a long day already."

She muttered something and hefted the roasting pan from the oven. I avoided looking at it, lowering my gaze to Wilco, who had curled at her feet in front of the still-warm oven. Gran rubbed her stocking-covered foot down his back—he nestled even closer—as she busied herself spooning flour into a jar to make thickener for the gravy. A comforting warmth washed over me. My fondest memories were of Gran in the kitchen. She was happiest when nurturing her family. But her hands, freckled and veined, now fumbled as she tried to hold the jar under the faucet for just-enough water. And her shoulders, burdened with grief and guilt, seemed to bear the weight of the world.

This year had taken its toll on her: my mother's murder, Gramps' illness and death, and . . . Dublin Costello. Dublin. Simply missing according to the police, but long dead, at the hands of my own grandmother, his trailer burned to the ground and his body disposed of somewhere in the surrounding woods. His name was never spoken in our home, yet loomed over us like an ever-present dark cloud, threatening to unleash a fury of storms that would forever ruin our lives. That threat weighed heavily on both of us.

Gran turned to our main course. She stabbed the browned breast of the chicken with a fork, pale juices running freely. Her knife grated across the crisp skin with a snapping sound and then she heaped the still-steaming flesh on a plate. Visions of bloody feathers, lifeless carcasses, withered combs, and eyes glazed over with death . . . all came rushing back at once. I gulped at my whiskey, the hot liquid pooling with the acid churning in my gut. "No chicken for me tonight, Gran. Just bread and vegetables."

"No appetite?"

"Just a rough day at work." I pulled my eyes from the platter and grabbed Wilco's bowl, filled it with kibble to set on the floor.

She frowned. "Knew this job would be too much."

"I love what I'm doing, Gran." I took another sip and closed my eyes, willing my muscles to unknot and my stomach to stop rolling.

"Don't see how you can like doing that job."

"It's what I do. What I'm trained for. Both Wilco and me. What? Would you have me going back to cleaning toilets at the Sleep Sleazy?"

She frowned at my use of the local slang for our town's only motel, the Sleep Easy. "It was a respectable job."

"So is this."

She plunked down at the table and crossed herself for a prayer, her brows furrowing in concentration. Less, I was sure, in thanksgiving for another meal, and more in petition for my salvation from what she'd deemed as an unholy foray into the settled world.

I waited until she finished. "Did you stop in on Ona today?"

Her shoulders shriveled even more.

"What is it, Gran?"

"I went to see her. To pay my respects. But she refused to let me inside." Gran pushed food around her plate, but didn't take a bite. Between the two of us, tonight's dinner was going to waste.

"Because of Eddie?"

She put down her fork. "That boy will never be right again. He's lost sight in one of his eyes."

"He ran from us, Gran. When we found him . . . well, we did everything we could."

"How's he going to work half blind like that? And Ona, widowed with no one but her son to support her. And her only daughter . . ."

"That's what we're trying to do. To find her daughter's killer. Bring justice to Maura."

"Eddie had nothin' to do with that. He's her twin. They've always been close."

"I don't think he had anything to do with it, Gran." I regretted the words right away. I knew better than to discuss my work with her. Especially a case that involved our people.

"Why'd you hunt him down like a rabid dog, then?"

"We didn't. We'd gone to question Nevan Meath, and someone ran from their camper. We thought it was Nevan, but it turned out to be Eddie."

"Question Nevan? Why? He loved that girl. They were getting married." Her lips flattened. "You suspect him, don't ya?"

I made no comment.

"Listen up, child. The Meaths are well respected around here. I won't have you—"

"We just needed to question him. That's all." I drained the rest of my drink, surprised I was at the bottom of the glass already. I wanted more, but didn't dare, with Gran watching me. "It's procedure in a case like this."

"And are you *muskers* questioning any settled people?"

"Gran, please don't call me that." *Muskers* was a not-so-polite Pavee word for "police."

"It's what you are now." She sat back, her arms crossed over her thin frame. Her words, laced with disappointment and bitterness, cut to my core. She got up and scraped her dinner into the garbage. "Nothing's changed, has it? Us *gypsies* are going to get blamed for everything that goes wrong in this community. The *muskers* go after us when something goes wrong. Now you're doing the same. My own granddaughter. And people don't like what you're doing. That you're working for the cops. And I'm paying for it. My friends, they don't trust me no more." She slid her plate onto the counter and tossed the fork into the sink with a *clink,* and then stood with arms folded over her chest.

*Enough.* I crossed to the cupboard and took down the bottle again, felt her blazing eyes watch every move, but I said nothing, refused to be condemned for doing my job. Or having a drink.

I'd just filled my glass when the front door burst open. Meg rushed in, wearing a white T-shirt with tell-tale mustard stains from her shift at the diner. She carried something in her hand. Her face was flushed.

"What is it?" I snapped, then instantly regretted taking my feelings out on my cousin.

"This was at the diner, where we stash our coats and purses." She handed me a small composition book. I turned it over in my hands a couple times, unsure where she was going with this. "A journal," she said, "in Maura's cubby. I brought it here as soon as I found it."

I paused. Any recent entries in this journal could reveal Maura's mental state or any conflicts she might have had leading up to her murder. It needed to be turned in. Yet it was also the words of a Pavee girl. What was between these pages wasn't only the private words of a teenager, but could reveal aspects of clan life and attitudes that outsiders would find offensive. Seemingly damning secrets to those who didn't understand. I felt the weight of Gran's stare on my back.

I looked toward Meg. "Did you read it?"

She fidgeted with the tie on her apron.

I sighed and glanced at the wall clock. Not yet 6:00 P.M. Pusser was probably still in his office. I gave Meg a quick hug. "This is big. Thanks for bringing it to me. I'm going to take it in right now."

I got Wilco, ran the journal out to the trunk of my car, and slipped it into an evidence bag. Gran's words came back to me about Pavees always getting blamed for local crimes. She was right. Even now, Pusser was looking heavily at the clan.

I slipped on gloves, pulled out the journal.

I paged through the entries, about two dozen in all, from Christmas through the week she was killed. I took out my cell phone and snapped pictures of each page. Against department policy, sure, but once this journal was entered into evidence, I might not get a chance to see the whole thing. I was the only one on the force who could fully understand the writings of a young Pavee girl.

I read the first entry:

> *December 26*
> *Yesterday was one of the best Christmases ever. I remember thinking it might not be, since Dad couldn't be there with us, but Mom was all happy and everything. She didn't cry. Not once. And she even cooked ham for supper and we all got presents. I got this new journal from Nevan. He's so good to me. . . . I can't believe only a couple weeks ago I had doubts about Nevan and me being together. I was so stupid. I never should have doubted us—I love him so much.*

A flash of movement from the trailer caught my eye. I looked up. Gran's curtains parted, her tiny form illuminated against the backlit room. She looked my way, and I hoped for a brief smile or small wave. But she shook her head and yanked the curtains shut again, blocking out the outside world. Blocking out me.

Grabowski kicked back in a chair, while Pusser sat at his desk signing papers. The agent had a take-out burger in one hand and a framed photo in the other—the picture Pusser kept on his desk of a young lady with straight brown hair parted over a roundish face, soft eyes, and a slightly crooked smile. I'd asked Pusser about her

once. He'd ignored me and offered no explanation.
Pusser's past was an enigma, even to those who knew
him well, which weren't many. He outdated even the
oldest member of the force by twenty years. All I really
knew about him was that he'd lost his wife many years
back. Maybe this was a daughter. Strange that he'd
never talked about her.

Grabowski looked my way. "The chicken farm was
a bust. He's selling game fowl, alright, but the show
type, not the fighting type. And I don't think there was
a bird at that farm that would go for under a hundred
bucks."

I took the other seat. "Overpriced for our local occult?"

He slid the photo back onto Pusser's desk. "More
than likely." He pointed to the bag in my hand. "What's
that?"

I held it up. "My cousin worked with Maura at the
diner. She found this, says it's Maura's journal."

Pusser leaned forward and reached out. I handed it
over. He gave a quick once-over of what I'd written on
the outside of the bag, raised his brows, and punched a
number into his phone. "Cheryl. Send someone up
from the evidence room. I've got something that needs
to be processed and recorded."

He hung up and looked my way. "There were a few
empty bottles of beer in the back of Maura's vehicle.
We found a receipt on the floorboard for a convenience
store on Hampton."

"Lenny's?"

Pusser nodded, took a bite of cheeseburger, and
washed it down with a swig of iced tea. Supersweetened,
probably. Between the doughnuts and the fast food, he'd

packed on another five pounds this winter. "Yeah. Lenny's. I've got an officer over there now. The receipt was time-stamped for seven-thirty P.M., Friday. Either she bought it, or a friend did. If so, they might have been the last person to see her alive."

"The Joyce girl, maybe."

"Maybe," Pusser said. "Or the girl's baby daddy bought the beer."

An officer came in for the evidence bag. Pusser handed over the journal and turned back to me. "What did you know about the pregnancy?"

"Nothing. I was surprised by it."

Pusser squinted. "You think Meath knew he was going to be a daddy?"

"I don't know. Has anyone questioned Ona about it? Or the brother?" I pictured Eddie out in the woods, tears streaming down his face, his bloody eye swelling around the protruding twig.

Grabowski spoke up. "You should talk to Ona. She'd be more willing to open up to you than one of us."

Doubtful. Especially from what Gran had told me about Ona's sudden distrust of our family. But I wasn't going to attempt to explain clan dynamics to Grabowski. "I'll stop by their place first thing in the morning." I stood and motioned for Wilco. "I'm heading out."


The next morning, I put off going to Ona's house and headed to Mayor Anderson's place instead.

The mayor lived in a Norman Rockwell portrait: two stories of white brick, a deep columned front porch and snow-covered shakes. This was the real Americana, baby. Only I knew Mr. Mayor had cultivated a lie. The home, the luxury SUV, the beautiful wife, and two overachieving kiddos . . . they were really hollow-chocolate-bunny people—solid-looking on the outside, until you bite through the sweet, shiny exterior and discover there's nothing but empty air inside. Maura must have figured that out the hard way after she ended up pregnant by the mayor's boy:

> *February 2*
> *Everything is such a mess. I saw Nevan in the hall and couldn't hug him or anything. I know he's hurt and can't do a thing to help. It's all my fault, anyway. Being in love is so hard.*
> *Nevan found out today that it's Hatch's baby. So stupid! Plus Mama knows and is taking the news hard. She's been crying a lot. I don't know if the other kids at school know about the baby or not. It doesn't really matter. They all hate us, anyway.*
> *I know Nevan still loves me. I just don't see how we can be together now, after what's happening.*

It was just one of the couple dozen entries, but the only one that mentioned the father of her baby by name. I dialed Pusser's cell. He answered on the second ring. "You at the Keenes' place?"

I'd planned to talk to Ona first thing, but after reading the journal, talking to Hatch seemed more pressing. "No. I'm—"

"That's okay. It can wait. We got a positive ID on the

kid who bought the beer. He's on surveillance. It was the mayor's kid."

I blew out a long breath and told him about the journal entry I'd read.

"Yeah. I figured you checked out the journal before you turned it in." Checked out, not photographed. Pusser would be ticked if he knew the whole truth.

He continued. "The kid's been nothing but trouble. What a screwup. Vandalism, shoplifting, possession . . ."

"And the mayor runs interference. Keeps his name out of the papers and his offenses off the records."

"Yup."

"Murder is too big for that."

"You're jumping to conclusions."

"He was possibly the last person to see Maura alive, and I figure . . ." The front door to the mayor's house opened. Hatch swaggered out, a book bag slung over his shoulder. Tall, athletically built, with blond hair framing chiseled features, he was every young girl's dream. And quite possibly Maura Keene's nightmare.

"I'll let you know what I find out." I hit END, pocketed my phone, and got out of the car, leaving Wilco in the back seat for now. No need to escalate things. Just get a few answers. "Hatch Anderson? Deputy Callahan, McCreary County Sheriff's Department. I need to ask you some questions about Maura Keene."

Hatch pulled a key fob from his jeans, aimed, pressed, and popped the locks of a sleek black Range Rover several feet away from him. "I don't have anything to say about her."

"Nothing to say? She's dead. Murdered. You two were friends. Good friends."

He widened his stance and looked down at me, blue eyes intense and piercing under a flop of yellow bang. "You don't know nothing about Maura and me."

"I know you were having sex with her."

"Yeah. We had sex. So?" He admitted it without the tiniest bit of shame, the way someone might admit he had a blister on his foot.

"I don't get it, Hatch. How'd you two connect?"

He rocked back on his heels, his eyes shifting to the side. I could see him remembering the day they met, maybe a party, maybe at school, how it all came about. He opened his mouth, about to say something, when the front door opened. The mother, Gina Anderson, crossed the yard, a plastic smile on her Botoxed face, sleek hair, and designer jacket. "Get in the car, Hatch." She turned to me, all polite-like with blindingly white teeth smiling down at me, friendly on the surface, but without any actual warmth. "What can I do for you?"

"I have a few questions for your son about Maura Keene."

"I'm sorry, it'll have to wait. We're superbusy this morning." She waved her son toward the car, but he still didn't move.

"Well, this is *super*important. It concerns a murder investigation. And it can't wait."

"I'll have my husband call you. Set something up." Hatch still lingered. She scowled. "I told you to get in the car, Hatch."

I stayed on him. "When did you see Maura last?"

"We're not answering these questions." Gina grabbed her son and turned him toward the car, then wheeled on me. "This is ridiculous. Harassing my son like this." All pretense of civility gone, she got in my face. "What's your name again?"

"Callahan. Deputy Callahan. I was just—"

"You are just leaving."


Twenty minutes later, I was at the station, catching hell from Pusser. "What were you thinking?"

"Just doing my job. Trying to get some information from the kid."

"The mayor's kid."

I bristled. Wilco sauntered over and lay next to my chair. "Why does that matter? He's a viable suspect. He could be the governor's kid, for all I care. I don't play favorites."

"*Play favorites?* That's what you think this is? Me kissing up to the mayor?"

*Yes.* "Sounds like you've done a lot of puckering around the mayor's kid already. You said it yourself. He's been in trouble for about everything, but nothing ever comes of it. The mayor's boy must be above the law."

We stopped talking, Pusser staring me down, me squirming in my seat, running my fingertips back and forth along Wilco's spine. A vision of Gina Anderson flashed through my mind, those bleached-out teeth of hers sneering at me while I sat in the hot seat getting my butt chewed out by my boss. To her, I was a pesky fly, annoying, troublesome, something to squish and brush off. . . .

The phone rang. Pusser yanked out his toothpick and answered. "Tell him to hold." He slammed down the receiver and pushed back from his desk. "You're such a screwup, Callahan. Letting your personal crap influence the case, like this."

"What are you talking about?"

"You're paranoid. You think everyone is out to get you because you're a 'Pavee.'" He made quote marks with his fingers. "Like it's all about persecuting your people. You talk about me running interference for the mayor's kid? You run interference for those Bone Gap people all the time. That's what you were doing today, wasn't it?"

"No. I was just trying to get some—"

"Bull. You drove over there this morning because you figured I wouldn't do anything about it because he's an Anderson. That I'd be trying to pin it on a Pavee. 'Cuz in your mind, that's how all us cops operate. Congratulations, Callahan. You're just as prejudiced as us 'settled' people."

I tried to think of the right thing to say. Couldn't. Pusser was right. I'd read Maura's handwritten journal last night and found out about Hatch. The mayor's kid. How would the sheriff respond? I'd tossed in bed all night thinking about it. This morning, I should have gone to Ona's, like I was told, but I'd done what I thought was needed. For the truth. *My* truth.

"FYI," Pusser said, "I already had something in the works. After the convenience store video showed his connection to the Keene girl, I put an officer on him. At eleven last night, he purchased a sizeable bag of pot from one of our undercover cops. It's still in his vehicle. Harris was in position to pull him over for a traffic stop this morning and bring him in on a possession charge. That way, we could get him alone. Away from his parents. You blew that for us. What do you wanna bet he cleaned out that pot the moment you left."

I tensed, heat rising in my cheeks. Blew it; I sure as hell did. "I didn't know."

He pointed to the phone. "That was the kid's attorney. They'll be in this afternoon for an interview."

"I'd like to be in on it."

"You won't be here."

*Yeah, well, hell, no surprise there. I was canned from my last three jobs, why not this one, too? At least Gran wouldn't have to deal with—*

"You're heading back out to the crime scene." I shot a look at him. He shuffled through a stack of papers. "You and your dog. Parks will go with you. I want every inch of earth within a two-mile radius sniffed out."

"Why? We already—"

"Because." He tossed a printout my way. "This came in over the transom. A Jefferson County girl, Addy Barton, same age, same basic physical description, went missing Friday."

"The same day as Maura."

"Yes. Grabowski is heading down to talk to her family, but we need to make sure we didn't miss anything up there in those mountains."

"She could be anywhere. There might not even be a connection." This felt contrived. Like Pusser was working extra hard to get me out of town while he handled the mayor's boy. It was better than being fired, but . . . "There's better ways I could be spending my time."

"No. There's not. I need you up there with your dog." He nodded toward the paper. "There's a connection, alright. Read the trace report on her credit card."

I scanned the document. Her last charge was made on Friday, the same day that Maura disappeared: $7.54 at the McCreary Diner.

# CHAPTER 7

I straddled his backside, clamping my knees around his neck and pulling his head upward, flinging off my glove and sticking my fingernail into his left nostril, digging deep, going for gold. My knuckle brushed against his soft, spongy snout as I flicked out the impacted muck. There was nothing easy about picking my dog's nose.

I went for the other nostril. He wriggled away, backed up, and stomped the snow, prancing and clawing while thrashing his head. I moved back in for another try, got ahold of his collar and leaned in just as he raised his head and let out a sneeze. Dog snot and debris sprayed the front of my parka. I jumped back and swiped the front of my coat. Gooey blobs morphed into two brownish streaks running along either side of my zipper like racing stripes.

Parks scrunched her nose at my fingertips. I swiped my hands through the snow a few times, rubbed them along the side of my jeans, and held them out for her inspection. "All clean now."

She didn't look convinced.

We continued our search, Wilco working ahead, us following, snow crunching like broken potato chips under our boots. A cold breeze sighed through the barren tree branches overhead and my muscles loosened a bit. I'd always found a bit of peace in these hills. But like everything else, that was changing. Perhaps it was age, or the type of reluctant wisdom gained from encountering morbidity on a daily basis, but peaceful respites were slipping from my mind, replaced with gruesome memories of death and decay. What would Wilco find next? The Jefferson County girl? Another young woman left slaughtered and mutilated in a cold mountain cavern? I shuddered.

"You okay, Callahan?"

"Yeah. Fine." I threw back my shoulders, gulped the crisp air. A flock of birds released overhead, dark wings batting against the cold grayness.

"So, what do you think of Grabowski?" Parks asked. We'd already discussed her son's academic struggles, hubby's current obsession with basketball, a clogged septic line, her mother-in-law's pending visit, the extra ten pounds she'd gained over the holidays, on and on. . . . Now, apparently, she wanted to discuss Grabowski. I was used to working alone. All this talking made me crazy.

I glanced at the map and scanned ahead for my dog.

"Oookay," she sighed. "Guess I'll tell you what I think. I don't buy into all his psychoanalysis bullcrap. Like this perp. Grabowski's come up with some cockeyed profile on the killer. I mean, get this. Male. Organized. Which basically means the crime was pre-

meditated. Like we hadn't figured that out already."
She rolled her eyes. "Probably a first- or secondborn
child. Intelligent, but not well educated, socially inept,
lives rurally, cut off from the rest of society." She
grinned my way. "Sound like anyone you know?"

*Yeah. Every male Traveller in Bone Gap.*

"And there's something else," she continued. "Pusser
and him are buddies, I hear. Worked some big case together way back—"

"Hold up." I'd stopped. We were high on a ridge over-
looking a steep ravine. I had a visual on my dog. He'd
hesitated by a cluster of fallen trees, his tail flat and
rigid—he was on scent. We maintained our distance and
watched as he worked his way down the slope, his
nose etching a telltale tunnel through the snow-laden
forest floor. From our vantage point, I couldn't tell
where the scent was leading him.

Parks watched him work, fingering the cross around
her neck. "The Jefferson County girl." She shivered,
her eyes darting upward, then back, scanning the char-
coal dark tree trunks. A small breeze rattled the bare
branches, inciting the alarmed, high-pitched cry of a
nearby chickadee. His call echoed off the snowpacked
ground and pierced the frozen silence.

"I'm going to check it out," I said. "Stay here." I
started down, knees bent and leaning forward for balance. My feet slid out from under me, I grabbed a
sapling, and it snapped under my weight. I tumbled
back on my butt and slid a couple yards before regain-
ing control.

"Callahan?"

I clenched a tree and caught my breath. "I'm good!"

Down a ways, Wilco broke into rapid barking, alerting to a find. I scrambled back to my feet and hurried toward the sound. He was just ahead of me, standing in front of a cluster of trees. Something was there, but I couldn't see from my vantage point. I started down, slid some more, and came to a stop a few feet from my dog. He went schizo, prancing and pawing, then shooting off again on another scent. I rolled over and stood up. Pain shot through my rib cage and down my right hip. "Stupid dog." I swiped at the mud and snow that caked my face. My hand came away with blood.

Parks came down to where I was. "You've got a nasty gash on your temple. You gonna be able to walk back out of here?"

"I've walked away from worse than . . ." My voice tailed off. Parks's gaze was trained over my shoulder. I turned and saw what she saw: the back end of an overturned ATV.

We surveyed the wreckage. The vehicle was covered in a thick layer of mud and snow, the front end sunken into the soft ground. Rounded packets of dried grass and twigs stuck out of the wheel wells, where mice and other small rodents had built their nests. Another animal had sharpened its claws on the vinyl seat, leaving it hanging in shreds. Lodged under the wheel was a piece of material, a torn piece of clothing, or a rag, discolored from exposure and the elements, and stained dark black along the edge where it'd wicked up someone's blood. A small stain, but enough for Wilco's nose to detect.

Parks chipped caked mud off the broken license

plate, revealing a couple numbers. The rest were gone. "The plate's damaged. But we've got a partial. Looks like this happened a while ago."

I tensed, jerked back. *A while ago, yes. Last fall, to be exact, when the leaves had turned orange and yellow and dirty blood russet and . . .*

Parks sensed something. "What is it?"

"Nothing."

She scanned the ridge above us. "No one could drive through this gulley. Someone must've drove it off the ridge."

*Or pushed it off.*

"The driver didn't walk away from this accident." She reached for her radio. "I'll call in the plate number."

*No need. I can tell her who the victim was.* Nausea rose in the back of my throat. Of all the places, all the areas it could have been . . . it was here.

Parks lowered the radio and shot me a curious look. "You okay? Do I need to request medics?"

"No. I'm good." I cocked my thumb uphill. "My dog took off. I've got to go find him." At the top of the hill, Wilco spied me and bounded back. Relief washed over me at finding him, then fear. My dog had unburied and exposed a secret that was about to turn my life upside down.

He sensed my emotion, bristled, and lowered his head. But just for a second before his nose twitched and his focus switched back to his work. He bounded uphill, his tail tensed and curled as he raised his nose and peered at a couple tree trunks, then lowered it again and continued upward. I gulped in air, my head spinning as I dragged myself behind him.

He alerted again. This time his bark echoed from inside a rocky cavern.

"What is it? What's he found?" Parks had come back up the hill and stood next to me.

I unclipped the lead leash secured to my belt and headed for my dog. "Wait here," I told Parks. "I need to get my dog out of there first."

I bent over and shuffle-stepped toward the back of the cavern, secured Wilco's leash and drew him backward, away from his quarry. He pranced proudly at my feet while I bounced the beam of my flashlight over his find. Not a body, but a skull and bones. And some other items: pieces of deteriorated clothing, a shoe, just one, and a pocketknife . . . and . . . and a bullet.

My stomach sank. *If this is who I think it is . . . No, it is. It has to be.* I'd never known where the body was hidden, but how many times had I seen that very ATV tearing around Bone Gap? This had to be him. And if it was . . .

I bent down and plucked the bullet from between two rib bones.

"Is it another girl?" I startled, slid the slug into my pocket, and glanced back. Parks stood at the entrance of the cavern, leaning over and peering inside. She cocked her head, trying to see around me, nervous fingers once again caressing the cross that hung around her neck.

"No. It's not a girl." Part of me—an ugly, selfish part of me—wished it were the Jefferson County girl.

I turned back and stared at the skeleton, nothing more than a heap of dirt-covered bones, really. Shocks of dread and fear coursed through my body. A ghost from the past had come back to haunt me. A man who, in life, had tormented and brutalized me, and now, in death, was going to completely destroy everyone I held dear.

*Dublin Costello.* That dark cloud that had hung over my family this last year was about to pour its acid rain on us.

# CHAPTER 8

My phone screen glowed bright in the dark night air. I leaned against my car and scrolled through my photos, trying to focus on each and ignore the sound of my dog peeing on my front tire. The Lurchers caged in the backyard caught a whiff of Wilco's scent and erupted into a raucous spurt of barking. They didn't appreciate a canine intruder in their territory.

Things had calmed down at Ona's. I'd arrived at her camper twenty minutes earlier and found only Colm's vehicle parked outside. The good priest consoling the bereaved, I assumed. Or perhaps finalizing plans for Maura's funeral. In either case, I thought it prudent not to interrupt them, so I passed the time by scrolling through more pictures I'd taken of Maura's journal.

> *January 1*
> *Nevan and me snuck out and went to a New Year's party last night at an old farmhouse. A bunch of kids from school were there. I got knackered on rum and Cokes and puked*

*on the floor. So embarrassing! Especially at midnight when Nevan and me snuck a New Year's kiss. My mouth probably tasted like puke.*

Not much different than my New Year's Eve, minus the kiss. And the party. I'd spent the night with Wilco and a fresh bottle, passed out on the sofa before the ball dropped in Times Square, woke up two hours later cold, alone, and wondering if living through another year was worth it. I must've decided it was. Here I am. Still cold, still alone. I zipped my parka over my chin, looked at the trailer, then back at my phone. I scrolled through to her final entries.

*February 6*
*Mother's heart is broken. I've never seen her cry so much. She said the baby will bring us shame and embarrassment. And now she says she's going to try to talk Nevan into going through with the marriage, just to make things look right. She says it would be the best thing for the family. I hate my life. I wish I was normal, not some freak Pavee. I don't fit in anywhere.*

This was dated a few days before her death. I already knew the baby was Hatch's, or at least Maura had thought it was. What had happened during the time between the first part of January and this entry? She'd gone from being in love with Nevan to having another guy's child?

A flash of movement from the house drew my attention upward. Colm stepped out and made his way toward me. I slid my phone into my pocket. "Hey there." My eyes were immediately drawn to his neck. Instead of his usual white collar, he wore a wool scarf tucked under a heavy black fleece jacket. A knit hat was pulled low over his forehead. Somehow he looked younger. More like the old Colm I used to know. And loved. Maybe still did. I lowered my eyes. "How's Ona doing today?"

"Not well. I'm worried about her."

She'd lost her only daughter. What did he expect? I met his gaze, saw his worry. "What do you mean by 'not well'?"

"I work with grieving people all the time. She's especially distraught."

"How's that?"

He searched the air for answers. "I'm not sure I can explain it. It's as if there's more there than just sorrow."

"Like what?"

"Fear. That's what I'm sensing from her. She's scared of something. She wouldn't talk about it. Actually, she hardly talked at all. I tried to pin her down on funeral arrangements tonight, but she was too upset. I'll try again tomorrow."

Metal cages clanked and rattled in the backyard. The Lurchers were going crazy. I craned my neck and saw Eddie out back, tossing scraps onto the concrete floors of their pens.

"How's the investigation going?" Colm asked.

He meant about Maura's death, not knowing about the remains I'd just discovered. I rocked forward on my toes, opened my mouth, then shut it again. We'd never discussed it, but Colm knew about Dublin Costello. He also knew that my grandmother had killed the man. Gran herself had told him, in a confession that I'd happened to overhear. Now Dublin's body had been discovered and I'd stolen evidence from the scene. Right or wrong, guilt wracked my conscience. I wanted to confide my transgression. Get his opinion, or approval—was I justified, for the sake of protecting my family, or not? But could I trust Colm?

"Brynn, what is it?"

"Nothing." I took a step back and crossed my arms over my chest. He was a priest, yes, meaning he could be trusted with anything. Or at least he could now. But I'd trusted him once, years before he became Father Colm, and he'd betrayed that trust. Seemed to be a pattern in my life. I'd loved my mother; she'd abandoned me. I'd loved Colm; he did the same. And most recently I'd opened up to another man, Kevin Doogan. He'd left me behind, too. Then there was Gramps, the one man who should have protected me, but in the end loved his ideals more than his own granddaughter. There was only Gran. She'd given up so much to protect me. I owed her the same. Didn't I?

"Brynn?" Colm looked worried. "Something is obviously wrong. Let me help you." He stepped forward, close enough for me to see a tiny scar under his jawline. I didn't remember it being there when we . . .

I took a deep breath and changed gears. "There is something bothering me. There's been a new development. The autopsy showed that Maura was pregnant."

Sadness shot through his eyes. "Oh, no. A double homicide then."

"She was only eight weeks along, but, yes, Tennessee law rules it as a double homicide, no matter the gestational age."

"The way I see it, it would be a double murder at any stage of pregnancy, no matter where the mother lived." I nodded and he glanced back at the trailer. "Does Ona know?"

"I believe so."

"Do you think the killer knew she was pregnant?"

"Maybe. I don't think Maura was chosen randomly, the killing is too personal for that. She knew the killer."

"That means you should be able to narrow down the list of suspects. If she wasn't that far along, she probably hadn't told many people."

"Even if she told one person, and that person told another . . ."

"Anyone could have heard about it." He nodded. "The Jezebel reference . . ."

I shrugged. Nothing could be certain at this point.

I decided to tell him about the latest turn in the case. "There's another girl missing."

"What?"

"Not a local girl. She's from south of here. Jefferson County."

"You think it's connected to Maura's murder?"

"We don't know yet. They've put out an alert."

"Let's pray she's found safely."

"You pray. I'm more of the take-action type."

"You could do both."

I bristled and looked away. He sighed. "Well, I've got to get going. A delivery is coming in for the food pantry tonight. I need to help unload the truck." He said good-bye and turned away. I watched him leave and regretted my decision not to confide in him. He knew what Dublin had done to me all those years ago. And he knew that Gran had killed Dublin in self-defense. He knew the whole story, but it'd come to him in a confession. Anything I said to him now would be held sacred and private as well. And Colm wasn't the type to break the rules.

Unlike me.

I shoved my hands into the pocket of my parka, my fingers nudging against the cold steel of the bullet nestled deep in the folds of fabric along with a half-dozen chalky pills.

Guilt and relief, all in one pocket.

# CHAPTER 9

Maura Keene's funeral was the next morning. Outside, the crusted snow sparkled like diamonds in the morning rays of the sun. Inside, the church dampened the senses with sullen mosaics of suffering saints and bleeding hearts. Mourners sat with heads bent, hands clasped respectfully, and shoulders trembling with emotion. I'd come in late. Gran and Meg were a few pews ahead of me. The woman next to me smelled of jasmine perfume and cigarettes and a tangy undercut of lasagna. Early-morning baking. Comfort and nourishment for the bereaved. How thoughtful.

The procession commenced as bagpipes emanated haunting tones of "Danny Boy" as the family followed behind the pall-draped casket. Ona and Eddie were first behind the coffin. She wore a clingy black chiffon dress stretched tight over her breasts and hips, perhaps pulled from the back of the closet, or borrowed from a thinner friend. The rosary beads, twined between the fingers of her left hand, clinked as she walked, keeping time with the sound of her heeled footsteps, her right hand grasped under Eddie's arm for support; not for herself, but for him. His lips trembled, his unpatched eye blinked tears that landed in wet, puckered stains against his polyester suit. Midaisle he swayed, Ona stopping to grasp him quickly with both hands. A collective gasp echoed throughout the sanctuary. "His twin," the lady next to me whispered, and then nodded, as if that said it all.

Opening prayers mumbled through the sanctuary, a reading and another, all probably poignant and meaningful, had I been able to focus. My thoughts wandered in and out, my eyes taking in every mourner as a possible suspect. The church was segregated: Travellers and settled, two easily distinguishable groups. Pavee men in black suits, hair slicked back, gold crucifixes on thick chains, and arms protectively around their women, who sat pretty in their hats over teased hair and garishly applied makeup. They needed to look their best as if, by association, this tribute elevated Maura's status as she approached the Pearly Gates, seeking entry. A sharp contrast to the monotone, conservatively groomed group of settled mourners tightly huddled in the back pew: the principal from McCreary High, a few teachers, Maura's boss from the diner, and a couple others, too. The rest were kids—classmates, I assumed. They sat with their heads hung in sadness, or was it shame? How many had actually been nice to the weird girl? A gypsy freak from Bone Gap.

I sat in my jeans and a sweater, neither somber nor garish, the perpetual observer, never an insider to either front.

As we rustled to stand once more for another offered prayer, two pews up, Riana Meath turned and waggled her fingers my way.

All this time, since my return to Bone Gap, we'd been avoiding each other. Lately she'd acted like we were best friends again. Maybe she'd changed. Tragedy often did that to people. Nothing changed a person like death and mortality slapping you in the face.

"Today the world feels dark." I peeled my eyes from Riana and focused on Colm as he began his homily. "A brightness, a true light in our lives, has been extinguished. We face unbearable grief, but yet we do not weep alone. . . ."

*Wrong.* I glanced to the front. Ona wept alone.

Drawn into a tight bundle of sadness, she sat at the edge of the pew, shaking off Eddie's, or anyone's, attempts to comfort her. Chin down, she bore her anguish with periods of whimpers broken by short pauses of shallow, desperate recovery breaths, before breaking into more wrenching sobs. I'd seen this before. Ona had just begun walking the path of grief, a journey burdened by the heavy load of denial, anger, bitter loss, and all the raw wounds of a mother who'd loved and lost.

She wept alone, she'd walk alone, and in the end, she would mourn alone. There was no avoiding it.

Without his mother to comfort, Eddie wavered: Which way to go, what to do? He fidgeted uncomfortably, turning around in the pew several times, his one good eye darting about like a loose pinball, blinking angry tears as he searched the crowd. *For whom?* I wondered.

He turned back around as Colm wrapped up the

homily with one final platitude. "Our faith offers us hope. For as devastating as this loss is, we can take comfort in the fact that in the end, love conquers death."

The woman next to me sighed and dabbed her eyes.

I bit my lip. *"Love conquers death"? Really? Just how's that working for Ona? Love might sweeten life. But only justice avenges death.*

On the way out, I got caught up in a black clump of perfume-infused mourners and emerged into the stark daylight breathless and a bit dizzy. A small number of press dotted the sidewalk, for a change keeping a respectful distance. Few in number now, but still an unwelcomed sight. IRISH GYPSY GIRL MUTILATED BY DEMON WORSHIPERS was too good of a story to let stand. Bloody occult killings made for titilating, juicy stuff. The Bone Gap gypsies had sizzled hot in the headlines for days, finally eclipsed by an even riper story: a familicide in a tiny rural town south of Nashville. The father blew the brains out of his wife and three kids before mouthing the barrel himself.

I cringed at reveling in another family's misery, but such a horrific story would dominate the next edition of the papers and hopefully push us to the back page. Or at least someplace midcopy. We could use the reprieve.

They put Maura Keene's casket in a grave next to her father's. Our culture and faith taught that the body corrupts, but the soul is immortal, never ceasing to exist. Our loved ones are but resting, waiting for us, until we're reunited again. Death does not mark the end.

The sun peaked in the midday sky as the first handfuls of dirt were thrown and condolences uttered. The shadow of her father's tombstone crept over Maura's open grave—the Shadow of Death.

It all seemed very final to me.

# CHAPTER 10

Meg told me not to accept Riana's invitation. I should have listened to her. But the opportunity to get this close to the Meaths, to Nevan's sister, was too good to pass up. Anything to help the case.

So here I was, sitting in Riana's mobile home, sipping wine from plastic cups with "my girls." Riana's phrase, not mine. She'd said it a dozen times so far: *my girls* this and *my girls* that. "I've sure missed my girls," and—big hugs and gushes all around—"I'm so glad to be here with all my girls."

The wine soured on my tongue. I'd ceased being one of Riana's girls, one of the old gang, the night they held me down and shaved off my hair.

Had they completely forgotten?

At least Leena seemed to remember. A quick, painful glimpse at my hair sent her silently brooding over a fashion magazine. She gave the ads her full attention, not looking up again. Bogged down by guilt perhaps. Or regret. Her own auburn curls had been shaven off amidst recent chemo treatments. Easier, she'd confided, than constantly cleaning clumps of hair off the bathroom floor. The story had run through the grapevine: "So sad"; "Too young for breast cancer, poor thing"; "She'd had such beautiful hair." Had she thought of me when the hairdresser ran the shears over her scalp? Karma bites.

Then there was Noreen, or Nora as we *girls* called her, who'd always been the nerd of the group. No more. She'd lost her glasses, dropped ten pounds, and learned to play up her assets, which generously bulged between her elbows as she leaned over the polished wood table. She'd married up, I learned (whispered in my ear from Riana), to a Pavee man from a clan down south, who made a fortune in the "insurance" business. Which in lay terms meant he purchased large policies on family members and collected big payouts when they kicked the bucket. Not illegal, yet not completely ethical, either. Anyway, it looked like Nora's bustline had benefited from the family business.

Shy Shannon had folded herself neatly in a nearby chair. Close enough to hear our conversation, but still hovering on the peripheral edge. A glance her way would get you a quiet smile and perhaps a shrug, a nervous little giggle and a flash of a dimple, but rarely much else. She'd always been that way. A filler, of sorts, in the gap between Riana and the rest of us, a minion. There, but in the background, holding my feet as the others shaved my head. As if out of sight meant out of mind. *Not for me, Shannon. Not for me.*

By Traveller standards, Riana was the one who'd fared the best, as was fitting for the ringleader. She'd married Pete Riley, a big shot in the clan, even back in our day. A semifamous boxer, he'd travelled the country making a name for himself in the bare-knuckle fighting circuit. Word was that some bigwig coach from the WBA was courting him, and a major contract was in the works. Yes, Riana had done well for herself.

A lot better than if she'd married her first love—Dublin Costello.

Way back when, she'd been in love with Dub. Most Pavee girls were, or at least considered him quite the catch. Which is why it was such a shock when he set his sights on me, a stigmatized mixed girl from a family with few assets. Gramps, never one to miss a moneymaking opportunity, swooped in and took advantage of Dub's interest by negotiating a profitable backroom deal that sealed my future as Mrs. Dublin Costello. I was expected to accept my fate. Arranged marriages were, and always had been, an acceptable, even cherished part of our culture.

What neither Gramps, nor anyone, had taken into consideration was the fact that I would refuse to marry Dub. I shocked the clan. Most of all, Riana. I'd turned down the man who'd scorned her. As if she didn't hate me enough because Dublin had chosen me over her, I'd dared to reject him. All the more reason to condemn me, single me out, and teach me a lesson. What she never knew, what she would never know, was that shaving my head, which might, under normal circumstances, have been humiliating, was child's play compared to what Dub Costello had done to me.

And here we were, a decade later. Pretending nothing had ever happened.

Kids and husbands and home decoration dominated our inane discussion for the first twenty minutes. More wine, a nibble of cheese here and there, and the discussion progressed to diet plans, and the latest fashion trends, parties and socials: *How could so and so have worn the same dress to two events? What was she thinking? And did you know that Little Petey's teachers think he's gifted?* Then a pouty face and a big sigh from Riana: *Poor Ona. How can she bear losing a child? And my Nevan, my poor little heartbroken brother. Poor Nevan. Poor me. Me. Me. Me . . .*

And then all eyes turned to me.

"You don't honestly think Nevan could have killed Maura, do you?" Riana batted innocent lamb eyes my way. *Finally the wolf in sheep's clothing emerges.*

"I can't really discuss the case."

"We won't tell," Nora promised. She leaned her ample bosom forward as she poured more wine into my cup.

"That's right," Riana said. "We're all just friends here. Friends don't keep secrets from one another, do they, Shannon?"

Shannon glanced sideways and grinned, noncommittal, but not objecting. *Not out of sight, Shannon.*

I took a gulp of wine. "Right now, we're looking at everybody." The "everybody" lingered as I batted my own eyelashes at *the girls.*

Leena looked up from the magazine. "But you can't really think it's one of us?"

I offered my best noncommittal little shrug. "I just do what my boss tells me."

"Settled law," Riana sneered. I remember that sneer from our teen years. It still sent shivers up my spine. "I never would have guessed you for one of *them.*"

"I never would have guessed any of us to be where we are now." I tipped my glass in her direction. "You, for example, Riana."

"What about me?"

Time to pour it on. "Mrs. Pete Riley. He's practically famous. And you have a brood of boys, too." They had five boys, at last count. In fact, they'd parked another mobile home behind this one and connected them with a wooden breezeway. As a bonus, Kitty and Nevan lived right next door. Free babysitting, too. "Lucky you."

She twirled a strand of blond hair, gloating, but tense, as if uncertain if this was a compliment. "I do feel very fortunate."

Leena looked on longingly. Chemo must have killed her chances for a passel of noisy brats.

"Rory and I haven't been able to have any children," Nora whimpered. "We've tried everything."

"Mission style." Shannon blushed. "With a pillow under your hips so the spermies don't have to swim too hard."

"Tried that."

"Honey," someone said.

Leena's brows crept up her bald head. "Eat it or smear it on each other's bodies?"

Giggles.

Riana grinned wickedly. "Smear it, then eat it."

More giggles and the tension evaporated as we unscrewed another bottle of wine.

I needed to ask questions, extract some useful information, but instead I'd just lost my questioning advantage to sticky-sex imagery.

I sipped my wine and glanced around the room. We were back to just a bunch of girls enjoying each other's company and having a good time. Except Riana. Her laughter now felt forced, undercut by hatred, or something more. Fear? The bully afraid? That was a switch. What did she fear I'd bring out in the conversation now?

Riana suddenly stood and reached into one of the kitchen cabinets. "Shhh . . . my secret hiding spot." She held up a joint.

Shannon's reaction surprised me as she quickly rose to crank open a window, then joined us around the table. A closet pothead? She beamed expectantly at the group for approval. Enthusiastic nods ensued.

Except from me. "No thanks." I was a cop. I couldn't participate. Besides, pot wasn't my thing. Just booze and illicit opiates, but only when I was alone.

Silence choked the room and I felt myself transported right back to the old days. Always the party pooper, I was. I went to take another sip. My cup was empty. No one offered me a refill.

"Uh-oh." Riana dramatically placed her hand over her heart in mock concern. "We're in trouble now, girls. Brynn the copper might arrest us."

Shannon swallowed, looked like she might burst into tears. "I didn't do nothing."

I chuckled. "Relax. No one's in trouble."

Riana lowered her chin and looked up at me. "You mean, you're not going to turn us in? Aren't you the *law*? Isn't this *illegal*?" She waved the joint in my face.

I bristled. "What's your problem?"

"I don't have a problem, Brynn. You do."

"Oh yeah? How's that?"

"Seems to me that you can't decide where your loyalties fall."

"*Loyalty?* How about enough loyalty to want to find

the sick bastard who butchered and killed one of *the girls* in the clan!"

Screw them. What was I thinking? I wasn't going to get anything useful from these girls. I pushed back from the table and headed for the door, turned back at the last moment and leveled my gaze on Riana. "If you see Nevan, tell him I'm looking for him."

# CHAPTER 11

"I don't have to talk to you. You're not welcome here. Leave." Ona's angry face glared through the narrow opening of her door. Colm had said she was upset, so I'd waited a day before calling on her, but I couldn't wait any longer. I needed answers.

"Maura's autopsy showed a pregnancy," I blurted before she could get the door shut.

She reacted as if I'd just slapped her, flinching, her eyes darting about nervously.

I pushed: "But you already knew about the baby, didn't you?" She steadied her gaze on me. The darkness in her eyes sent shivers through me. "Let me come inside, Ona. So we can talk about this." I was glad I'd caged Wilco back in the cruiser. Ona would be reluctant to let me in with a sixty-pound police dog at my side.

"No. I don't want you in here."

"Why? We've always been friendly." I would have said, "We'd always been friends," but that wasn't quite true. Ona, at least fifteen years older than me, was closer in age to my mother than me. Widowed young, with two children, her life had been one struggle after another. Still, she carried an air of superiority about her. I'd always had the feeling she looked down on me for being only part Pavee and a child of an unwed mother. Like many in the clan, she'd labeled me as a half-breed. And now that I'd joined forces with settled people, and was a cop, I'd picked up another label: *graansha.* Outsider.

All that was fine. I could take it. But anger welled inside me as I thought of Gran and the hurt in her eyes as she talked about being shut out from Ona yesterday. I fought to temper it, keep it from interfering with the job before me. "You can't deny the pregnancy, Ona. The medical examiner's report proves it."

Her gaze was defiant, but her lower lip quivered. Was it fear, like Colm thought, or something else?

"I don't believe Nevan was the baby's father. There was someone else, wasn't there?" The irony wasn't lost on me. This woman had spent a lifetime adhering to her strict moral ideals, working hard to instill those very morals in her children, probably using people like me as an example of how not to be, and then her own daughter, Maura, betrayed everything she'd worked so hard to cultivate.

*Pride comes before the fall.*

I pressed harder. I needed her to crack, open up, and give me information. "She got pregnant by a settled boy. And you knew—"

"No! My Maura wasn't like that!" She tried to slam the door shut, but I'd anticipated that and had already stuck my foot against the jamb.

"Like what, Ona?" *Like my mother?*

Her eyes popped. Tears sprang along the edges. "Get off my property!"

I leaned forward. "Did Nevan know he wasn't the baby's father?"

A tremor rippled through her muscles. I saw it. Plain as day. The fear Colm referred to. What was it that had her so scared? "Ona, what is it you're not telling me? Has someone threatened you?"

"Leave her alone." The voice, angry and masculine, came from directly behind me. I startled. My foot drew back; the door slammed shut. The lock clicked.

I turned. "Eddie." He stood not five feet from me, his hand gripping a leash. The Lurcher on the other end curled its lips and snarled. Inside my car, Wilco went nuts, barking and scratching at the window. I tensed, but kept my gaze steady on Eddie's one good eye. The other was patched like a pirate's. "How are you feeling, Eddie?"

"What do you think? I'm half blind now."

"I'm sorry."

"No you're not. You couldn't care less. You're out to get us like all the other damned coppers. Your own people. Everyone says you're a traitor."

"I'm doing my job, Eddie. Trying to bring Maura's killer to justice. That's what you want, right?"

"Leave Nevan alone. He wouldn't hurt anyone. Especially not Maura."

"Did Nevan tell you about the baby?"

He turned away, walking toward the back of the house.

I followed. He went to the cages, unleashed the Lurcher, and guided it into one of the pens. I waited until the pen door was secured before stepping in closer. "Did Maura tell you that Nevan wasn't the father?"

He whipped around. "Are you saying my sister was a *limmer*?"

No, I didn't think she was a slut, but had she been in love with Hatch Anderson? Or had he taken advantage of her? From somewhere across the yard, I heard what sounded like a rooster crow. "What was that?"

Eddie's eyes darted toward an old shed in the far corner of the yard. I headed that way. He trailed close behind. "You can't just walk all over my yard without a warrant."

I continued around to the back of the shed. A five-foot chain-link fence surrounded a stack of small cages. Most were filled with rabbits or hares. Probably for hare-coursing training for his dogs. But a couple cages contained roosters. "What a coincidence. We just busted a cockfight up at Jack's. You know the place?"

"Yeah. I've been there. I don't know about no cock-fighting, though."

"Oh, I see. You're raising these two roosters for a special 4-H project, aren't ya? Because I don't see any hens. If you had hens, I might understand why you needed the males. But just two cockerels? Seems strange to me, Eddie." Or maybe he did have hens at one time. Maybe he whacked off their heads and hung their bodies from trees. "One of the guys we busted seemed to know your buddy Nevan. You two into the cockfights? Is that how you turn an extra buck or two?"

His jaw jutted out. "You can't prove nothin'."

"What about Maura? Did she approve of Nevan's extracurricular activities?"

Eddie busied himself scooping pellets into the rabbit cages.

I kept on him. "Maybe she was in on it. With a baby coming and all, she probably needed the extra cash."

I knew from the journal entry that Ona was going to talk to Nevan to try to convince him to go through with the wedding in order to save Maura's reputation. I didn't know if that conversation had happened or not. I was about to ask, when my cell buzzed. I stepped aside and answered.

It was Pusser. "The remains are at the morgue. There wasn't much to process at the scene. They're working on getting the ATV out of the ravine now."

My mouth went dry. "Good."

"We've got a name on the license number. You won't believe this."

*Unfortunately, I would.*

"It came back registered to Dublin Costello."

*"Costello?"* I hoped I sounded surprised. "What do you think we're looking at?"

"Too soon to tell. We'll know more tomorrow after the examination."

I was sure we would. I disconnected and turned back, but Eddie had already disappeared inside the camper. I let him go. I had a more pressing issue to deal with now.

My grandmother.

"I need to know exactly what happened the night you killed Dub Costello." I placed a cup of coffee in front of her and took the seat across the table, Wilco curled at Gran's feet, his snout resting on her slipper. "You can't leave out anything, Gran."

She held the mug between trembling fingers and took a sip. "I've told you most everything there is to say about it."

"Tell me again. Start with why you went to Dub's trailer that night. And why you had your gun with you."

She put her mug down and leaned back. "Your granddad was so sick back then. The cancer, all the medicines he took, and then his mind started to fail. You remember how he'd forget things. I could tell him something and two seconds later it was gone. But things from a long time ago . . ."

"I remember, Gran." Lung cancer had eaten away at his lungs, stolen his ability to breathe, but the dementia took his mind. I couldn't decide which was crueler.

Gran took a long sip of coffee before speaking again. "That night, he was so upset. At first, I thought it was your mother's death. How we'd just learned she was killed and left out there in those woods."

I squeezed my eyes and tried to block out the images flashing across my memory. I'd found her body, or what was left of it, dumped up in the mountains, rotting and ravaged by animals, picked over beyond recognition.

"It happened that very night of her funeral, remember? Fergus had been in bed all day, unable to go to our own daughter's funeral. Not that he really understood what was happening. By then, his mind was about gone." Her eyes widened, her mouth drooped. "Maybe that was a blessing. God's way of protecting him in his last moments."

I gave her hand an encouraging pat. "I know this is

hard, but I need you to tell me the story again. Just in case there's something you forgot to mention before."

"I haven't forgotten anything about that night. It's etched in my memory forever." The words came as barely a sigh. Gran never complained. Never displayed her grief like many widows. After Gramps passed, she went on, stronger than ever, always helpful and outwardly cheerful. But I sensed the toll her grief had taken. I saw it in the small things: dull eyes, weak posture, laughter that didn't quite meet her eyes. Or like now, pale and ashen, a sheen of sweat on her face as she recalled Gramps' last moments.

Maybe I was wrong to press her like this. She'd suffered enough. But if I didn't get to the truth, there could be much more suffering to come. "Are you okay?"

"Yes. I'm okay." She sat a little straighter and continued the story. "Fergus was babbling a bunch of nonsense that night, living in the past like he always did. At first, he was talking about your mother, remembering the good old days and all. Then he got real upset. He started ranting on about you and how you could never follow our rules, and then he told me about Dub and how he'd . . . you know."

"Raped me." The words had festered inside me all these years, like a poisoned cyst, and, now released, they burst out of me, hot and vile. I closed my eyes, swallowed my own emotions; I had to get from Gran the story that only she could tell.

"Yes. And I was so angry. All those years and I hadn't known what had really happened that night you left Bone Gap." She clenched her fist. "I've never felt so angry in my entire life."

"The gun. What made you grab your gun?"

"I didn't. I took my purse. I don't know why, but I did. The gun was in my purse, like it always was. You remember how your grandfather bought me that gun when all those attacks were going on."

That was true. Several of our women had been attacked and roughed up. The law never got to the bottom of it. Never really tried, according to Gran and Gramps. That's when Gramps got her a gun and told her to keep it with her at all times. Was it registered? Traceable? "So you went to Dub's trailer. With your purse."

"Yes. I confronted him. Told him I knew what he'd done to you all those years ago. And he laughed. He said you owed it to him. He felt no remorse for what he'd done. I couldn't believe what I was hearing. I became so angry, told him he would pay for his sins and that I was going to see to it. And he . . . he exploded. Lord, but I'd never seen a man so angry. He started shaking me . . . and he . . . he had me backed against the kitchen counter. He was hitting me." She raised her hands, staring at them like they were foreign appendages. "That's when I cracked. My purse was right there. I got to my gun, and . . ."

She swiped at her eyes. Her skin went from ashen to a splotchy red flush.

"Then what, Gran?"

"I couldn't believe what I'd done. I ran home. Kevin Doogan was outside and he saw me. Asked me what was wrong and I told him everything. He told me to go inside. Wash up. Change my clothes and to not tell anyone. Not your grandfather, not you. No one. He said he'd take care of everything. I didn't see him again after that. The next thing I knew, Dub's place burned to the ground."

Doogan had done that. He disposed of Dub's body and burned his place to the ground in order to cover any evidence that might lead back to my grandmother. Over the past months, I'd wondered, over and over, about what compelled him to risk everything for Gran. A woman who wasn't even family. One answer returned time and again, however unlikely. We'd only known each other for a few days as I'd helped him discover the fate of his sister. Then I'd shared my story with him, a story I'd shared with no one before. And that night in his arms, I'd seen it and felt it: an intimacy borne from an understanding and connection few people share. Doogan would risk anything to protect me.

"How many times did you shoot him, Gran?"

"I . . . I don't know. . . ." She used her napkin to wipe her forehead.

"It's important. How many? Just once?"

Her lower lip trembled. "No. More than that. I just kept pulling the trigger."

It was a little snub-nose revolver—S&W Model 36, with distinct engravings on the metal grip. She may have unloaded the whole cylinder into him. Five rounds, if it was fully loaded. "Do you know how many bullets were in the gun?"

"No. Your grandfather loaded it for me."

None had been recovered from Dub's burned-out trailer, and I'd only found one by the remains. There could still be more rounds. Had Doogan picked up some at Dub's place and gotten rid of them? Had I missed something at the scene? It was possible that bullets had embedded in other parts of the body and been dragged off or ingested by predators. There were too many variables. "And the gun? You'd told me that Doogan took it from you."

"Yes. But I don't know what he did with it. Like I said, he told me to go inside and wash up. I didn't see him after that."

The gun tied Gran to the murder. If Doogan dumped it somewhere near the body and it was found . . . "Gran, what is it?"

She doubled over the table, grasping her temples and letting out a deep, body-rattling groan that set my nerves on fire. I shot out of my chair. Wilco scrambled out from under the table and began whining and sniffing at Gran's face. I pushed him away and wrapped my arms over her shoulders. "Gran!"

She started to tell me something, but her words came out garbled and slurred. I knelt down, grasped her cheeks. The left side of her face drooped slightly.

"No! Oh, God, what have I done?" I dialed 911 and gave the operator my address. "Please hurry. It's my grandmother. She's having a stroke."

# CHAPTER 12

The doctor delivered the news in the same manner as one might place a drive-through order—brief and to the point. "She's had a ministroke, or, in medical terms, a transient ischemic attack. The good news is that a TIA usually doesn't cause permanent disabilities."

"The bad news?"

"It's a warning. A bigger, more serious stroke could be coming. She'll need to make some lifestyle changes."

*Prison would be a huge lifestyle change. . . .*

"I want to keep her for observation and more testing. Then after she's discharged, she'll have follow-up appointments and medications to take. She'll need someone at home with her for a while."

There were more questions I should've asked, but shock had slowed my mind. The doctor left and I went back into the room to sit with Gran. She looked frail and small under the thin hospital blankets, tubes running from her veins to an IV bag and monitors. Flashbacks of

Gramps ran through my mind. Even with the best care and Gran's loving touch, he'd deteriorated quickly.

Meg sat by Gran's bedside. Her hands shook as she smoothed back a piece of Gran's hair. "I can't believe this is happening. First Gramps, now Gran."

"She's going to be fine." A brave front, but inside, I wasn't so sure. I'd been there and seen the change that came over her so suddenly. Fine one minute, and then the next minute, she was slumped over in her chair, confused, weak, one side of her face slack. It'd happened so fast and without warning. It could happen again at any time. Only the next time it could be bigger. Deadly.

Lifestyle changes, the doctor had said. *No problem there, Doc.* A trial, prosecution, jail time, the rest of her years endured in an institute . . . lifestyle changes didn't come any bigger than that. I couldn't bear to see Gran's life end in such misery. I'd do anything to prevent that from happening. Including tampering with evidence. And so much more, if I had to.

"Brynn." Meg's voice, a mixed bag of annoyance and concern, cut through my thoughts. I blinked and focused. Meg looked on with strained eyes. "You're exhausted," she said. "Go home. Get some rest. I'll stay through the night."

Thank God for Meg. Steady and loyal, she was always there when I needed her the most. I'd questioned my loyalties in the past: the law or my family. But seeing Gran's fragile state now, knowing that I could have lost her tonight . . . there was no question in my mind. Family would always come first.

I took Meg up on her offer, but I had no intention of going home and resting.


Wilco turned, lifted his stub, and relieved himself on the old tire propped outside Doogan's back door. I jumped back, but not quick enough to avoid getting my boot doused. *Lovely.* I shook my foot, scowled, and went back to looking for the spare key Doogan kept under his back steps.

I hadn't liked Doogan when we first met. He was too egocentric, too aggressive. I'd had enough of those guys in the Marines—the ones who were all "we'll take control, do what we want, when we want"—or at least I thought I had. One night with Doogan changed my mind. Except that night ended short and then he disappeared. I hadn't heard from him since. But maybe it was for the best. Doogan was a Traveller and I'd long ago decided that a relationship with a Pavee would never work for me. Pavee women were expected to stay home, tend to the children, and follow their husbands' lead. A concept that worked for some, I guessed, but snotty noses and dirty diapers weren't my thing. Neither was being subordinate to a man. Something I'd discovered long ago, the hard way.

I found the keys taped under the top step and let myself inside, flipped on my flashlight, and made my way through the trailer. The old man Doogan rented from had died a few weeks after Doogan fled Bone Gap. That was over eighteen months ago. The trailer had stood vacant and locked up since then. Long enough for smells to accumulate and multiply. The stench hit Wilco the hardest. He hovered at my feet, nervous and fidgety, his nose working the air like crazy.

The cops had done a job on the place. The day before Dublin Costello's house burned to the ground and he went missing, Doogan had confronted Dub in the streets, accusing him of murdering his sister. It got nasty and the cops had to break them up, making Doogan the perfect suspect. They'd aggressively sought him ever since, starting with this trailer. Cabinets and drawers were open, the garbage can spilled over, rugs pulled up. A pizza carton was left open on the counter near the sink. White fuzzy mold smothered its contents. I clamped my hand over my nose and mouth and turned away. You'd think a little moldy pizza wouldn't bother someone used to the stench of days-old human flesh. But, hey, I liked pizza. And I hadn't eaten.

Add to duty list: Get a pizza. Without white fuzz.

I'd start my search in the bedroom. A room I recalled all too well.

I'd only been in it once before, but the memory of that single night had ignited my dreams many a night over the last year and a half. It had started with a visceral hunger for each other's bodies and could have ended blissfully if we'd gone to his bedroom at the outset. But we hadn't made it past the living room before our passions took over . . . and then the memories of another cold living-room floor—Dublin Costello's floor, where he'd brutally raped me as a teenager—had flooded my brain, crippling me. What happened after that still amazed me. Doogan could have taken advantage of the situation—I'd known men like that—but instead his once-eager hands gently rocked me. He shushed me and pulled the truth from my past. We'd made it to his bed, yes. But for a night of comfort and peace in the arms of a man who cradled me like the small child I'd become from reliving my pent-up fears and revealing past cruelties.

One night, we didn't even get past first base. And yet Doogan had then turned his life upside down to protect Gran from a crime against the man who had taken my innocence and destroyed my life. I owed Doogan. And I still wanted him.

Add a note to duty list: Find Doogan. With a clear path to home plate.

I forced my gaze away from the rumpled sheets on the bed, looked for any clues to his whereabouts. Doogan lived lean. His dresser drawers contained little more than the essentials: T-shirts, a couple pairs of jeans, socks, and underwear. It appeared he hadn't returned to take anything at all after dumping Dub's body. I rummaged around a bit more, went to the closet, and found a trunk on the back of the floor. The contents had already been rifled through and the lid shoved back on top. If there had been anything of interest inside, the cops had probably taken it. Still, I took it to the bed and pulled out the contents one by one: owners' manuals, electricity bills, a car magazine with a couple pages marked. Nothing that gave me any clue to where he might have gone. Pusser had tracked down his family in Augusta, but no one claimed to have seen him. No surprise there. Pavees never turned on one another.

As I replaced the items, a photo slipped out of the magazine. I turned it over and the air expelled from my lungs. A picture of Doogan, in front of a church altar, with his arm around the shoulders of a beautiful woman with a baby in her arms. The baby wore a baptismal gown. Two other children stood in front of them, a boy and a girl. The boy looked to be about ten. He wore jeans and an untucked shirt. A shock of dark hair fell forward over his defiant eyes. He was wiry, with the same chiseled features as his father. I crumpled the photo, jammed it in my pocket, and turned my back to the bed.

Doogan had children. And a wife.

No wonder he'd left. He had a family. Wife, children . . . another life. He'd satisfied his needs here. He'd gotten answers about his sister's death, seen her killer avenged. He'd protected an elderly Pavee woman from the crime. Then returned to his family. Simple. *It didn't ever really include you, did it, Brynn?*

Wilco pressed against my legs. I brushed him aside and paced the length of the room. I'd thought I'd found someone who cared and took my side . . . now this. My skin prickled with sweat. Wilco nudged me again. I jerked back and kneed him away. He let out a little yelp, but didn't budge. I looked into his eyes, still trained on me—loyal and loving—and felt a sharp twinge in my gut.

*Don't take it out on your dog, Brynn.*

One hand reached out to pet him and the other itched for a drink. A bit of comfort in each hand; that's what I needed.

Doogan had kept a bottle in his cupboard. Would it be there now? I found it, tossed the top on the way back through his trailer, and took a swig. Hot liquid burned down my throat and hit my stomach, radiating

numbing heat outward through my tense muscles.
Another long swig and I felt the sharp edges of my
emotions start to blur and soften.

I plopped on his sofa, dust clouding the air, and
leaned back against the cushion and jammed my hand
into my pocket and pulled out a pill. Just a little extra
something to numb that part of my brain that the
whiskey could never reach. There were four pills left. I
took them all.

Wilco hopped onto the sofa and wriggled his way
onto my lap, nestling his warm nose into the crook of
my neck. We stayed like that for a few minutes, wrapped
up together, and soon my own breathing slowed to match
the steady rhythm of his. I closed my eyes and felt the
Vicodin take effect. It loosened my tense muscles, eased
the pounding in my temples. Noises began to fade
away: a motorcycle engine, distant music, a car horn.
The sounds of Bone Gap were swallowed by the heavy
purple curtain of drug-induced calmness. I exhaled and
let myself go. *I'm staring down at a dead soldier. His
helmet is split open. Brown hair flutters across his
shrapnel-peppered forehead. A gold band shimmers on
his finger. Someone is a widow. I hope they don't have
kids. Mortar shells slice the air and explode nearby.
Wilco whines. A man touches my arm and points to the
waiting stretcher off to the side. I don't want to, but I
grasp the dead soldier's ankles. One boot is missing,
his lower pant legs a jumble of fabric soaked with
blood. A missile whistles through the air. I duck as dust
and rubble rain down and hit my skin like splattered
grease from a hot frying pan. Gran's in the kitchen,
making fried chicken for dinner. I want to go home. I
tighten my grip. The other man gives the signal and*

*we lift. The load is too light. I look down. The soldier is still on the ground . . . but . . . I look at my hands. My throat constricts. A scream pierces the air. My scream. Two bloodied legs—white bones gleaming through mangled flesh—dangle from my grip. . . .*

My cell erupted. I bolted upright, sweat soaked and foggy, my first clear thoughts were of Gran. *Please don't let this be about Gran.*

It wasn't. It was Pusser. "You up?"

I pushed a sleepy Wilco to the side. "Sort of." I flipped my cell over and snuck a peek. It was a little after 5:00 A.M. now. I put it back to my ear.

"I'm at Buck Road Cemetery. I need you and your dog out here now."

"Right now? Why?" My head was swimming. The pills still hadn't worn off. Why did I take so many?

"Just get out here. We've got a problem. A big problem."

# CHAPTER 13

Buck Road Cemetery was a small, private family plot tucked alongside a winding mountain draw. Most of the graves were over a century old, the names and dates barely legible, as was the case in most of these old family plots. Over the years, mourners had joined the buried, leaving few behind to care for the fading tombstones.

"Took you long enough to get here." Pusser walked over from the cemetery's entrance as I opened my car door.

After Pusser's call, I'd downed a couple cups of coffee and taken a hot shower, trying to clear the haze in my brain. It'd been almost a full hour since I got the call. I was still only half sober.

As I got out, I gripped the door, a rush of dizziness hitting me. His hand flew to my shoulder. "Easy, Callahan. You okay?"

"Fine. Just tired. You find a body?" My words were labored, slower than usual. Pusser didn't seem to notice.

"Not yet. Half the graves have been vandalized.

Spray-painted. Same type of symbols that we saw at the cave where Maura was found." He nodded toward an adjacent tree line. "I want you and your dog to work those woods back there."

The sound of a car drew our eyes back to the road. A news van had pulled up, followed by another car, a sedan. The sedan driver raised a camera and snapped off a few shots. Pusser frowned. "Local press for now. But what we've got here is a damn freak show. Dug-up graves and ritualistic killings. That type of stuff sells papers, boosts television ratings. Hell, I'm surprised we haven't already made national news."

"Is Grabowski here?"

"He's on his way."

I pointed at one of the techs, who was photographing a spot not far from an overturned tombstone. Another tech wore a mask and squatted over a camp stove, stirring sulfur cement for casting. "You find some tracks?"

Pusser nodded. "Tire imprint. Looks like they used a motorcycle to push over the grave marker. There's a good shoe print next to it. The rider probably sat idling for a while with his foot on the ground for balance. The heat from the exhaust softened the ground enough to make deep impressions. We're working on other prints, too, but this is a public place—it'll take a while to narrow the field." He squinted up at the sun. "And it's warming up. We'll be screwed if it heats up enough to start melting this snow." He indicated toward my vehicle. "Get your dog out and get started in those woods back there. I want to know if any skeletal remains are still around, or if this sick bastard carried them home for his own personal collection."

I did as I was told. As soon as Wilco's nose hit the cemetery air, he became anxious. His muscles rippled with anticipation. The smell of death. It enticed my dog like nothing else. And Wilco was capable of ferreting all levels of decay, even ancient remnants. Although we'd never trained on historic human remains, I'd seen his abilities firsthand in Iraq while on a recovery mission. It'd happened in Mosul, at an area outside a Badush prison, sometime after the area was occupied by the Islamic State. Wilco and I were on a recovery mission, but instead of finding a soldier, he hit on something else—over seventy Shias massacred and buried in a shallow mass grave over thirty years ago during the rise of the Saddam regime. Hundred-year-old decay wouldn't be an obstacle, either.

Wilco pulled toward a clump of trees off to the left. "What's he doing? The grave's over there."

I gripped the leash tighter. He's drawn to the highest concentration of odors. Low areas, like the grooves around tree roots, gathered more scent. A sudden jerk on the leash pulled me forward. My knees hit the ground hard. I recovered quickly, stood, and brushed the snow from my knees with my free hand. Pusser stared at me. *What's his problem?* I'd stumbled in the snow. Big deal. It was slippery. I was tired. My dog yanked me off balance.

*Focus, Brynn. You can handle this.* I sucked in the cold air, willed my head to clear. I knew better. I could tolerate my liquor, it was the pills that always got me. Or the pills with the liquor. A deadly combination, some doc had told me. Not for me, apparently. *Straighten up, girl. Get a grip, smile.* I frowned. No, that's not right. Nix the smile. Never smile when you look for bodies. I shook my head, tried to look . . . what? Serious? In control? *Right.*

I turned my focus back to Wilco and gave him some slack. He zipped toward the trees, doubling back here and there, scooping up scents and gulping at the odor-laden air. Nothing here. Nothing there. A little something here. Another fifteen yards and he hesitated again, flipped back on himself, raised his snout, and beelined for an old hemlock.

There was a hollow spot at the base of the hemlock's trunk. As a kid, I went through a stage where every nook and cranny in a tree would become a fairy house! A piece of flat bark was the bed; a spent spool of thread became a table; Popsicle sticks were for the door. But that was back before a bed was a lumpy cot, tables served for impromptu autopsies, and Popsicle sticks became tongue depressors that peered down dead men's throats to determine new enemy poisons. So much for the innocence of childhood fantasies.

Wilco ran his nose along the rough edges of the bark, more enthusiastic with every sniff. I bent down and peered closer at the snow-encrusted leaves and twigs that'd gathered in the cavity. Nothing. I straightened my knees. My head spun. I pitched forward and caught myself against the tree.

And dropped the lead rope.

I bent to get it, but Wilco had moved on, his snout sniffing a frenzied line toward the crime scene techs. The leash slithered away like a retreating snake. "Stop." *You idiot—he's deaf!* I motioned my command. He was too engrossed in his task to notice. I went after him, struggled to move in a straight line, got close, tried to snatch his fur, but fell again.

By the time I fumbled to my feet, Wilco had penetrated the crime scene. Several deputies jumped into action, yelling and grabbing for him. Wilco darted from their reach, trampling over the scene area, then back toward me.

Pusser's voice cut through the chaos. "Get your dog, Callahan."

Harris got into the mix. Running at Wilco and waving his hands like an idiot. "Git! Git, dog!" Wilco dodged out of the way, shimmied sideways, and ended up in the print casting, his feet trampling away any semblance of prints below the casting goo.

"Damn it, Callahan. Get your dog!"

I reached him and clipped his lead, ripped off my scarf and started frantically wiping the mixture from his feet. Anxiety over Wilco's feet vanished as I wiped off the goo, swished his feet in the snow and realized he'd be okay. My relief also vanished as hot stares burned into my back. *What to do? What to do?* Embarrassment blazed inside me, but with everyone's eyes glued on my next move, I forced anger to swell and erupt. I snatched Wilco by the back of the neck and got in his face. "Bad boy, bad boy!" My words were for the onlookers, not for my deaf dog.

Wilco lowered himself, his brown eyes darting about nervously. I let go, stood erect. My heart sank. The casting, perhaps the only solid lead we'd take away from this scene, was ruined. Compromised because of me, not my dog. I was the one who'd lost control of the leash. Wilco was only doing his job. Following the scent.

This was my fault.

And Pusser knew it. He drew me aside. "You're frickin' stoned out of your mind, aren't you? Aren't you?"

I couldn't answer.

"Damn you, Callahan. Do you realize what you've done?"

"I'm sorry. I'm—"

"You're *sorry*? Not good enough. That print may have been our best chance to track this perp. It's gone now. A murderer may get off because of you. Or worse yet, he may murder again." His head snapped upward, his eyes narrowing in on one of the reporters and his cameraman, whose lens had taken in every action at the crime scene. "And guess what? This whole fiasco is going to play out on the evening news."

# CHAPTER 14

*January 4*
*School sucks. The settled kids think I'm a*
*freak. Only a few of them will talk to me and*
*that's only because they're bottom-feeders*
*like me. I can't wait for us to get out of here.*
*I almost have enough money now. Just a lit-*
*tle more and I can take Nevan someplace*
*far away where we can live happily ever*
*after. . . .*

Nothing about high school ever changes. The same
sounds, the same smells, the same gray lockers and
off-white linoleum floors. A trophy case, classrooms, a
squeaky-floor gym with side bleachers caked with
dried chewing gum under each bench seat. The kids
were the same, too: the geeks, the jocks, the thespians,
and the mean girls. The preps in their cardigans and the
Goths whose black garb expressed their inner angst.
Then there were the fringers—on the outside, whether
by choice or from being pushed out of the normal

clique groups. They walked alone, kept their heads down, dressed to blend in, and worked hard to get through each day unnoticed. Their route through high school was the most difficult and loneliest to navigate. I'd been a fringer. Maura was a fringer. All Travellers, by default, are fringers. And because we don't conform to the norm, we're easy targets.

Had Maura been an easy target? Or did she go down fighting?

The journal entry brought back buried emotions for me. I knew how Maura felt. A Pavee girl in a public high school was no easy deal. I'd suffered the same angst in high school, worked hard to escape this place, all of Bone Gap, actually.

Yet, here I was again.

My eyes roamed the hallway. Nothing had really changed. "I hated high school." The words were out before I could stop them.

Grabowski looked my way, a slight curl playing along the edges of his lips. We sat outside the high-school counselor's office on a hard bench, waiting to do an interview. Wilco was on lead and seated at my feet, sucking up the attention thrown his way by passing students. "Let me guess," Grabowski said. "You didn't quite fit in with the popular crowd."

I closed my mouth. *Great job, Brynn. Misfit, fringer, loner . . . just one more tidbit of information for Grabowski to use in his profile of me. Right after druggie and all-around screwup.*

Pusser had tasked Grabowski with babysitting me after my all-too-public destruction of the cemetery crime scene. I would have objected, but Pusser clearly didn't want me in his sight anymore that morning.

Maybe never again. My primary job was to act as handler of a human-remains tracking dog and I'd failed Wilco miserably. Not to mention the department. And in front of cameras that could—

". . . something's missing," Grabowski said.

"What?"

"Anger."

"Oh." I tried to wrap my head around what he'd been talking about—and what I should be thinking about—the case. We'd just left the same fast-food joint we'd eaten at the other morning, and a stack of hotcakes and a gallon of hot coffee later my leftover pill buzz had worn off. Only my misery over screwing up my job still had me distracted. *Get it together, Brynn. Find a plausible lead and you just might save your drunken ass yet.* "So, what could be angrier than stabbing someone's heart out with a sticking knife?"

Grabowski paused. I glanced sideways, studying him. He sported a two-day growth on his face, which was more hair than he had on his head. On certain guys, bald was sexy. Not on Grabowski. His skull was speckled and rippled with wrinkles like an overly ripe cantaloupe. Besides the crappy bluegrass music he'd foisted on me and Wilco in his Crown Vic driving over here, I knew little about him. Married? Had a family? Mr. Profiler had my full number, especially after this morning; I didn't even know his first digit.

Finally he said, "I assume most of what you dealt with in the military were casualties. The motive is usually obvious."

"Yeah. Kill or get killed."

"Exactly. I've investigated a lot of homicides. Some

stand out as angry. Repetitious wounds like multiple stabs to the heart, mutilated genitals, gouged-out eyes . . . those are the types of wounds that indicate anger. A single, well-placed stab wound to the heart seems deliberate, not angry. That's why I don't think the Anderson kid is our guy."

"I'm not following you."

"Hatch's motive would be anger, right? She was pregnant. She'd trapped him."

"Maybe Hatch wasn't so much angry, just running scared. Trying to cover his tracks. A smart kid could figure the occult angle as a cover-up. Plan it out."

Grabowski shook his head. "He lives an entitled life, right?"

"Yeah."

"Gets away with everything. Mommy and Daddy make sure of it."

I agreed.

"That type of kid is used to being in control, or being able to manipulate his way out of things. But a pregnancy is the woman's deal. If she wanted to have the baby, she would, and she could tell the whole world it was his kid, prove it even, and tie him up for years with child support payments. For the first time in his life, he'd have lost all control. He'd be angry about that, believe me."

"Maybe." What he was saying made sense, but I liked Hatch for this crime. Period.

The school counselor's office door opened and a secretary ushered us inside. We were searching for a link between the killer and Maura, and the best way to do that was to dig into her life, especially the time leading up to her disappearance. If we could piece together a timeline, we'd be one step closer to finding the perp.

But we got zilch from the counselor. Maura was a mediocre student, he'd told us. Never a behavior problem, but not academically motivated, either. She was quiet, kept to herself, a bit of a loner, one of those kids who flew under the radar. We'd heard the same from most of the school staff. Some hadn't really considered her much until her death. Like she was simply a shadow, slipping in and out of their days, visible but not really noticed. Maura the wallflower.

Until she wasn't.


Most of these kids hated cops. Evident by the cold stares we got as we moved through the hallways and out to the crowded parking lot, packed with kids heading out for lunch. High schoolers, especially minority youths, mistrusted the police. I got that. I was a minority, of sorts, and had grown up constantly exposed to that sentiment of mistrust. Pavees had always viewed the police as more of enforcers than protectors, and many cops had earned that negative attitude. But not all. Stereotypes. I'd lived with them my whole life and I'd come to understand that, whether propagated by skin color, age, affluence, or ethnic background, the need for superiority over others was an unabashed universal truth. Cop or civilian, black, white, brown, settled, gypsy, straight, gay, Jew or Christian, it didn't matter. Bigotry transcended all divisions. Haters were going to hate. Get used to it. But a few students reached out to pet Wilco as we walked toward the car. Wilco would be all Mr. Happy, getting his pats and soaking up any "pretty boy" cooed his way. He was, by far, the department's best public-relations tool.

We cut through a row of parked cars to avoid the crowds. A mistake on my part. The temptation proved too much for my dog. Three cars in, he stopped, turned his backside on an old Buick's rear tire, and peed. I yanked his leash. Two feet later, he turned again. I yanked again.

Grabowski fidgeted with his keys. "Is he going to hit every tire, or what?"

I gave Wilco another impatient tug. He ignored me, straining instead to reach another tire. I gave up and let him pull me that way. He'd eventually run dry.

While he left his pee-mail behind, I scanned the lot. My eye caught some movement off in the distance by the football bleachers. I craned my neck and squinted. Just some kid messing around. But something made me look closer. Not just some kid, but Winnie Joyce. She was talking animatedly to someone, but a bank of bleachers obscured my view. Who was she talking with? "Hey. You see that? It's the Joyce girl . . . ," but Grabowski had already moved on, didn't hear me.

I looked back. Winnie had shrunk down into her puffy coat, her blond braid swinging back and forth as she shook her head. She was scared. *Something isn't right. What's going on?* I headed across the lot and toward the field, pulling Wilco with me. He resisted, reluctant to leave any dry tires behind, but I reined him in and dragged him along. I was about fifty yards away when Hatch Anderson popped into my view. He loomed over Winnie, his gestures exaggerated with anger. I picked up my pace. People around me were busy going about their business: talking, laughing, getting into their cars . . .

Hatch grabbed Winnie by the collar. He was in her face, his features twisted with anger as he shook her. My blood boiled. Years of encounters with abusive men—in the Marines, in the clan, in my own home, even—worked their way to the surface. *Breathe.* That's what my VA docs told me to do. *Control your inner monster.*

*Screw them.* I moved faster, ready to put the little jerk in his place.

Ten yards away. He squeezed her throat. "You crazy bitch. How could you?"

I dropped Wilco's leash and charged in. "Stop!"

He turned, his fist raised. I grabbed his arm and twisted it backward, reached for my cuffs. He resisted, yanking me off balance. I fell against his car, rammed my elbow, and dropped the cuffs. Wilco scurried under my feet, snapping and snarling, ready to tear into the guy. I recovered and reached for Hatch again.

Out of nowhere, Grabowski appeared and jerked Winnie out of the way before coming after Hatch from behind. Hatch anticipated his move, threw an elbow, and connected to Grabowski's jaw. He went down hard.

*I'm really ticked now.* I lunged forward, got a piece of Hatch's jacket this time, yanked the SOB forward, and slammed my forehead into his nose. *Crack.*

He clasped his hands around his nose and went dull-eyed. Blood trickled between his fingers. He sank to the ground and hunched forward. Blood ran from his left nostril and down his ski jacket like red spidery veins. I snatched the cuffs from the ground and locked him down.

I looked up. We'd drawn a crowd. A dozen kids had closed in on the scene. They heckled and called out names: "Police brutality!" "Frickin' sow!" Cell phones were aimed my way.

Grabowski slowly stood, shaking his head and rubbing his jaw.

"You okay?" I asked.

He worked his jaw a couple times and leaned in, just inches from my ear, his eyes darting between Hatch and the cell phones, then back to me. "You're really in trouble now, Callahan. Did you have to head-butt the mayor's kid?"

"What? He resisted arrest, assaulted a cop. Was I supposed to play nice? Besides, it's your fault, you know."

"And how's that?"

"You were supposed to be babysitting me. Remember?"

# CHAPTER 15

Winnie slouched in the straight-back chair, sucking on a strand of stringy brown hair. Grabowski and I sat across from her, Grabowski all serious-like, pen in hand, ready and capable. Me? I licked my lips and let them curl into a Cheshire cat grin, not even feeling a teensy-weensy bit guilty as I'd replayed the sickening *thunk* of cracking bone in my mind. It'd felt good, damn good, to bust that scumbag's nose. I'd do it again in a heartbeat.

Hatch had been transported to the hospital and witnesses interviewed. They all claimed police brutality. No doubt I was in trouble. I expected it to catch up to me at any moment. Until then, I wanted to get as much out of Winnie as possible. "Hatch was pushing you around. Why?"

She picked at a piece of loose laminate on the edge of the table.

"Come on, Winnie. He was choking you."

Her knees bounced. Her eyes darted toward Grabowski. Nervous and twitchy, she was like a caged animal. And a man, or more accurately a settled man, a cop, made her feel uncomfortable. I understood. So did Grabowski. He grabbed his chair and moved out of her line of sight to the corner of the room. I changed my approach and kept talking, softer this time, small talk about this and that, until her shoulders relaxed and her hands quieted. I reached out and touched her arm. "Why was Hatch so angry at you?"

Pick, pick, pick. She worked the laminate.

I glanced back at Grabowski's self-satisfied, smug look, one that said, "See, I was right." He'd already pegged Hatch as the angry type. Too angry to be our killer. In Grabowski's analytical mind, Maura's killing was too methodical, too calculated, for someone harboring rage. Maybe so. But to me, most killings were about anger in some form: revenge, jealousy, hate. Murderers were angry people. Period.

"Listen, Winnie. You and Maura grew up together."

Tears built along the edges of her eyes, she quit picking and started twirling a strand of hair. Back into her mouth it went.

"Hatch isn't even one of us." My tone was hushed, Pavee to Pavee. "You don't owe him anything. But Maura? She was your best friend."

"I know. I know." Tears flowed now.

She knew something, I could sense it, but what? Could Hatch have used the occult symbols to try to cover his crime? Did Winnie know something about that, and had Hatch been trying to shut her up?

"Are you into the occult?"

Her eyes widened. "The what?"

"Occult. Devil worship."

"No. Of course not." Her eyes darted to the door. I'd touched a nerve.

"Kids your age sometimes mess around with stuff like that. You know, Ouija boards and things. Just for fun."

"Maybe other kids, but not me. I don't do that type of stuff." Her voice turned high and whiney, words clotting in the back of her throat. "Why are you asking me this?"

Grabowski cleared his throat. I changed directions. "Tell me what happened that night."

She swiped her cheek and looked away.

"You're scared. I get it. But you need to tell me what you know, Winnie. More girls could die."

Her shoulders opened up and she turned slightly in her chair, fully facing me. I'd found a soft spot. "Maura and me, we told our mothers we were going shopping that Friday after school and then sleeping over at each other's houses, but we went out to Stoners' Draw. You know the place?"

I gave her a jittery nod, memories flooding my brain. Oh, yes, I knew Stoners' Draw well. Stoners' Draw, which was really Old Fire Tower Road, a bit off Old Highway 2, but over the years, it'd become a popular spot for kids smoking pot and whatever else it took to get stoned. Hence the name. Also the spot where, at fifteen, I went halfies on a bottle of whiskey with Jimmy what's-his-name, pierced my navel, and danced half naked in the moonlight. Years ago, a decade and a half before any of the real humiliations of life had caught up with me.

"Just you and Maura?"

"No. Hatch went up there, too."

"Did he bring anything?"

"Just some beer." She shrugged and looked away.

I lowered my chin, captured her gaze again. *Soft, Brynn. Be soft.* "And what else?"

She started crying again. Wrenching sobs. I rubbed the back of my neck. If he'd brought something else, I wasn't going to get it out of her. Not yet, anyway. What I needed in here was Wilco, not Grabowski hunkering like a vulture in the corner. Wilco recognized grief and pain and had his way of reacting, with a look or nudge or a sympathetic whimper, that calmed anyone. But he was so keyed up after the Hatch incident: pacing, lying down, getting up and pacing again, whining. . . . I finally walked him down the hall to visit Parks for a while. She had a giant bowl of doggy biscuits on her desk. He was happy and scttlcd; still, I wished he were here to soothe Winnie, and me. I shifted in my seat and glanced around the room: the floor, the ceiling, the wall, the hole in the wall where a felon had punched his fist through. And people think I have anger issues. I looked back to Winnie; she was still crying.

I tugged her arm, trying to bring her back around. "So you three partied for a while."

"Yes. And Maura and Hatch . . . they . . ."

"They paired up."

Her expression changed. Her lips pressed thin, her nostrils flared. She'd gone from misery to . . . to what? Rage? It dawned on me. "You like Hatch, don't you, Winnie?"

Her eyes bore into mine.

I sat back. A high-school love triangle. Girl likes boy, boy likes girl's best friend. I should have seen this coming.

"And Maura knew I liked him. I couldn't believe she'd do that to me. And she already had a boyfriend. A fiancé. But she didn't care. She was like that. She got a rush out of flirting with him." Snot dripped between her nose and lips. She swiped it away with her shirtsleeve.

"Had she been with Hatch before?"

She met my gaze with a bewildered look. No doubt Hatch and Maura had been together before. More than likely, Hatch was the baby's father, at least Maura thought so. Winnie's best friend had been messing around with her boy crush for a while, and she had no clue. *Better to back down from this before she puts it together and gets all worked up again.* "Why was Hatch so angry with you?"

"He told me to lie. He didn't want the cops to know that he and Maura were together that night."

"But you decided to tell the truth. Why?"

"I thought with Maura gone, and if I covered for him, he'd see . . ."

He'd appreciate her. Like her, even. Poor kid. She had a long ways to go when it came to understanding men. "But he didn't."

Her lips tightened. "No. He ate lunch today with Shelby Reynolds. She was practically sitting on his lap. He kept touching her butt."

*Out with the old, in with the new.* "So you planned to rat him out to the cops."

She clamped her mouth shut. *Uh-oh. Too much,*

*Brynn.* I sighed and sat back for the next couple minutes while she vacillated between seething and sobbing.

This girl was a tornado of emotions. Seventeen, the age where teen angst and womanly desire collide to make or break the young female. Some navigate this time gracefully; others turn into manipulative snarks and spend a lifetime striking out at any female they see as a threat. It sounded like Maura was that type of girl, throwing herself at Winnie's would-be love. Had Winnie had enough? Had she been pushed too far? Did she know Maura was pregnant, possibly with Hatch's baby?

*Time to get serious.* "Did you take a baseball bat to Maura's car?"

Her jaw went slack. "No. Why? What do you mean?"

"Someone vandalized her car that evening."

"It wasn't me."

"She was making out with the boy she knew you liked. You must've been angry."

She lowered her eyes. Something wasn't adding up.

"It was cold out that night, Winnie. Snowing. Where were Maura and Hatch making out?"

"In the back seat."

"With you in the car?"

She looked disgusted. "No. I got out and went for a walk." She shifted in her seat. "I took the bottle of beer and left."

"You left? Where'd you go?" Stoners' Draw was an isolated stretch of mountain road. There's only one way up and one way down. The ideal park-and-party spot for kids in the area, but not so great if you were on foot.

"I went to a friend's house. He lives up that way."

*Really?* There used to be a few houses up that way, but most of them were long-ago abandoned. "What friend?"

"You don't know him."

I let it go for now. She continued: "When I got there, I called Nevan and told him where he could find his fiancée." A little smirk played along the corner of her lips. She enjoyed causing trouble. Gone was the withering flower, replaced by little Ms. Mean Girl. Who was the real Winnie? I had no idea. This interrogation was giving me mental whiplash.

"Did Nevan go up there?"

Her expression changed. Yet again. "I . . . I don't know. I stayed with my friend for a while. We drank and played video games, and then he drove me home."

"So you don't know if Nevan showed up."

"I . . . I wish I knew." Her eyes rounded with worry.

*Give me a break, girl.* I slid the legal pad and pen her way. "Write down this friend's name. We'll need to verify your statement."

She scribbled the name and passed the paper back to me.

*Jacob Fisher.*

# CHAPTER 16

Parks sat at her desk, with Wilco curled around her feet. "Harris just came by. He was talking about you."

"Yeah? You don't actually listen to that dumb ass, do you??"

"That you busted the mayor's boy's nose."

"He deserved it."

"No doubt. Still . . ."

"How's my dog?" I pulled up a seat next to her.

She held up an empty bag of doggy treats. "He's not a dog. He's a pig."

I squinted. Chicken Chews. *Great.* Chicken still turned my stomach, but my dog? Inside Wilco's contented stomach, chicken chews churned into chicken farts. "I just got done interviewing the Joyce girl."

"I did that already."

"I know. She lied to you."

"Figures. They all lie to me. I must look easy."

I glanced at her profile. Hardly what most suspects would call "easy," let alone what guys might refer to that way. Hair cinched into a tight bun, a creased uniform, an even gaze, and a serious set to her jaw, a straight talker. Yet chubby cheeks and laugh lines hurt her tough don't-mess-with-me image. A capable cop, but did she have the guts to press suspects where it hurts? Doubtful. I skimmed the monitor in front of her. The Tennessee Incident Based Report System (TIBRS) was up on her screen. "What are you searching?"

"Pusser has me double-checking evidence from the crime scene you and Wilco turned up the other day."

"They found something?"

"A bullet. Pulled from the skull. Thirty-eight Special ammo. So I'm thinking a small revolver, a .38 or 357." She clicked on the keyboard. "I'm going back about five years in the database, just to see what turns up. A long shot. Probably a waste of time. But you never know."

Gran's gun was a nickel-plated Smith & Wesson 36 J Frame, chambered with .38 Special ammo. Easy for her small hands and compact enough to carry in her purse, or pocket, if needed. There might be cases with similar guns. I hoped there would be—anything to derail this investigation. But nothing would turn up linking the gun to Gran. She hadn't fired it before plugging Doogan full of bullets. Or . . . had she? Had she used it in the years I was away? I'd have to ask her if anyone had ever seen her . . . *Damn!* Last year, when the press was hounding us, Gran waved her gun in front of the cameras. Did that air on the news segment? I'd never seen it. Meg told me it took Uncle Paddy and Jarvis stepping in to finally get the cameras to back off, but had they been rolling when Gran stuck her gun in their faces? I had to know. Was that the television station out of Greenville? *Ah, crap.* The local paper ran the story, too; that nosey reporter and her camerman had been glued to the porch that day as well. Not that it was proof of anything. Just the kind of connection that slaps handcuffs on Travellers. A Pavee with a small revolver that took .38 Special ammo. Another Pavee murdered with .38 Special ammo. To settled law, that kind of "one plus one" equaled "case closed."

"Brynn? You okay?"

I blinked. "Yeah. Why?"

"I was talking to you. The Joyce girl? You said there was something—" Her focus shifted across the room. I turned. Pusser was coming my way. Mayor Anderson shadowed him, slightly off step, his thick gut straining his shirt's buttons. Out of nowhere, Harris appeared, coffee mug in hand and a stupid grin on his face, anticipating the drama about to unfold, no doubt. Maybe I should've asked him if he needed a doughnut to go along with his coffee, just a little snack for enjoying the show. Or a scone perhaps? Or a smack in the mouth. I stood and faced the approaching entourage head-on, my good-soldier face ready for the assault. Fearless. Stoic.

My stomach churned.

Three months. Three lousy months on the force and I was getting canned. Temper issues, flashbacks, can't play well with others . . . Why can't I get my act together? Hell, I'd blown a job as a security guard at a stupid storage facility in only one month. Three months looked like a lifetime career by my current standards. But this job . . . I really needed this job. No, I *wanted* it. And I'd be damned if I was giving it up without a fight.

Pusser stopped a few feet in front of me. Behind him, Mayor Anderson stared me down, arms crossed, face flushed. I scrambled for something, anything. "Some more info just came in regarding the case. We should probably talk in private before—"

He ignored my words and, with a jerk of his head for me to follow, he moved toward his office, Mayor Anderson on his heels. I followed. Behind my back, Harris laughed.

Inside his office, Pusser started with a slick lead-in. "Deputy Callahan, the mayor wanted to meet with you to discuss—"

"You broke my son's nose."

I looked to Pusser for help. Nothing. A regular Mr. Poker Face.

"I said, you broke my son's frickin' nose. You don't have anything to say about that?" His jowls quivered, spittle on his fat lips.

"I'm sorry?" My words came out more like a question than an apology.

He slammed his fist down on Pusser's desk like he wanted to drive his knuckles through my skull. "Bullshit. This is the second time you've gone after my boy. You got something against us, some sort of personal vendetta? You had no right to go to his school and—"

"Your son resisted arrest! He took a swing at me. I had every right to defend myself."

Pusser's head swiveled. "Careful what you say, Callahan. The altercation was recorded on a dozen cell phones."

"Good. Then you'll see that what I'm saying is true." I looked at the mayor. "Hatch brought this on himself. He was out of control, dangerous. He assaulted another officer. I was justified in using force."

Mayor Anderson jabbed his index finger in my direction. "I want her dismissed."

Pusser's jaw tightened. "No."

"What?" Anderson's eyes bulged. He turned red jowls on the sheriff.

"No. I'll have DOJ review the recordings. If they rule that Officer Callahan used excessive force, I'll take appropriate action."

"I'm warning you, Frank. Get rid of her. Didn't you watch last night's news? She lost control of her dog. Compromised evidence at the scene. It was all over the television. An embarrassment to *your* department. To *my* town. She's a hothead. A drunk. A liability."

My jaw clenched. I'd been called worse. I could handle any hateful smear. Trouble was, in this case, I couldn't argue with it.

Pusser leaned forward, his tone cold. "A drunk? Really? You got proof of that?"

Anderson turned beet red. "My son's no killer. He had nothing to do with this. If you people pursue this, you'll be—"

"Pursue what? The truth? That's our job."

Anderson stood. "We're done discussing this, Frank. From here on out, you can talk to my attorney."

He slammed the door on his way out.

I blew out a long breath. "Thanks for defending me, boss."

"Don't thank me." He sat back in his chair, his voice even colder now as he looked up at me. "I agree with the mayor. You're a drunk. And probably an addict, too."

I swallowed hard. It wasn't like that. He didn't get it. Drinking was . . . My throat felt dry, begging for a belt of Black Label or a cold beer. I forced myself not to lick my lips. Okay. So maybe I drank a bit. But the meds? The doctors prescribed those for me. At least they used to. My usual VA doc wanted me off them, so I found another one who understood me better. Or I thought he did. Last visit, he mentioned something about a new pain-pill policy, how I might have to taper off the meds or look at alternative therapy. What a crock. As if acupuncture or yoga was going to touch my pain. *No, Doc, there is no alternative for vets like me. We're home, but we're still fighting a war: the scarring, the physical pain, the anxiety that comes with the flashbacks.*

The VA docs didn't get it. Pusser didn't get it. No one got it. I avoided his accusations, looked him straight on. "I have info for you," I said. A lead. A way to redeem myself. "Winnie gave up the whole story." I sat and relayed what she'd said about Hatch and Maura making out. How she took off and met up with the Fisher kid. Everything.

"Good work." His tone was flat.

"You're going to question Hatch about it, right? He lied before, he was with her that night. The night she disappeared. We need to know if the Meath kid actually showed up. My guess is that the mayor's kid—"

"I'll take care of it."

"And Jacob Fisher?"

"I'll put Parks on the Fisher kid. See what he knows. Maybe he'll confirm some of what the Joyce girl told you. Or maybe she's an unreliable witness."

I bristled. "Because she's a Pavee."

"No. Because she's already lied once."

I shifted in my chair. "If it's all the same, I'd like to question the Fisher kid."

"No. Parks will do it. I want you to take the afternoon off. Go visit your grandmother."

"My cousin is with her. I don't need the afternoon off."

"Take it, anyway." He shuffled a few papers. "And you're going to see a shrink. I'm going to get an evaluation set up."

*"An evaluation?"*

"Yeah. See if you're fit for duty."

A decorated combat veteran, body maimed and brain fried from service to my country, and I get this kind of crap thrown at me? *Cool it, Brynn.* "Hey, it was just a little booze. I'd tossed a few back before bed. My grandmother just had a stroke. We're in the middle of a gruesome killing of young women. Who wouldn't have a drink? And the call came in early. That's all that was. I'm a good cop. You know that."

He didn't bother looking up from his papers. "Go home, Callahan."

# CHAPTER 17

I called the hospital to check on Gran. The nurse told me she'd been discharged, so I headed home. Meg met me in the front room. I made no mention of my work problems. I could picture her shooting me one of those vindicated looks and launching into another lecture about the booze and pills. I'd just got that from Pusser. I couldn't take much more. Especially not from Meg. I kept things on neutral ground. "They discharged Gran early?"

"Her tests came back okay. The doctor thinks she'd recover better at home. She's sleeping now. And don't you dare go wake her. It took me most of an hour to get her settled down." The lines around her eyes were more pronounced than usual.

"You look exhausted." Wilco pranced at my feet, wanting food. I brushed him aside with my foot.

"I am. You didn't check in today. Weren't you worried about her?"

"Of course I was. I just got tied up with work stuff. And I knew you were with her." My eyes darted toward the back room. "Is there something you're not telling me?"

Meg backed down a little. "No, she's better. Physically."

"*Physically?* What's that mean?"

"She's upset."

"I understand. This whole thing must be upsetting to her. And she'll have to make some changes: diet, exercise—"

"That's not what I mean. She's upset about you."

*Not this again.* I rolled my eyes and pushed past her to the kitchen, where I scooped a cupful of kibble for Wilco. He pranced around his bowl, eager to eat.

Meg pursued me. "Don't you want to know why?"

"Let me guess. I drink too much." How much more of this did I have to put up with today? I threw it in her face by retrieving my usual bottle of Jack from the cupboard. I skipped the ice and poured. Hell, if I'm admitting I'm a drunk, I might as well have a drink on it.

Meg watched me with a look I'd seen a lot of lately, smug and judgmental. She'd always been my antithesis: pretty and delicate to my strong features and dark looks, dutiful to my rebellious nature, sober to my drunkenness . . . It went on and on. I threw back my drink, let the heat of the amber liquid follow down its all-too-familiar path.

She shook her head in disgust.

I chuckled, poured another, and carried it to the front window, sipping while I took in the neighborhood. A new couple had recently moved into the trailer across from us. Older, childless. She was nice enough, but he was a crotchety old bastard. They never drew their curtains, or maybe they didn't like curtains. Whatever.

I could see the old man in his recliner. His hand tucked inside his waistband, his head bobbing with sleep. There was a rhythm to his head bobs, a sort of swaying roll punctuated by a chin bounce against his chest. I watched and sipped, the Jack's warm balm spreading to my limbs, softening the tension. I was tired, too. It'd been a long day. I simply wanted to drink, go to bed . . .

Meg was relentless. "Gran's upset about what you're doing to the Meaths."

I squeezed my eyes shut for a second. *Oh, that.*

"Everyone's talking, Brynn. They say you're betraying us. Your own people."

There must have been a noise next door. The old man startled, sat forward, looked around. He wiped at his nose, then dug in knuckle deep, extracting his finger and studying it curiously, before wiping it along the side of his jeans, sitting back and nodding back off.

*The things people do when they think no one is watching.*

"Are you listening?"

"Yeah. I heard you. Nevan is a suspect. I'm just doing my job."

"That's the problem. *Your job.*"

"I'm a cop. It's what I do. It's what I did before, back in the Marines. Nobody cared then."

"That was different."

"How's that?" I didn't need this conversation. I needed to sleep.

"You weren't going after Pavees then."

"Nevan Meath isn't the only one we're looking at."

"Still, you said it yourself, he's a suspect. How could you even think one of your own could do something so evil?"

I turned and glared. "Have you forgotten what happened last year, Meg?"

She flinched. Two murders, and she was almost the third, and a Pavee with the victims' blood on his hands.

"Don't be stupid, Meg. Evil permeates every facet of society. Even ours. Especially ours." I'd experienced it firsthand. So had she, but she chose to deny it. She'd erected a wall in her own head, a barrier against the ugliness of reality. I understood. I'd spent a lifetime trying to build walls in my mind.

They always crumbled under the weight of truth.

I took another sip of whiskey. *Forget blocking the pain. It's much easier to drown it.*

She continued speaking. "It's your choice, Brynn. Call it what you want. Your duty, justice . . . whatever. Just know that Gran is paying for your decisions."

I stared down at my glass. My drink was already gone. I wanted another. "You think I did this to her? Caused her illness?" *Go ahead, Meg. Say it.* Guilt ate at my gut enough already, considering our conversation when she'd collapsed: her murder of Dublin, Doogan's help to cover up for her. The gun . . . Oh yeah . . . the gun. And now they were looking for that, and—

"She didn't get invited to Violet Ferrin's baby shower."

I laughed. "The Ferrins have always been snobs."

"And nobody called on her at the hospital. Her own best friend won't even talk to her. These people are all she has."

"She has us. We're her family." The words half caught in my throat. I hadn't called in on Gran today. Too busy waking up sloshed, screwing up a crime scene, breaking the friggin' mayor's son's nose, and getting called on the carpet by my boss. Maybe she was right: Gran could count on her community better than on me. And now I'd screwed that up for her as well.

"She feels like an outcast."

"What do you want me to do? Go back to working at the Sleep Easy?" After my colossal screwup, that's what I might end up doing, anyway.

"She was lucky. This could have been so much worse. It might be a full stroke next time."

I gripped my glass tighter. "Don't you think I know that?" I turned away, set my glass down on the coffee table. "I'm going out for a while. I'll be back in a couple hours."

She followed me into the kitchen, where I roused Wilco from his full-stomach, deep sleep. "Where are you going?"

"Out."

"To the bar, no doubt. Go ahead, Brynn. Go lose yourself in a bottle. Don't worry. I'll take care of things here." She crossed her arms snug against her model-perfect figure, her red curls jostled on her shoulder, and that pathetic look of self-righteousness on that pretty face of hers. God knows I wanted to hate her.

I grabbed my grubby parka and my dog and headed out the door.

# CHAPTER 18

I pulled out the photo taken at the church and turned it over in my hand. I'd looked at it a half-dozen times since I'd found it. Each time, my eyes were drawn to the woman in the photo—long hair, even features, porcelain skin—my fingers traced the crumpled skin on my own neck and my cheeks burned with embarrassment and a hot flush of anger. That night, the time Doogan and I had shared together, I thought . . . I wanted to believe . . . but no, it hadn't meant anything to him.

Wilco whined and climbed from the back seat to sit next to me. He panted and stared at me, his ears spiked like two black horns and his warm doggy breath filling the car. Meg was wrong. I wasn't heading to the pub. Not yet, anyway. I was heading up to Stoners' Draw, the last place where Maura had been seen alive.

*Get over yourself, Brynn. Separate your emotions.* That's what they'd taught us in the Marines. And that's what I'd do now. Forget what could have been and focus on the case. Protect my grandmother. Save my job. Simple.

I smoothed the photo over my dash. I'd realized earlier that I recognized the church. I'd been there several times for weddings and baptisms of distant cousins who lived in the North Augusta area. There was a huge Pavee settlement there. More than likely, Doogan's wife was part of that clan. She could lead me to Doogan, and eventually to the gun. I needed her address, but I couldn't use anyone in the department to help me get it. Too risky. But maybe Colm could help me. I snapped a photo and sent it his way.

I parked my vehicle at the end of Stoners' Draw and let Wilco out. He took a quick pee and followed me the rest of the way uphill to where the old fire tower loomed on the horizon. It was originally erected in the early 1900s when most of this area was designated Cherokee National Forest land. Some twenty years ago, the land transferred to private ownership. After that, the tower was abandoned and neglected. The harsh elements had beaten it down to a mere ghostly skeleton of its original structure. Now this area was nothing more than a party spot for local teens.

I moved quickly. There was only about an hour and a half of sunlight left, which meant that if Pusser was going to send someone out to investigate the scene today, they'd be here soon. Not that he'd be able to tell much. Probably a dozen or more kids had been up here partying since the night Maura disappeared. Any evidence would be compromised. But Pusser was thorough. And as soon as he read the report of my interview with Winnie, he'd send someone out to secure the area until he could conduct a search at daybreak.

He'd be ticked if he knew I was here. Not that it mattered at this point. He was already mad at me. Besides, this was my case and Maura Keene was one of my own. Telling me to stand down was like a slap in the face. Pusser always relied on me to run interference between the Travellers and settled law. Tensions had never been higher. The sooner this case was resolved, the better.

I had a theory. I didn't want to be right, but I needed to know for sure. Unfortunately, I found it. A large oil spot on the edge of the clearing near the head of a trail. A black smudge on the frozen tundra of garbage and waste: beer cans, broken bottles, fast-food packaging, spent condoms. According to the perp from the cockfight, Nevan's truck leaked oil. I crouched down and took a closer look. The oil could've come from any car, but my instinct told me that Nevan was here that night. This oil was from his truck.

Wilco brushed against my thigh and started nosing around the spot. I pushed him away and stood. I had what I came for; what I hadn't wanted to find, and I needed to get out of here. I bent to tap my dog on the head, then stopped. He'd moved on toward a large stone cropping up ahead, happily scooping up benign scents as he went: dog urine here and there, a whiff of snowshoe hare, maybe, and animal scat. Who knew what smells his powerhouse of a nose detected? He drew closer and closer to the outlook rock. Several footpaths ran down the mountainside from there, like veins from an artery. It was easy to underestimate the severity of these trails, but I'd hiked this area as a kid. They started off as a gentle slope, but farther down the mountain, the trail morphed into steep rock faces, narrow ledges, and loose rocks that made for a difficult trek under the best conditions. Add snow and ice, and the trails became treacherous. One slip could be fatal. And Wilco's nose was leading him in that direction.

Snow crunched beneath my feet like dry crackers as I hurried toward him. Wilco's fawn-colored body snaked away from me, his black-masked face hovering centimeters above the frozen ground. I quickened my pace and caught up to him just as he reached the rocky shelf that hung about a hundred feet above the canyon below. I attached his lead and crouched down next to him, delivering whispers on deaf ears. "Good boy, good boy. You need to be more careful."

I stood and looked out over the valley. The sky was big and blue and clear up here. Sunlight poured down and transformed the white landscape into a blanket of thousands of sparkly diamonds. A glimpse of "Heaven on Earth." And for a second, I became caught up in the beauty, and the constant tension that hummed through me dissipated. I felt peaceful and whole and clean. But then a cold wind whipped around me and the day rushed back over me: Gran's illness, the mayor's allegations, the look on Pusser's face when he sent me home. *Home.* Where Meg and Gran judged my every move. Questioned my loyalty and judged my choices.

I pulled my parka tighter against my body, closed my eyes, and squeezed out the beauty around me. I remembered who I was, where I'd been, what I'd seen, and what I'd done . . . and not just in war, because the things I'd seen and done in those foreign lands were commissioned, ordered, expected. . . . It was the other things I'd experienced since then. Ugliness seeped into the recesses of my mind: rotting flesh, bloodied bodies . . .

death and more death. It continuously swooped into my life like a rider on a pale horse, stealing my sanity, and robbing me of any hope for peace. . . .

No one understood. As a young Pavee, I'd lost my innocence; as a Marine, I'd lost my mind. The only peace I'd found since then was at the bottom of a bottle. And now, they were trying to take that away from me, too.

I opened my eyes. I was standing too close to the edge. A chill of danger fingered my spine even as I laughed and my voice echoed back at me. It sounded weird, tired, too thin.

*Back away, Brynn. This isn't safe.*

But I didnt. I found the edge alluring. Fascinating. I always have.

*A couple more steps. That's all it'll take.*

Several of my Marine sisters had already taken the final leap. At times, I envied them. I'd tried eating my gun, slitting my wrist, swallowing it all away with . . . but I'd always backed out.

*Coward! Well, here's another chance.*

The sparkling snow below beckoned. So beautiful. So peaceful. Why not embrace that peace? Because Gran needed me? Or did she? All the stress I caused her, the worry, the tension . . . no wonder she'd had a stroke. And she had Meg, anyway, a good Pavee girl, to stay by her side.

*She'd be better off without me. Everyone would.*

I closed my eyes again and raised my hands out to my sides like wings.

*One more step, Brynn. One more step.*

I lifted my arms a bit higher, leaned, and something brushed my leg. Wilco's lead.

I startled and opened my eyes. My dog had circled in front of me, his lead draped across my feet and his lone back leg now positioned precariously on the rock's ledge. He started to slip, whining and scampering forward, clawing with his front legs.

*Wilco! Wilco!*

I thrust out my hand, sank my fingers into his flesh, and yanked him back. We fell against the cold rock and I pulled him close, clenching him to my body. "I'm sorry. I'm sorry," I breathed into his ears. How could I have been so selfish that I hadn't even thought about the lead, about what would have . . .

"What are you doing, Callahan?"

It was Harris. I let go of my dog and stood. How long had he been there? How much had he seen? I busied myself with brushing off my pants as I swallowed hard, tried to get it together. "Pusser gave me the afternoon off. I decided to come up here and admire the scenery. Maybe go for a short hike."

"Like hell. Pusser told you to go home. And stay there."

"What do you know about it, Harris?"

"I just talked to him. Saw your vehicle parked up there, so I called him on the radio and told him you were here."

"Couldn't wait to rat me out, could you?"

He came down to where I was and looked around. "Like it matters. Frickin' waste of time coming out here. We ain't going to find nothing. Too much goes on out here. Probably a couple dozen kids been up this way since last week. Just a couple days ago, I busted a couple having sex. They were so into it, they didn't even see me coming."

*Sicko.* "Probably the closest you've been to getting any. Did it make you feel all tingly?"

"At least I don't sleep with my cousins." He was in my face, a smug grin.

"You don't know crap, Harris."

"Don't bet on it, Callahan. You might be surprised by what I know."

My insides clenched. *What does that mean?*

He smirked and lifted his chin, looking over my shoulder. "That's a long ways down, ain't it? You know, a couple years ago, a kid came out here and got pumped up on meth. He started hallucinating. Thought he was being attacked by flesh-eating bugs. Ran himself right off this cliff. Such a sad thing. Took us three whole days to find him down there. Course, we didn't have your dog at that time."

Acid stung the back of my throat. Even if I hadn't held the lead and I'd . . . Would they use Wilco? My stomach roiled.

Harris opened his mouth, sucked, snorting through his nose, turned his head, and hocked a green glob of spit. It glowed iridescently against the white snow. "You hear the latest?"

I felt sick.

He went on: "Pusser got a statement from Hatch Anderson's attorney. Hatch claims that Nevan Meath showed up that night with a baseball bat and smashed up Maura's car. We're getting a warrant now to search the Meath trailer."

*The engine oil.* Nevan might have been up here, maybe he even bashed up Maura's headlights. Still . . . "And you buy that? Come on, Harris. You're not that stupid. Why's Hatch just now telling us this?"

He ignored me, his mind already working out the details of a guilty Pavee. It was always the same for us: tried without proof, culpable without merit. "That dirty knacker probably did in the car and then went after his preggie girlfriend."

"You'd like that, wouldn't ya, Harris?"

"You bet. Ask me, all you people belong behind bars." He took a step closer. I held my ground. He was just inches from my face. "Know what I've been wonderin'?"

"Why you're so butt ugly?"

"Been asking myself why someone went to all the trouble to shoot Dublin Costello, hide his body, then burn down his trailer?"

I swallowed hard again. Wilco came to my side and circled my feet. He'd picked up on my distress. If my dog had picked up on it, Harris probably had, too. *Stay calm, Brynn. Stay calm.* I shrugged. "Pusser seems to think it was the Mexicans, that Costello was in on the drug pipeline and knew too much."

"Ever known a gangbanger to bother hiding the body? Drive-bys, walk-bys, or a bullet to the brain, execution style. Kill and retreat, that's how they operate. The body's their trophy, a souvenir of their handiwork. Not something they'd hide." He leaned in even closer. The stench of stale coffee steamed the cold air. "But it's the trailer that really bothers me."

"Why's that?"

"Come on, Callahan. 'You're not that stupid.'" He sneered the repeat of my earlier words.

An ugly brew of fear and anger boiled inside me: hot, acidic, potent . . . flooding my mind, blurring my vision. I'd been too long without food, too long without a drink, and had way too many reasons for bile to fill my gut. *Keep calm, girl. Don't let him see ya sweat.*

He stared intensely, taking in every emotion that crossed my face. "Think about it. Out of all those trashy trailers you people live in, someone knew exactly which one belonged to Costello. He never would have let the Mexicans into his territory. He wouldn't have been that stupid. Still, someone knew. You know why? Because it was an inside job, that's why. All I have to do is figure out which one of you gypsies had motive and the weapon."

The roots of my hair dampened with moist fear. A high-pitched buzzing echoed between my ears. I was going to puke.

Harris noticed. A sly smile crept onto his face. "You're not looking so good, Callahan."

# CHAPTER 19

I left Harris on the trail and headed back down the mountain just as the sun slipped under the horizon. About a half mile down the road, my cell service kicked in again. Five missed calls from Pusser. I should have pulled over and called him back. I didn't. I kept driving, my anxiety ratcheting up as the trees whizzed by outside my window. I flipped the radio off, then on again. I wasn't much in the mood for music, but I couldn't stand the silence, either.

Farther down the road, my headlights reflected on Deputy Parks's cruiser next to an old farmhouse. I pulled up and looked around. Her vehicle was empty and there was no sign of activity anywhere.

I tapped my fingers on the steering wheel. *Where are you, Parks?*

The house looked abandoned. Peeled white paint exposed rotting wood planks, the front porch was partially collapsed, and many of the windows were cracked or boarded over with plywood. The whole place seemed about to collapse from exhaustion. I looked off in the distance where a large barn stood. It must have been something in its glory days, but was now practically see-through. I squinted, wondering if Parks might be over there. I hesitated. The fire tower I could explain: hiking, enjoying some fresh air, whatever, but my presence on a suspect's property was a direct violation of Pusser's orders. Grounds for dismissal. But a litany of possible tragedies swirled through my mind. And none of them boded well for Parks.

Screw Pusser. I was here and I wasn't leaving until I knew Parks was okay.

I cut the engine, but kept my headlights trained on the front of the darkened house. I opened the car door, listening, then attached Wilco's lead and got out with my dog.

"Looking for me?"

I wheeled around. "Parks. I saw your cruiser, but—"

"I was behind the barn. I didn't even hear you pull in. You're still in uniform."

"Yeah. Haven't really had time to change yet. What is this place?"

"Jacob Fisher's address."

I looked back at the dilapidated house, the trash in the yard, for any sign of life. Nothing. I heard a rustling sound from the barren bushes by the porch. Probably a coon, or some other critter. Wilco strained against his lead. I clamped down. *Easy, easy!* I was in enough trouble as it was, without my dog getting out of control again.

"No one's home, but I found something interesting. Back by the barn, there's an old chicken coop."

"Chickens?"

"No. Just feathers. A lot of feathers."

"No birds?"

"Nope. Not a one." She fingered her cross necklace again.

"Could be they killed them all and hung them from that tree up by the cave." I yanked back again on Wilco's leash. *Behave, dog!* Again I glanced around the property, shook my head. "I can't believe how these people live. It doesn't look like there's any electricity or propane hooked up. I'm not sure how they're heating the place. And do you smell that?"

"Yeah. Raw sewage. And my kids complain when I put a limit on how much television they can watch. They don't know how good they got it." She looked at me. "Pusser's not happy with you."

"Nothing new there."

"I'm serious, Brynn. Harris told him you were just up at the party site."

"Harris has a big mouth."

"Still, you shouldn't have been there. Or here."

"I only came here because I was driving by and saw your vehicle. I thought you might need help. Pusser doesn't even need to know I was here." I opened the car door to get back in. "Maybe I should get going."

"Don't worry. I'm not going to tell him. But I wouldn't push your luck with him. He's been in a piss-poor mood lately."

"I've noticed. Worse than usual."

"Yeah, well, it's that time of year."

"What do you mean?" I motioned for Wilco to get

in. He hopped up and took his normal position in the passenger seat. My constant copilot.

"Guess you haven't been around him long enough to know, but every year around this time, Pusser gets in a mood. No one knows why. But some years it's pretty bad. We've just all come to expect it. We know to stay out of his way. He usually gets okay again in a couple weeks."

A shadow darted around the edge of the house. I startled. "You see that?"

"No. What?"

In the still night air, the creek of the porch boards sounded like a wounded animal's cry, high-pitched and hollow and mournful. Something I'd heard before. I looked through the car window at my dog. Something I never wanted to hear again. "Someone's here."

"I checked the place out already. No one's—"

A twig snapped.

She turned, her hand moving to her gun; with her other hand, she pointed across the yard to a giant oak. "It came from over there, behind that tree."

I squinted. My headlights barely illuminated the tree's bare branches. "I don't see anything."

Another snapping sound. This one from the opposite direction. Parks took cover behind the front bumper, crouching low and drawing her gun. "It's those devil people. I know it is."

I'd joined her behind the bumper. "It's not devil people, Parks. Calm down." The voice of reason, yet I squeezed my sweat-slicked palm around the grip of my own gun and eyed my dog. He was whining and pawing at the window. He was no use to us locked inside the car, but I couldn't risk leaving cover to get to him.

Parks cupped a hand to her mouth. "Who's out there? Show yourself!"

My heart pounded against my ribs.

She yelled again. "Who's there?"

A high-pitched half cackle, half whisper, like a shrill and evil taunt, pierced the air and echoed around us. I rotated and caught a flash of movement to the right, raised my gun, and panned the yard. Nothing. "What the hell?"

Next to me, Parks trembled. "Devil people."

Darkness and shadows, strange noises, the games our minds play. I knew them all too well. The most normal things become instant nightmares. "Probably just . . ." The shadow darted between the house and a nearby tree. I trained my weapon, finger on the trigger, then jerked it away. The shadow was small and darting around playful-like. It was a kid, just a kid.

I holstered my gun, my hand shaking now. "It's a couple kids," I managed to tell Parks.

*Kids. Just kids.* Like before. In Kabul.

Sweat dribbled along my hairline. I turned away from the car's headlights, hoping to hide the physical change coming over me. A familiar dread churned in my gut, I knew what was next. *Stop. Stop . . . don't go there.*

But I did.


A dark veil descended on my mind, and the line between now and then blurred.

*He's there. On the ground. His glazed brown eyes stare lifelessly from an impish face. There's a smudge of dirt on his cheek. And blood. A lot of blood.*

*That's because I shot him in the head.*

*I shot a kid.*

*"Marine, clear out!"*

*I shot a kid.*

*An explosion rips through the air. Debris rains down around us. Someone calls for the TacSat radio. My dog barks and pulls at his lead. I don't move. Corporal shakes me. "I said move out, Callahan!"*

*I can't pull my eyes away. He's just a boy. Bony and thin, the kufi he wears swallows him whole. His hands, small, brown, with dirt-encrusted nails, grip an M16. . . .*

*I'm shoved from behind. "Forget him, Callahan. He was gunning for us. Kill or be killed. Now move!"*

*Bullets spray the area. Someone's talking into the radio. "Two down, call for MERT!"*

*Corporal shakes me. "Damn it, Callahan! Get your head in the game."*

"Brynn? Brynn?" It was Parks. She shook my arm, her eyes wide with worry. "Are you okay?"

I looked around. "Sorry. I . . . I . . . What were you saying?"

Parks was standing next to me. She'd already holstered her weapon. She tilted her head my way, shifted her stance, unsure of what had happened. I was unsure too. Sometimes what seemed like an eternity in my distressed mind was only a few seconds of real time. I blinked, my mind racing for a cover story.

None was needed. A noise from the road spun us both around. An old Ford pickup turned in and rumbled down the driveway, a single silhouette outlined behind the wheel.

"This must be Jacob," Parks said.

A teenage boy got out of the truck. Black hair and pale skin . . . but nothing in particular struck me about his features beyond the fact that he gave off an aura of cold indifference. "What are you cops doing here?"

Parks stepped forward. "Jacob Fisher?"

"Yeah." He looked around. "What'd you do with my brothers?"

"Your brothers?"

"Elijah and Levi."

Parks and I exchanged a look. Parks fired off the first question. "Are your parents home?"

"It's just our mother. She's on a business trip."

Parks stared him down. "Where?"

"Atlanta."

I rolled my shoulders, keeping quiet and letting Parks ask all the questions. Anxiety zinged through my body; my fingers itched for a pill—a little pop of relief. I ached to climb into my cruiser and take refuge with my dog.

Parks was still asking questions. "When's she coming home?"

"In a few days."

"How old are your brothers?"

"Eleven. They're twins."

Parks switched gears. "We're here to ask a few questions about last Thursday. The night Maura Keene went missing."

Jacob's expression remained flat. "What would I know about that?"

"What were you doing last Friday evening?"

"Nothing. I came home after school and stayed here."

"You didn't go out?"

"No." He reached into the bed of the truck and pulled out a box marked PERISHABLE. Food-pantry boxes.

"Anyone come over?"

He narrowed his eyes. "Yeah. Maybe."

"Who?"

He didn't answer.

Parks pushed it. "We're trying to piece together everything that happened that night. Who came to see you?"

"A friend. Her name's Winnie. I know her from school."

"What time did she get here?"

He shrugged. "I dunno. Late. It'd been dark for a while."

"What did you do?"

"Not much. Talked. Messed around a little. She was mostly drinking and talking on her phone. I got bored and took her home."

"She say anything about Maura?"

He looked toward the house. "I gotta take the food inside and put it away."

Parks cocked her head. "Did Winnie say anything about Maura?"

"No . . . I don't know. She was mad at her, I guess. Maura hooked up with some guy she liked."

"Hatch Anderson?"

He nodded. Parks pressed on. "Did you see Maura's fiancé that night? Nevan's his name."

"Nope." He shifted the box in his hands. "Look, I'm sorry about what happened to Maura. But that's all I know. I've got to get this stuff put away."

I stepped in front of him. "Officer Parks noticed that you're missing some chickens."

His eyes darted toward the barn, back at my car and my dog, and back to me. He shrugged. "Something got into the pen. Killed them all. It happens."

Giggles. Not taunts by devil people, but children's giggles—that's what we'd heard earlier. This time from the front porch. I looked, but even with the headlights shining that way, I couldn't see anyone. I glanced at Parks. She shook her head.

I turned back and locked stares with Jacob. His eyes were two dark pits of inky oil that drew me in and held me captive. His gaze moved down my face and settled on my neck. A little light sparked in his expression. He'd found a weakness. He tilted his head and smirked. He wanted me to know that he knew. He wanted to unnerve me. This kid seemed okay on the surface, but was hard and cold, through and through. A part of me shivered, recoiled at his gaze, fell right into the power trip he wanted to have over me. Yet a little piece of my heart went out to him, too. *Just a kid,* I reminded myself. A child who, judging by his living conditions, had probably suffered years of neglect, if not abuse. No wonder.

I forced myself to remain still. We stood like that, for what seemed like a full minute: him staring; me feeling exposed and vulnerable. But I didn't flinch. And finally he turned away.

He crossed the yard and climbed the porch steps. As he neared the door, two small boys popped out of the shadows and followed him into the house, their high-pitched giggles lingering behind them.

# CHAPTER 20

It was 10:00 p.m. by the time I pulled into Bone Gap. Red and blue lights glowed above the east end of the trailer park. Several officers were standing outside the Meaths' place. I got out of my vehicle. It was noisy: people shouting, car doors slamming, dogs barking. I let Wilco out and he beelined for the Lurcher kennels in the back of the property—another chance to torment his caged friends.

I approached a huddle of uniformed officers. "Is the sheriff inside?"

One of the officers turned my way. I'd seen him around before, but couldn't recall his name. "Yeah. Sheriff's inside, but we're not supposed to let anyone else in."

Two more officers walked the perimeter of the trailer, shining lights around the trailer's axels. I folded my arms and waited. Shadows passed back and forth behind the curtained windows. Out front, Mrs. Meath stood in a heavy robe cinched over a nightgown, and boots on her feet. She was agitated. Her voice cut over the noise of the crowd, shrill and panicked. "You damn *muskers* have no right to be in there. This is my home. *My home.* You hear me?"

I went to her and placed my hand on her shoulder. "Take it easy, Kitty. You're getting too upset—"

She pushed me away. "Don't touch me. You're one of them now. Course you've never really been one of us, have you? You Callahans never could follow the clan code, could you? Not your whorin' mama, not you."

I drew back, dazed. I looked around for help from my neighbors, people I'd known all my life. Their contemptuous stares caught me off guard. I recoiled and felt completely alone in the world. Is this how Gran felt?

"Over here! We found something."

I turned back to the trailer. An officer was crouched down in the evergreen shrubs that ran along the base of the trailer, his flashlight focused on one particular spot. "Someone get the sheriff. I found it."

Silence fell over the crowd. Pusser emerged from inside the trailer, shot me a glaring look, and joined the officers. "Yup. That's what we're looking for. Document it and bag it."

He walked over and held out another bag. "Care to tell me what this is, Mrs. Meath?" The bag held an address scrawled onto a piece of scratch paper.

She clamped her lips tight.

"This is an Augusta address. Is this where your son is?" Pusser yanked the toothpick from his mouth and tossed it aside. "Answer me, Mrs. Meath."

"Most of these knackers got kin down that way." It was one of the officers. Pusser shot him a look.

Kitty turned her eyes my way. They were wet now, but her jaw jutted out firmly, her mouth nothing more than a mere slash across her face. A mother would do anything to protect her child. But was she protecting him from prejudices and unjustified accusations, or did she know that her son was a killer?

Pusser spoke to the officer. "Take her in. We'll question her at the department."

"What?" I latched onto Kitty's arm. "Don't do this, Pusser. It isn't necessary."

"It's my call to make, Callahan. Not yours." He lowered his chin until his mouth was just inches from my face. "Not that that ever seems to matter to you."

His gaze bore into the side of my face. I stood my ground, but fought back the dread rising in me. His breath was hot against my ear. "I've got things to take care of now, but later, you and me, we're going to talk about what happened today."

He broke away and motioned to the officer, who clamped cuffs on Kitty's wrists and turned her toward his cruiser. Her body went slack. I stepped in and reached out, afraid that she might collapse, but she righted herself. Her body stiffened with anger and her features distorted into an ugly mask. She strained against the cuffs, leaning down and spitting at my feet. She raised crazed eyes and met my gaze. She uttered one word: "Traitor."

Pusser called me at eight the next morning. "The Augusta police have Nevan Meath in custody."

I slid my coffee mug onto the kitchen counter. "Is he talking?"

"No. But he will. I'm counting on you to make that happen."

I glanced over my shoulder. Meg was at the counter, buttering her toast. Her eyes darted my way.

"And what about Hatch?"

"He claims the Meath kid came up there with the baseball bat and went ballistic, threatened to kill him, and bashed the hell out of the Keenes' car. That's when Hatch left."

"He left Maura up there alone with Nevan?"

"I can't arrest him for being an asshole."

"What'd he say about the pregnancy?"

"He admits that the kid could be his, even agreed to DNA testing. He says he would have stepped up to the plate. Taken responsibility for the kid."

"You believe that?"

"Doesn't matter. We can't prove it one way or the other. But the bat has paint on it, and it looks to be a color match for Maura Keene's car. It's being analyzed now."

"That bat was out in the shrubs. Anyone could have planted it there. Hatch could have done that."

"You're grasping at straws, Callahan. Is that because Nevan's a Pavee?"

I gritted my teeth. "You're making assumptions. Is that because he is a Pavee?"

Pusser moved on. "We've got a team up at Stoners' Draw now. Probably a waste of time, but I'm going to have them collect what they can. See if there's anything to tie Nevan to the crime scene."

"There is." I told him about the engine oil. "Could be his. Maybe not, though."

Silence on Pusser's end of the line. I hadn't hesitated to tell him what I'd found—even though it could implicate a Pavee. He got my point.

Finally, "I'll alert the techs. It still wouldn't prove that he was up there that exact night. But we have witness testimony for that."

"I'm not sure how reliable Hatch is as a witness," I offered.

"It's what we got for now," he replied.

"Anything on the other missing girl?"

"No. Nothing substantial yet."

There was a pause in the conversation. I braced myself. I knew what was coming.

"You've been walking a thin line with me, Callahan. I was going to fire you yesterday, but it looks like I'll need you for this Meath thing."

"What do you mean?" Although I knew what he meant. My only useful skill was that I was a Pavee, someone to keep around for times like these when my ethnicity came in handy.

"I'm sending you and Grabowski to Augusta to bring the Meath kid back. I need you along for the ride, you know, Pavee with Pavee. I wouldn't want the kid screaming prejudice later."

"I understand."

"I'm sure you do. So get packed. I need you two on the road first thing this afternoon. I got your psych eval scheduled for Tuesday morning."

"Fine."

"You'll take a urine test, too."

My mind raced. A urine test?

"Just a precaution. No big deal, right? You'll pass?"

The booze wasn't a problem. It'd be out of my system by then. But the Vicodin? I'd just taken a couple to kick the day off. "This Tuesday? I don't know if I can—"

"You don't have a choice, Callahan. Make it work."

# CHAPTER 21

*February 7*
*Things are getting really bad. Everything is out of control. It was a mistake to tell, and Nevan is paying for my mistake. I can't even trust leaving my journal around here. I can't wait to leave this place.*

"What do you think of this?" I turned down the radio and read the entry to Grabowski. After nearly three hours of pumped-up banjos and mandolins, the silence was blissful.

He glanced sideways at my phone. "I thought there was a new department policy prohibiting the use of private phones for police business."

"You've never broken a rule before?"

"Have you ever actually followed a rule before?"

"What are we missing here? This entry is dated the seventh. By then, she'd already told Nevan, her mother, her brother, and even Hatch knew. So did she mean one of those people, or did she confide in someone new? Why was Maura worried about Nevan here?"

"I wondered the same thing. It's possible she went to someone outside her normal circle. According to you, Traveller girls don't normally end up in that sort of trouble."

I watched the road signs whisking past us. Willed myself to ignore the obvious signs of our Pavee transgressions. My own youthful sexual fling that strayed far from acceptable Pavee morals. Premarital sex, and with a settled boy, no less. Sin topped with sin. I knew neither of our actions reflected Pavee standards. But . . . there was more to Maura than just being another young Traveller girl in trouble.

I remembered what Winnie had said, that Maura got a rush out of leading Hatch on. Maybe she led on other guys, too. And the journal showed another side to Maura. A manipulative side: lying to her mother so she could go out partying, sleeping with one man while engaged to another. And Winnie also said she threw Hatch's affection in her face. . . . Who else might she have infuriated with her manipulations?

"We need to dig more into Maura's social circle. Maybe look more at the Fisher kid, see how well he knew Maura."

"Waste of time. Frank seems to think Nevan's the guy."

"His logic is clouded by his prejudices."

"If he's so prejudiced against Travellers, then why'd he hire you?"

"I come in handy in cases like these. It looks good to have a Pavee on the force." I thumbed toward the seat behind us. The department's SUV had come automatically equipped with a K9 cage in the far back. "And I came with a dog. He loves Wilco." All I was to Pusser was a dumb Pavee with a smart dog.

Grabowski glanced in the rearview mirror. "That's true. Frank loves your dog. We all love your dog. He might be your only redeeming quality."

"Thanks." He had no idea how close to home that statement hit. And hurt.

He chuckled, then sobered. "The way I see it, you're the one with the prejudice problem."

"How's that?"

"You're ignoring the facts. Probably because Nevan is a Pavee. Think about it. He was the last person to see Maura alive. A witness saw him vandalize Maura's car. . . ."

"Hatch isn't exactly what I'd call a reliable witness."

"Maybe not, but the bat was found at Nevan's residence. And he ran. Why run if he wasn't guilty of something?"

And there was the oil stain, which, if it tested positive, would put him at the abduction scene. "Simple. Pavees never trust the law."

Grabowski didn't respond. I knew it sounded like an excuse. I didn't bother to say the bat might have been planted—that really reeked of defensiveness. Was Grabowski right? If Nevan wasn't a Pavee, would I be eager to pin this on him?

I turned and looked out the window. It was getting close to sunset and we were still about an hour north of the South Carolina border. We'd gotten a late start and it'd be dark when we got there, so Grabowski and I planned to get hotel rooms tonight and get Nevan first thing in the morning. I had a plan of my own, too: shake off Grabowski as soon as possible and go to the address Colm had given me for Doogan's family. I glanced down at my hands. My fingers trembled slightly. It'd been about five hours since my last pill. Is that a long time? I didn't know. I'd been on the take-as-needed regimen for the past couple years, popping a pill when the pain got to be too much. Or the anxiety. Or the stress. Or just when I needed to chill.

"I've known Frank a long time," Grabowski continued. "He's a good guy. A good cop. No way he'd let anything influence his judgment on a case."

"Guess I haven't known him as long as you. Every time something goes wrong, he looks our way. All cops do. That's the way it's always been." Why was I saying this? Pusser had always treated me and my family fairly. Why was I so eager to sell him out? "I didn't really mean that."

"What *did* you mean?"

"It's hard for me to trust people. Even Pusser." *Fit for duty? Urine test? The ungrateful SOB. And after all my dog and I had done for him.* Five hours since my last pill. I'd spent most of that time feeling pissed at the world, second-guessing myself, my job, whether I should beg off from this assignment, finally deciding to push through. I'd done this before, the first day was hard, but nothing like the second and third day. We'd be back by then. I'd take a day or two off. Get through this.

Grabowski was still talking. "Give him a chance. He's a good guy. This case is hard for him. It reminds him of something from his past."

"The girl in the picture?"

A nod. "Her name was Josephine. Jo. Their only child."

My mouth went dry. *Pusser's daughter.* "Where is she? Is she dead?"

"Probably. She was a senior in high school when she went missing. The same age as Maura."

"But that must have been . . ." I tried to put together a timeline in my head, but my brain was turning at half speed.

"Twenty-two years ago, this month."

My chest heaved. Everything rushed in on me at once: things I'd said, things Pusser had said, the way his eyes clouded with sadness at times. . . . "I didn't know."

"His wife went crazy with grief. She died exactly two years after Jo went missing."

"How?"

"Suicide."

I swallowed hard. Standing on that cliff, I'd relished only my selfish release from my miseries, without a thought to the pain I'd inflict on others if I jumped. Pain like the ghostly images that haunted Pusser every day of his life from a missing child, a wife gone forever. *Selfish, selfish.* Pusser had needed his wife to help bear their burdens. And Wilco and Gran needed me. Gran especially. She needed me to take care of her, provide for her. I quickly slid my hands under my legs, hiding the shakes from Grabowski.

His eyes stayed steady on the road. "Frank always thought her boyfriend had something to do with it. He was no good. The type of guy you hate to see your daughter with. Frank had forbidden her to see him, but she snuck around. He knew it at the time. Cops' kids can't get away with anything. All the guys in the department kept an eye out for each other's kids. But

Pusser let it go. He figured she'd come to her senses about the guy."

"Why didn't Pusser like the boyfriend? What was wrong with him?"

"Oh, you know. Always in trouble. Shoplifting, underage drinking, small-time vandalism . . . minor stuff compared to what kids are into these days. But after Jo went missing . . . well, you'd have to understand what that type of thing would do to a parent."

"I can't imagine."

"Frank spent every waking moment searching for Jo. And he hounded the boyfriend. Put patrol on him twenty-four/seven and harassed him every chance he got."

"Where is he now?"

"In the state pen. He's been in for fifteen years. Armed robbery. He's probably in his late thirties or early forties now. He's up for parole in six months."

"Pusser must be crazy knowing that he's going to get out. What's his name?"

"Jack Doherty."

*"Doherty?"* I knew the name. A cold dread etched my spine. "Was he a—"

"Yes. He was from Bone Gap."

# CHAPTER 22

We pulled into Augusta a little after eight, got a couple bags of fast-food burgers to go, and checked into the local flophouse, adjoining rooms on the first floor. As Grabowski headed to his room, I asked for the keys to the cruiser to run a few personal errands. He didn't ask what type of errands and I didn't offer an explanation. More than anything, I wanted a hot shower and bed. I was nearing thirteen hours without my meds, an intense aching had settled into my muscles. Still tolerable now, but I knew it was going to get worse. Much worse. But this was my only chance to see Doogan, so I headed out of the lobby, tossing the grease-soaked bag in the trash on my way. Couldn't stomach even the smell, but hadn't wanted Grabowski to suspect anything was off. From the car, Wilco looked longingly at the tossed bag, but he'd wolfed down his plain burger patty before we'd left the drive-through's parking lot.

Colm had contacted the priest at the church where the photo was taken and got not only an address, but the name of the woman in the picture—Katie Doogan. She lived in a large community of Travellers outside North Augusta. Years ago, a reality TV show was filmed here. People had watched that show and assumed that all Travellers lived the same, but our clan lived nothing like these people. They'd integrated more, opting to live in large traditional homes, while we maintained more mobile residences: trailers and, for some, manufactured homes like Gran's, larger and more comfortable for the older set, but still moveable. In short, our clan was still wheeled. These folks were rooted in place. Travellers who no longer travelled, but Pavees nonetheless.

Many of the homes in this area were mansions by anyone's standards, but the address I had was for a more modest brick home tucked along a side street off Kildare Road. My pulse kicked up a notch when I spied Doogan's bike in the driveway. I parked next to it and huddled in the front seat with Wilco, willing my heart rate to slow. My eyes took in every detail of this place as I tried to steady my nerves.

I flipped down my visor and looked in the mirror. My scar stood out, dark and splotchy against my all-too-pale skin. My face was drawn; my eyes were flat and hollow; my nose red and dribbling. . . . The shakes had returned. Not just my hands, but my whole body trembled. I was a wreck. I thought again of the beautiful woman in the photo. *No wonder he left.* I shook it off. None of that mattered. I was here for only one thing: to find out about the gun. The one loose end that could tie my grandmother to Dublin Costello's murder. Nothing more.

The woman in the picture answered the door. She wore a deep green silk scarf around her neck. My fingers flew to my own neck and my scar, bare and exposed. Her eyes were a golden-hazel color that seemed to look right through me.

"I'm Brynn Calla—"

"I know who you are."

Such a simple statement, but it said so much. She knew. Doogan must have told her about me. Had he told her everything? My mind raced for words. I had none.

Doogan appeared at her side, placing his hand on the small of her back. He looked down at Wilco, a brief smile crossing his lips, then up at me. His smile faded. "Hello, Brynn."

I'd mentally prepared myself for this moment, telling myself that I wouldn't react to him, but the second I saw him, my breath caught and a familiar tingling burst through me. I couldn't control it. My med-deprived blood held my pituitary gland at gunpoint, demanding a shot of endorphins that a certain sexual release could bring. . . . I lowered my gaze and forced myself to talk. "I have to speak to you about something. In private."

The woman clenched his arm. Her expression turned icy cold.

I looked to Doogan for any indication of what he was going to do. "How did you find me?" he asked.

"Through a mutual friend."

"Who?"

"It doesn't matter. I need to talk to you about my grandmother. Something's come up. It's important."

He turned to the woman. "It's okay, Katie. I'll only be a couple minutes."

"No. I don't want you to talk to—"

"It'll only take a minute. I'll be right back inside."

She shook him off, wheeling and storming away. He watched her go. His jaw tightened and then relaxed, but when he turned my way, a look of sadness crept into his eyes. But the sadness quickly changed to something else as his gaze swept hungrily over my body.

Every nerve in my body sprang to life. *Withdrawals,* I reminded myself, *that's all this is, just my body playing tricks on me.* I cleared my throat. "Your wife?"

His expression hardened. He pushed past me and walked toward the side of the house. I followed, speaking to his back. "And you have children."

"Yes. Three."

So it was true. "You were married when we . . . we . . ." He turned and faced me. I searched his face, wanting answers. "Why?"

"I comforted you. We comforted each other. That's all."

"We almost . . ."

"But we didn't. We didn't take it that far."

"Only because I . . . I had a flashback."

He raked his hands through his hair. Hands that had traced my naked body, hands that I wanted even now to . . . I shook myself, barely heard his answer. "We got caught up in the moment. It was a mistake."

*A mistake? That's how you've reconciled it?* "You seemed pretty intent on making it happen."

"You came on to me. Remember?"

I remembered the longing—no, the need—and that same urge inflamed my body even now. *Stay on point,* I told myself again. "I had no idea you were married. You never mentioned a wife. Or kids."

"It wasn't like that."

"Like what? You weren't married?" I laughed. "Come on, Doogan. The wife and kids didn't just magically appear out of nowhere. How long have you been married?"

"I was nineteen when we married."

"Ah . . . I see. Too young to know better. So that makes it okay for you to screw around on your wife?"

His eyes flashed with anger. "Just hear me out, okay?"

"I'm listening."

"Katie was only seventeen when we were married and she got pregnant right away. It was hard. Really hard. I was messed up back then. I told you about it before. The gang. The drugs."

"Yeah. You told me." *More lies, probably.* My right hand shook and I held it still with the left.

"I got caught up in the easy money. I wasn't big-time or nothing. Mostly just pot. A little here and there to friends. Never kids."

*People can find a way to justify just about anything. Damn, if I didn't need a pill right now.*

"But it wasn't enough. My supplier kept pushing for me to sell harder stuff. Katie tried to talk me out of it. She wanted to move. Get away from the crowd I was running with and start over. But I couldn't get out. They wouldn't let me. I ended up getting busted and sent to the state pen. I did seven years. And Katie and the kids, just the two at the time . . ." He ran his hand through his hair again, and I forced myself not to look. "Johnny was almost eight when I finally got out. We tried to make it work, Katie and me, she even got pregnant again, but . . . we fought all the time. Then my little sister went missing. That's when I went up to Tennessee. I had to look for her."

"You were married, Doogan. Married. And you didn't tell me." Anger sparked inside me. Pavees screwing around before marriage was unacceptable, but desecrating a marriage with adultery? *Another new low for you, Brynn. Add home wrecker to your sins. But the blame for this sin shouldn't have landed on my lap.* "You lied to me. Would have taken advantage of me. Then you left with no explanation. I trusted you."

"I thought my marriage was over. I never would have—"

"Shut the hell up, Doogan." I crossed my arms over my chest, conscious of my heated breasts as they strained for him. I pulled my arms into myself, trying to keep the shakes and my endorphin-deprived hormones under control. "I don't care. I really don't care. I came here about the gun. I need to know what you did with it." I blurted out about Maura's murder and the other girl who was missing and my current case and the body Wilco found in the cave. How they'd figured out that it was Dublin's bones up there in that cave, the bullet casings . . . everything. "That gun ties my grandmother to the crime. Where is it?"

"I tossed it."

"Where?"

"I don't know. I can't remember. Someplace up on the mountain."

"Think, Doogan. Where on the mountain?"

"They're not going to find it. Even if they do, they won't tie it to her. I wiped it clean before I tossed it."

"Before or after you dumped his body in the cave?"

"After."

"So, near the cave?" I prodded. I cocked my head to catch his gaze.

"Yeah. I think so." He lowered his head and paced. "I dumped the body and the four-wheeler and headed out of the woods on foot. I went south toward the highway. I stopped about halfway, cleaned it and tossed it. I remember there was a big tree, an oak, a widow-maker."

"How could you have been so stupid?"

He stepped closer. His body tense with anger. Wilco sensed the shift in his mood and pressed closer to me, alert and on guard. Doogan didn't seem to notice, his anger building with every word. "Look. I did you and your family a favor. I put myself at risk. If the cops find out, I'll be back in the pen."

He was so close, I could feel the heat of his temper. I'd felt heat from him before, only not from anger, but desire. I lost focus, my mind travelling elsewhere. The image of that night together, the strength of his embrace, the way our bodies fit together. . . . Something inside me shifted and stirred. A hotness unfurled inside my belly and moved lower.

He leaned down, even closer. "Is that what you want? Are you so angry that you want to see me go back to the pen?"

"No. That's not what I want." The words came out the wrong way, wanton and suggestive. *What is wrong with me? This guy's a user. A player. Back off, Brynn.*

But I didn't.

His gaze became more intense, his lips curling upward. "What is it you want then?"

My back arched, I looked up and met his gaze. *Him. I wanted him.*

A strange mix of desire and disgust washed over me. How could I want a man who thought so little of women, of me, of his wife? *Back away. Move. Leave.*

But I stayed. The surge through my bloodstream of narcotic-deprived craving for something, anything, to fill me with the hormones to take the edge off my withdrawals. *That's all this is. Shake it off.*

Yet, there was more, could be more; I knew that. He was willing, if I was. What would it be? Secret meetings, cheap hotel rooms, a quick roll in the hay when he was in the area?

He was like all the other men I'd known. Users. Cheats. I should have never trusted him. Yet, I wanted him. That night, back in the trailer, he'd awakened an instinct in me, something that had lain dormant for years, something I'd pushed aside since the rape. It hadn't felt anything like the shallow relationships I'd experienced during my time in the service. I'd trusted Doogan with my body. My scarred and maimed and ripe and desperate body. It'd felt good to trust, to be held again. I wanted that more than anything. I wanted to be loved.

*But not like this.*

I squirmed free of my desires and forced myself to step back. My peripheral vision caught on something. I looked closer. A slight part in the front-window curtains of the house. The face of a young boy peered out at us. I gave a little laugh, trying to cover my frustration and shame. "I don't want anything from you. Good-bye, Doogan."

# CHAPTER 23

By seven-thirty the next morning, we had Nevan Meath processed, signed out, and secured in the back seat of the cruiser, Wilco caged in the cargo area. We were cruising north on Highway 25. The Osborne Brothers were playing on the radio and I was sipping bottled water. So far, Nevan hadn't said a word. Neither had I. The night before, my med-impoverished brain had kicked into overdrive, amping up my anxieties until I thought I would explode. Then my nose started running. My eyes were tearing. I felt like I had the worst flu of my life, and, for all this suffering, I couldn't be completely sure the drugs would be out of my system by Tuesday morning.

Grabowski glanced over. "You look like crap."

"Thanks."

"Where'd you go last night? You didn't get in until late."

"Why so curious? Pusser put you back on babysitting duty?"

"No. I just wondered."

I shifted in my seat, trying to find a comfortable position, my every muscle jumpy or miserable. Or both. He turned his attention to Nevan. "Anything you care to tell us about, boy?"

He stared straight ahead, defiant. He wouldn't even look my way, hadn't since we'd picked him up at the Augusta Police Department. I didn't really care. I wanted to get this done and get home.

Grabowski glanced in the rearview mirror. "We've got a witness who saw you bash in Maura's car with a baseball bat. You must have a pretty bad anger problem to do something like that."

"Your witness is lying."

Grabowski looked in the rearview mirror. "You were the last person to see Maura alive."

"Says who?"

"Hatch Anderson."

Nevan's expression tightened. He turned and looked out the window.

Grabowski kept firing off questions. "We have another missing girl who was in the area at the time. You know anything about her?"

"No."

"How would you know? I haven't told you her name."

Nevan pressed his lips together.

"Addy. Addy Barton."

Nevan's jaw twitched.

"You know that name, boy?"

Nothing from Nevan. I wiped a bead of sweat from my forehead and scrolled my phone screen. "We found

Maura's journal. You might find some of it interesting. This one is dated just a few days before her death. It mentions you." I read it out loud.

> *February 3*
> *Nevan says he hates Bone Gap and his stu-*
> *pid family. I've never seen him so upset. I*
> *understand why. It's all so unfair. I'm angry,*
> *too, but not as mad as Nevan. Today we*
> *were in his truck and he freaked out about*
> *everything. He drove like an idiot and we*
> *went into the ditch. Then he started swear-*
> *ing and screaming like it was my fault. I*
> *was so scared.*

Grabowski let out a little whistle. "You did all that, boy? Makes it sound like you're on the edge, a violent guy."

"You don't understand—"

"Come on, Nevan. What's not to understand? She was carrying another man's child. That'd piss me off. She cheated. Disgraced you. She deserved to die, right?"

"Stupid-ass copper. You got it all wrong." I looked back at the boy. Just a boy. His face smooth, without a promise of a whisker for years, and fine-boned, nearly pretty-faced, like a Ken doll, only without a Barbie at his side anymore. He looked all wrong for playing the part of an enraged lover, jealous enough to kill.

Grabowski smirked. "Then tell us what happened, Nevan. Set me straight."

Nevan's eyes darted from me to Grabowski, then

settled outside the window again. Grabowski sighed. He'd pushed too hard and he knew it.

Suddenly my stomach reeled as if some vile stench filled the air. I could only hope it wasn't my own soured sweat. I swallowed hard and folded my arms across my chest. Grabowski turned up the music again. *Yeehaw* . . . I sat back, bit my lip, and wiped more sweat from my hairline. I closed my eyes, consciousness ebbed, I was vaguely aware of Grabowski's voice in the background, fading, fading. My mind released and swirled into darkness, punctuated with lucid images: dreams of flying through the clouds, Superman-like, up and up, higher and higher, closer to the sun. The heat sears my skin; on my arms, I see blisters bubble and pop, bubble and . . . I woke with a start and pulled a wad of toilet paper from my coat pocket. My face was soaked with tears and snot. My head zinged like I'd been hit with an electrical current. I dabbed at my eyes. "How much longer?"

"A couple hours." He looked me over, pressed his lips into a thin line, then went after Nevan again. "There's a lot of evidence stacked against you, boy. The bat and—"

"I don't know where that came from. I'd never seen it before."

"Hatch said he left you and Maura alone up there by the fire tower."

"He's lying. I went up there to see if she was okay. She was. She told me to leave. She wanted to be alone with Hatch. So I left."

Winnie left, he left, Hatch left—someone was lying.

"It didn't bother you that she was with another guy."

Silence.

Grabowski smirked. "Surprised you're so nonchalant about all this, Nevan. Your pretty little fiancée goes and gets knocked up by some guy outside the clan. A 'settled' guy, as you people say." He glanced in the mirror again. "Didn't it make you sick, boy? Thinking of his hands all over your girl."

More silence.

"Maybe you weren't man enough for her?"

A deep purple flush crept into the hollows of Nevan's cheeks. "You don't know shit, *musker.*"

Grabowski smirked and went for the jugular. "Or maybe it's true that gypsy girls are like that. You know. Easy lays."

My cell phone rang. Nevan's head snapped my way. He clamped his mouth shut, shifted back in the seat, and went quiet again. *Damn.*

After I finished the call, I turned to Grabowski. "A purse was found. The missing girl Addy Barton's purse. It was partially submerged in the river. They need my dog."

# CHAPTER 24

$A$ lot of things determine whether or not a dead body will float. Water replaces the air in the lungs of a drowning victim, making the body heavier and it sinks. But once bacteria begin their fleshly feast, decomposition creates gases that make the body lighter, and it floats to the surface. How long it takes for the bacteria to create enough noxious gases to reach that critical lift level depends on several factors: water temperature, ingested drugs and medications, body-fat percentages (fat floats better than muscle), the type of clothing worn, and even what food was last consumed.

For the Nolichucky River's most recent victim, the biggest concern was water temperature. This was February. Ice chunks floated on the water and gathered along the banks in large white conglomerates. With our current record low temperatures, it could take a body almost two weeks to float.

"A kid found her bag a couple hours ago." Pusser pointed up to a snowy area of the bank where a few picnic tables sat. It was late afternoon. We were at the

Gorge Campground, a popular destination for outdoor enthusiasts, even in the winter. After securing Nevan at the county jail, Grabowski and I came straight to the scene. "It still had her ID in it. And something else, too. A zip bag of white pills. We're analyzing it now."

I surveyed the river. "You're assuming she's in the water."

"It's all I have for now. The river runs pretty shallow along the banks, but there are some deep holes in the middle. Think your dog will find anything?"

I looked to where Wilco scurried back and forth along the river edges, dipping his head playfully at the floating ice. "If she's out there, Wilco will find her."

For a dog who'd served mostly in dry-desert conditions, water was a source of joy for him, never a hindrance. Nor was it for most HRD dogs. Bodies submerged in water still give off scent. It rises in the gases from the decomposition that bubble and pop along the surface of the water, dispersing a putrefied perfume easily detected by a trained dog. Decomposing bodies also release oils that rise and form greasy sheens along the water's surface. I'd seen Wilco hit off both of these phenomena twice before in the Badghis Province, where he detected the bodies of two internationals who'd drowned after trying to recover supplies that had fallen into the Murghab River. There we had some indication of where the men had gone down. Here we had no idea. No doubt Wilco could find this body, eventually, and with the right equipment. But with the amount of distance we had to cover, today was a bit of a long shot.

I slowly unpacked a bright orange immersion suit, something similar to what I'd worn in the Marines during cold-water survival maneuvers. It was heavy and cumbersome, my muscles rubbery and uncooperative, but in this frigid water, hypothermia could set in quickly. In this part of the gorge, the river smoothed out and mellowed into a few riffles and waves, leisurely compared to the downright suicidal rapids farther upstream. Still, I wasn't one to leave things to chance.

I bent to put my leg in, missed, and tried again. Next to me, Pusser chomped down hard on a toothpick and apprised me of his theory on the Barton girl. "Nothing seems to fit, does it?" he said. "Maura was stabbed and left whole to bleed out on a sacrificial altar. This girl, if she's out there, somehow ended up as fish bait."

I shivered. Pusser never sugarcoated things.

"So the only thing linking the two deaths is the timing. And the diner," he added. "We know from the trace on her charge card that she ate her last meal there. But that's not much to go on. That diner is the only real eating establishment on this side of the mountain. Most people travelling through end up there."

"Or she ate there regularly and knew Maura." I had both feet in the suit.

Pusser's eyes skimmed the surface of the water. "At this point, it doesn't really matter. There's a body somewhere, maybe out there, and we're responsible for finding it. Let's do what we can before the light's gone."

I glanced sideways. His stooped posture and distant, empty stare hinted at profound sadness. He was thinking of Jo. I wanted to say something, offer some words of condolence, comfort, but I wasn't supposed to know about his daughter.

I turned away, unable to bear his sadness, and

focused on working the rest of the way into the suit. Not easy. The shakes had momentarily subsided; they were probably the adrenaline rush of an upcoming search. But my muscles ached, and my limbs felt like a Gummy Bear's limbs. I was struggling to pull the heavy suit over my hips when noise drew our attention to a couple officers carrying a raft to the bank. Wilco noticed, knew what was coming, and declared his enthusiasm with a throaty affirmation that echoed through the canyon. Pusser looked his way and laughed. Wilco's timing was perfect, his enthusiasm soothed Pusser's sadness. Almost as if he knew. Maybe he did.

The raft was put in the water. I boarded with Wilco, huddled near the front, hunched over, sweating profusely, neoprene material clinging to my skin like plastic wrap on a steaming dish. Three more suited officers joined me. Wilco was climbing over all of us and positioning himself near the bowline. He knew his place. The other officers manned the paddles and oar, and off we pushed.

Expectations were low, given the breadth of the search area, water flow, the temperature, enormous depths of some of the water's pools, our lack of personnel and equipment. We needed divers, deepwater cameras, dragging equipment, sonar, a submersible robot. We had none of it. Just us and the dog. This was simply the initial pass. What I hoped for today was an alert. If Wilco alerted, we'd mark the area with buoys and bring in divers and equipment.

My stomach rolled and lurched with the raft. Twenty minutes in, and Wilco was already showing signs of impatience. That's the problem with water searches. My dog, despite his handicap—his missing leg had never slowed him down much—was an active searcher. He loved to romp through the woods, run and bounce over land obstacles, and push his snout along tree roots and rock outcrops, crevices, piles of debris, and anywhere else that held an enticing smell. Being trapped in a raft was pure torture. For my dog and my restless body. Not to mention that it was at least ten degrees colder on the water. At least my shakes might appear to be from the chilled air. Or so I hoped. I swallowed hard.

*Whiskey.* The thought of it popped into my mind and dwelled there for the next twenty minutes as we navigated the water in a grid, zigzagging back and forth in calculated distances upstream from the spot on the bank where the purse was found. We worked this way for over an hour, quietly and methodically, each of us immersed in our own thoughts. *A drink. A drink would warm me nicely about now. Still plenty of time to get it out of my system by Tuesday. No harm done, right? Wishful thinking!* I blinked, focused on my dog, watching his reactions closely. On land, I could easily tell when he was on scent; out here, the signs might be much subtler.

The first signal came about thirty minutes later. We'd rounded a bend in the river when Wilco dipped his head, whined, and clamored over us to the rear of the boat. He leaned over the edge, sniffed, and scurried back to the bow. He did this several times. Bow to stern, stern to bow.

"He's on scent." I looked at the officer manning the oar. "Narrow our zone." And to the others, "Slow and easy with the paddles."

Wilco stopped midway and frantically pawed at the bottom of the raft, as if he could dig straight through to the scent below. Thankfully the raft was hard-bottomed, with exposed rubber flotation only on the sides. He licked his lips, threw his head, whined, and clawed. I readied a buoy, planning to mark the spot, when Wilco lunged to the other side of the raft. The sudden movement spooked one of the officers; he cringed and covered himself, dropped his paddle. Wilco, hyperfocused, didn't flinch. Instead, he wedged himself between the officer and the edge of the raft, leaned over and snapped at the surface of the water, his jaws opening and clamping shut with a loud click. I instantly plunged to the other side, snatched his collar to keep him from jumping or falling. The noise and ferocity of his action was intimidating, even to me as I held him in place.

"I think this may be it."

"You think?" The officers chuckled.

I motioned to the officer, who set the marker, then said, "Let's pull away." I didn't want to risk Wilco going overboard. Frigid water and unpredictable currents could overwhelm even the strongest K9 swimmer.

A little ways downstream, after his praise reward, Wilco settled down with me at the bow of the boat. My emotions were a mixed bag of jubilant satisfaction over our success at a task well done and grief for the victim whose watery grave we'd just marked. It was always this way after a discovery. Conflict was a part of the job. Only today, it hit hard, the loss and misery, and I felt weak and cold and anxious. I wanted a drink, a pill, anything to quell my jittering nerves. Instead, I reached for my dog, wrapped my arms over his back, and caressed the soft underfur of his belly. Even through the heavy material of my immersion suit, I felt the strength of his muscles and the warm heat that radiated from his pelt. I placed my face on the back of his head and stayed that way, spooned behind him with my arms wrapped possessively around his body as our boat silently cut through the icy water.

# CHAPTER 25

As soon as I hit the shore with Wilco, I gave him another pat and ruffled his fur. Withdrawals had curbed my usual energy, but I looked him in the face and his eyes lit up at my pleased expression. Enough. We were done. I was nearing two days without my meds. The shakes and cold sweats were bad, but now the stomach cramps were starting. I wanted to get home, go to bed. Isolate myself.

Grabowski and Pusser stood nearby, watching. I glanced up at the men. "Wilco did good, didn't he? I didn't think he'd—" I stopped midsentence. Pusser looked concerned. "What's going on, boss?"

"A call came into the main dispatch from your cousin. She's trying to get ahold of you, wouldn't say what it was about. You're supposed to call home right away."

I tore at my suit. It wouldn't come off fast enough. "Do the cells—"

"No service here, just back at the main road. We can patch a call through the radio."

Pusser held my sleeve while I squirmed my arm free. "Don't panic, Callahan. It could be anything."

Meg called the office, meaning the police, people she mistrusts. She would never do that unless . . . "It could be my grandmother. She's not well. I should be home with her." The suit was off. I left it in a crumpled heap on the ground and headed straight for the Crown Vic. Grabowski followed, keys dangling in his hand. He helped get Wilco into the car and we hit the road.

As soon as we were in cell range, I saw there were several missed calls from Meg. I checked for messages, but my in-box was full. Damn it. No wonder she had to call into the department. I punched her number again and left a frantic message. "Meg, it's me. I'm sorry. I've got my phone now. Call me as soon as you get this."

I imagined Gran on her deathbed, Meg beside her, holding her hand, crying. . . .

"Can't reach her?"

I looked at Grabowski. "No. Go faster, will you?"

Grabowski sped up.

I punched Meg's number again. *Come on, Meg. Answer. Answer . . . damn it!* I disconnected and called the hospital, identifying myself and giving them Gran's name. The woman on the other end put me on hold. It took forever for her to come back and tell me that they had no record of Gran's admittance. No record of her admittance . . . that was a good sign, right? My heart sank. Or the worst sign. I tried Meg again. No answer. I gave up, clenching my phone on my lap; my hand was shaking, as well as my legs.

Outside, trees blurred past my window, a dark streak against a gray sky. My brain felt like it was knocking up against my eyeballs. Every bump, every sharp turn, rattled it more. Flashes of our olive-drab Humvee bouncing over rock-strewn Iraqi backroads on the way to retrieve . . . The last couple days came crashing in on me: the case, Gran, everything. My muscles ached, my mouth watered; I pressed my right palm against my pants pocket, craving my pills. Hopelessness washed over me. There was nothing to stop the tortured thoughts, the wracking guilt. "I didn't even call to check in today."

"Cut yourself some slack, Callahan. You've been a little busy."

"That's the thing. I'm always busy."

"You're in the middle of a homicide investigation."

"We're looking into one of the clan."

"It's your job. I'm sure your family understands."

"I'm betraying my own. That's all they understand."

"Yeah, but—"

"Forget it, okay?" *Nobody understands, Grabowski. Nobody understands anything about me.*

I ran my fingers through my hair. My scalp throbbed. "Just hurry."

Meg's right hand was wrapped in blood-soaked gauze. She used her other hand to pick at glass shards protruding like spikes from the shag pile of our front-room carpeting. The front window of our trailer was shattered. As soon as we walked in, she shot a dark look Grabowski's way. "I don't want him here."

I ignored her and grabbed Wilco's collar, pulling him aside before he sliced open one of his paws. "Where's Gran? Has she been hurt?"

"She's in bed. She's fine. Shook up, but okay." Meg pointed to a large brick on the floor. "Someone threw this through the window. She was in her chair when it happened." Gran's old blue recliner was just feet from the front window. It was covered in broken glass. I attached Wilco's lead and looped the other end to the knob on the front door.

"You can go now," Meg told Grabowski.

I scowled. "Could you possibly be any ruder?"

"There's no need for him to be here. We don't need him."

"Oh yeah! I can see that we've got it all under control here," I bit back at her, sweeping my hand toward the broken window.

Grabowski shuffled his feet. "Does anyone want to report this?"

Meg lifted her chin. "No. No reports. We'll take care of it ourselves."

He snapped on a pair of gloves. "Did you touch the brick, miss?"

"I moved it out of the way. Why?"

"I'd like to take it in to be processed for prints."

Meg's eyes flattened. "Not necessary, Officer. Like I said, we have our own ways of handling these things."

"This may be connected to our current case." He looked my way for validation and I saw a shift in his attitude, a sudden understanding of what I'd said in the car. I'm a Pavee investigating another of my clan in a murder. Many here resented me. That made me, and my family, connected to the case.

I took a hard stance. "Don't be stupid, Meg. You know people are angry that I'm investigating Nevan. This could be retaliation for his arrest. Someone's way of warning me to back off."

"No one here would do this to Gran." Her sharp glare silently finished the statement: *Not to Gran, but maybe to you.*

"Are you sure about that? Officer Grabowski is right, and if we connect this brick to someone, it might help find Maura's killer. You want that, right?"

She continued to glare at Grabowski.

"Grabowski has *my* permission to look around and take the brick." I hated the hurt look on Meg's face, but this was Gran's house. Which made it my house. Not Meg's.

Grabowski continued forward with gloved hands and retrieved the brick. I headed for the back of the trailer. "I'm going to check on Gran. Be right back."

The last slivers of daylight pierced the window and sliced across Gran's pale face. I went to her and adjusted the pillow behind her back, where she sat propped up. A smile lit up her face, but quickly faded. Her skin was sallow and drawn, blanched, her shoulders rounded and slumped forward. She swayed. My hand shot to her shoulder, adjusting her back in place. Anger welled in me. She'd been doing better. This had set her back. "Gran, are you okay?"

"Who would have done this? Who would have thrown a brick through our window?"

"I don't know." I took a handful of tissues from a box on her nightstand and lowered myself into bed with her, wiping at the sweat on my face. My ears rang, thin and high-pitched. I couldn't stop my legs from moving, as if someone had drained my blood and filled my veins with cherry soda, bubbly and red.

"You okay, child?"

I turned to my side, pushed a wiry hair from her

cheek, her breath hot and sweet on my face. I slid my hand down her arm, scooped her hand into mine, and rubbed my thumb over her thin, freckled skin. My body went still. Physical peace washed over me. I snuggled in closer, spoke in her ear. "Please don't worry, Gran. I'll find out who did this and they'll regret it, believe me."

Her eyes widened. "No. No. Just let it go, child."

"Someone threw a brick through our window. I can't let that go. No one has the right to destroy our property. You could have been hurt."

Her body stiffened, her lip trembled. *What am I doing? Trying to bring on another stroke? "Just let it go." She meant she couldn't face this right now. She isn't strong enough.* I took a deep breath and patted her hand. "I'm sorry, Gran. Please don't worry. It'll be okay."

Her eyes softened and moved over my shoulder. I turned to see Meg in the doorway. I raised up and sat on the edge of the bed. Meg came over and fussed with the blankets, adjusting them over Gran's legs. "Everything okay in here?" There was a false cheerfulness in her tone.

I frowned. "We're fine, Meg."

"Good. Your friend just left. He said he'd be in contact soon." She walked to the closet and removed a handful of blouses on hangers, placed them across the foot of the bed and started sorting them. A slow task with one hand bandaged.

"What are you doing?"

"I'm getting Gran packed. We're leaving in a couple days. Maybe tomorrow, if I can get someone to cover my shift at the diner."

"Leaving? Where are you going?"

Gran pulled her hand away and traced the delicate stitching of the detailed Celtic double-knot design atop her quilt. A wedding gift from her sister, its symbols meant to tie the lives of the married couple for eternity. It'd been on her bed as long as I could remember.

I ducked my head and caught her gaze. "Gran? Talk to me. Where are you going?"

"To your aunt Tinnie's place. She's got an extra room."

"But you have doctor appointments, and—"

"Tinnie's already been in contact with a doctor down there. She'll take good care of me."

"Okay." I put on my achingly polite voice. "Good." Yes, it was a good idea to get her away for a while, away from the stress—and from whoever just did this crime. "You could use a couple days away."

A thick silence settled over the room. I looked from Gran to Meg and then back to Gran. "What is it? What's going on?"

Gran's watery blue eyes grew more intense. "Child, this is no visit. I'm going to stay with Tinnie permanently."

"Did you put this idea into her head?" I leaned against the wall in the hallway, clutching my midsection. I was trembling again, from the withdrawals or anger, or both. "What the hell were you thinking, Meg?"

"I was thinking about Gran and what's best for her. One of us needs to think about her. I can't believe you. Would you really want her staying here now, with bricks flying at her?"

"Of course not. But once—"

"Once what, Brynn? This brick thing was just the last straw. She's been putting up with jeering and rude comments ever since you became a cop. None of her friends will talk to her. And now you're trying to pin Maura's murder on Nevan. How do you think that's going over?"

"It's my job." How many times had I said that this week? "And I'll fix it. Find out who killed Maura, and—"

"And nothing. She's already become an outcast in the clan. You know what that means. She can't return."

The words "can't return" tightened the scars in my neck into a crackle of ache as every fiber in me cringed. Darkness enveloped me, a thick black hole swallowing my soul as I knew Gran wouldn't be here for me in the searing burn of my nightmares of melting skin and shivering cold daylight of severed body parts and swollen maggot-covered carcasses. I wavered, legs unwilling to stand against one more abandonment in my life.

Meg's eyes widened with concern. She reached out, then dropped her arm. "You can go visit every weekend. Tinnie's only a couple hours from here."

"But I don't want her to go." The words came out tiny and weak even as they screamed through my brain. I needed Gran, now more than ever. How could she leave me?

# CHAPTER 26

I woke with a jolt, my heart racing, fuzzy remnants of my dream dissipating with every blink of my eye. My T-shirt clung in patches to my skin, wet and heavy. The flulike aches were back. They wracked my muscles. Snot dripped from my nose. I shook all over, uncontrollable shakes. My teeth chattered. I was freezing, but sweating.

Wilco whimpered and licked at my snot-stained cheeks. I lay back. More rest. That's what I needed, but a sudden pain shot through my abdomen. I shoved my dog aside and ran for the toilet. Shit and snot and sweat oozed and spurted from every orifice of my body until I was emptied.

I was nearing day three of no pills, no booze. Day one irritated me like a hundred mosquitos needling the brain and nerves, but clenched jaws quelled the jitters. Day two, the mosquitos morphed into a thousand razor-backed maggots crawling under my skin, and my jaw hurt from refusing to give in. But day three? A living hell as the vermin invaded every organ.

I called Pusser from the bathroom. I told him I was too sick to come into work. "Tuna sandwich from the gas station outside Augusta," I said.

"Damn gas-station food can kill you," he commiserated. As if the hell I was in had anything to do with salmonella or listeria. He knew better. We were both liars.

Exhausted and spent, I stood under a hot stream of water until the shakes stopped. *I can do this. I can do this. I have to do this.*

I wrapped myself in a towel and shuffled to the kitchen. Coffee would help. And something small to eat to ease the roiling in my stomach. I fumbled with the coffee filter, managed to fill the pot, turned it on. I shoved a handful of dry cereal into my mouth. Some missed and fell to the floor. It hurt to bend down. I left it there. It crunched under my bare feet. Wilco whined. "Shut up, you stupid dog!" I didn't mean that. "I'm so sorry, boy." I scratched his ears and begged forgiveness, as if he heard me, and waited for the coffee to be done. *Why does it take so long to brew?* I waited some more. The clock on the microwave said it was 8:06 A.M.

No job was worth this. Why couldn't Pusser just let it go? So I needed a little something to get me through every day. What I've seen, what I've done, what I've felt . . . I'm a damn war vet. I've earned it.

Coffee spurted into the pot like a liquid balm. A mug. I needed a mug, but opened the wrong cupboard door and my savior stared at me on the shelf. My gaze fixated on the square-sided, black-labeled shield that protected my sanity. I caressed the bottle, my fingers touching it like a lover's face. A lover that begged for my lips, always faithful, and always willing to fill my

basest desires. I thought of Doogan, the lover I didn't
have, the lover I'd never have. I wrapped my fingers
around the liquor bottle's hard neck, perfectly molded
with little indents to fit fingers, my fingers. My lips
twinged. Saliva formed on the edges of my tongue. I
swallowed. Anticipation zinged through every nerve in
my body.

One sip. Just one sip.

No! One day. Twenty-four stupid hours more and I
could piss in the cup and be done. Then I could drink.
Beat the system first, that's all I had to do. Beat the
frickin' system. I paced the floor and checked my
phone. 8:12 A.M. A team of divers was scheduled to
start searching at daybreak. I should be at the scene,
doing my job. Yet, here I was, trying to fight my way
out of hell.

I went to Gran's door. I stood there, with my hand
on the doorknob, heard her soft snores rise and fall
rhythmically. Every part of me wanted to go to Gran,
crawl into her bed, spoon myself into her like I did as a
child after a nightmare.

*My life is a nightmare. I can't let Gran see me like
this.*

I thought of the open suitcase on her dresser. Anxiety
kicked up and tiny pricks invaded my muscles, like a
thousand needles. The Vicodin had numbed me, but no
more. My body was a human pincushion, my mind like
a starving baby away from its mother's breast. And
Gran was leaving. But she had to go, I knew that. It
was dangerous for her here. Bone Gap was like a
fortress with invisible boundaries. We had no gates, no
guards, but strangers were spotted immediately within
our cloistered community. No stranger simply waltzed

in here and launched a brick through my grandmother's window. A Pavee did that. It wasn't a sudden illness that might take Gran from me, but prejudice and hate and antiquated ideals that no longer held true in today's world. I couldn't trust my own people.

I couldn't trust my own opiate-depleted mind.

I walked away from her door with limbs that felt lifeless and heavy as if the blood had drained from my veins. I thought of Maura, cold and truly bloodless, then thought of my pills. My pills. Relief. It'd be so easy. They weren't far away. Just a few steps away, in a Baggie and rolled into a sock that I stuffed in an old pair of shoes and placed on the top shelf of my closet. Out of sight, out of mind.

Only they weren't. Not now. Not ever.

They called to me. Just one, just one . . . *No! I can do this. I can do this. . . . Go back to bed. Not Gran's bed, mine.*

I slipped between cold sheets, shivering, nerves on fire, pricking, pricking. . . . I clenched my muscles as tight as I could, contracting them made the needles go away, if only for a second. Cold, so cold. Wilco joined me. His warm body felt good, comforting. I pulled him close, shut my eyes. Spinning, spinning. Hot, cold, hot. Sweat trickled and my head careened from the whirlwind in my brain. . . . *Fresh air. Away from my pills. That's what I need. Away from here . . .*

We ended up at St. Brigid's rectory.

It was mid-morning and a cold wind rushed under the small portico roof and swirled around my body. I shivered, pulled my sleeves over my hands, and hugged myself against the coldness. A concrete statue of Jesus reigned in the corner of the porch, along with a pot of dead geraniums and a pair of mud-crusted boots. My nose twitched with the smell of something foul, like soured milk or old cheese. I sniffed the air, looked at my dog, and then realized the smell came from me. *Great.*

Colm opened the door in sweatpants and a crumpled T-shirt. His expression shifted from surprise to concern. "What's going on? You don't look so good. Is it your grandmother? Is she okay?"

"No. Not really. Nothing is okay. I need to talk to you . . . about the case."

He invited me in and led me to his office. I shrugged out of my parka and slung it over the back of a chair, while he headed off to the kitchen. In the corner, a large oil painting of the Virgin Mary beckoned to me, arms open, palms outward in a welcoming gesture. An old heat radiator made a faint clacking as it wheezed hot air into the room. Wilco curled next to it, content to settle in for a nap. The room smelled of books and furniture polish and comfort. Something inside me shifted, the shakes subsided, my muscles smoothed. My breathing eased.

I shut my eyes and rested, opening them again when Colm returned. He handed me a mug of coffee.

"My grandmother is leaving," I blurted before he'd even settled behind his desk. What was I thinking? I hadn't come here with the intention of discussing anything personal.

*"Leaving?"*

I told him about the brick and how my part in the investigation had turned some in the clan against us.

"Gran's received the brunt of it. Her health issues, this brick . . . she's scared. She wants to leave Bone Gap."

"Where does she want to go?"

"Down south. To live with my aunt. Maybe forever."

His eyes widened.

"She's like a mother to me." My only mother, since my own abandoned me as an infant. "I'll be lost without her."

He let out a long breath. "Then, you're not going with her?"

"No, with this case, I can't take time to drive her down there right now. Meg said she'd take her, but—"

"No. That's not what I meant. I thought . . . Never mind." He shifted forward and put his elbows on his desk. "Once an arrest is made, things will settle down. She'll be back."

"Maybe. That's why I'm here. I need to ask you a couple questions. Get this case settled."

"Sure."

"Did Maura come see you the week before she died? Maybe to talk to you in private?"

"Why do you ask?"

I explained to him about the journal, took out my phone, and read the last entry to him. "I'm trying to figure out who she'd told about the pregnancy. I thought maybe she'd talked to you. A confession perhaps?"

He sat back, slid his hands off the desk to his lap. "Even if she did, I wouldn't be able to tell you. And I'm not saying she did."

"She's dead. What would it matter?"

"The seal of confession is absolute, even if the penitent passes away."

Rules. Everyone sucked up to the rules except me.

Even now, I was showing case evidence—which I had on my personal device—to a civilian. I shoved my phone into my back pocket and switched gears. "How about Jacob Fisher? Can you tell me anything about him?"

"I don't know a lot, except that the family is struggling. The mother is single, out of work, and trying to feed three kids."

"I think she has a job now. Jacob said she was out of town working."

"That's great. I'm surprised, though. She was having health issues."

I shifted and took a sip of coffee. Its hot bitter taste penetrated like a sharp jab to my tongue. "Maybe she's better."

He stared at my hands. "Are *you* feeling okay? You're trembling."

I slid my cup back onto the edge of his desk and slipped my fingers under my leg. "I noticed some food-pantry boxes in the back of Jacob's truck."

"He comes by the pantry once a week."

"How does he seem to you?"

"What do you mean?"

"What's your impression of him?"

Colm leaned back in his chair. "Is he a suspect?"

"Just one among several."

"I see. I've only recently met him. It used to be his mother who came in to collect food for the family. Since her illness, Jacob started showing up. He seems like a nice-enough kid. Quiet. I got to know them from the food-pantry days. I've never seen the family in church."

"Not churchgoers, huh?"

He shrugged. "I never see you in church, either."

"This isn't about me."

He studied me for a second, his eyes lingering on my face, then dropping to where I kept my hands tucked. I knew what he saw: paleness, dark circles, hollowed-out eyes, the shakes. I wasn't simply sick, and he knew it. "Maybe it should be," he said.

"Please. Spare me the lecture, Colm. I'm going through a lot right now."

"More than the case and your grandmother's illness?"

"Yeah. More than all that."

"What else are you going through, Brynn? Maybe I can help."

I pulled my hand from under my thigh, tried to rub away the horrible pain throbbing in my temples, my fingers thumping a percussion. "No one can help me."

"Try me."

"I'm fine. Really." I stood. He stood. Our eyes locked. He tried to hold my gaze. Shame made me look away. "I should go."

He sighed and nodded, but didn't make a move to show me out.

I ducked my head and went around him. "See you later then."

Outside in the hallway, a blaze of heat overwhelmed me, first igniting my face, then washing down my body like a bucket of hot oil, searing and viscid, had been poured over my head. When the heat reached my stomach, acid boiled up and rose to the back of my throat, my stomach reeled.

I bolted for the front door, but barely made it halfway

there before heaving. I sank to my knees, my stomach muscles purging its meager contents. My face burned from embarrassment. *Not here, not here. Oh, God.*

I sensed Colm behind me, felt his hand on my shoulder. "It's okay," he whispered. His voice came from far away, drowned out by the sound of blood rushing through my ears. My stomach cramped, another gush of vomit pushed its way up my throat. I gagged, and stomach slime sprayed the floor and splattered my cheeks. The acidic smell of puke burned my nostrils. *No, this is not okay. Nothing about this is okay. Please just go away. Please.*

His fingers brushed my cheeks, entwined themselves in my hair and pulled it away from my face. He stayed there, one hand on my back, the other holding my hair at the nape of my neck. I heaved again and again before my gut relaxed. I inhaled, wiped under my eyes, and sat back. Chunky orange fluid puddled on the hall rug and seeped into the crevices in the floorboards. Vomit streams, tiny off-colored tributaries flowing from a lake of puke.

Wilco appeared and began lapping it up. "No! Get!" I smacked his backside. He yelped and sauntered off, turning back with a hurt look.

I looked up at Colm. "I can't believe . . . I'm sorry . . . The rug . . ."

"It's okay. The rug is old, anyway. I'll get it cleaned up."

"No. I'll take care of it." I stood, swaying from the sudden rush to my head.

He caught my elbow. "Easy. Maybe you should sit down for a minute."

"Just get me something to clean the floor."

"We'll take care of this in a minute. Talk to me. What's going on?"

"Nothing. I'm not feeling well, that's all. Something I ate, probably."

"That's not what this is. I've known for a while, Brynn. You need help. You can't go this alone."

"You're wrong. I'm fine."

"Let me help. Let me be a friend to you."

"That's not possible and you know it."

His expression went blank.

"Don't act like you don't know what I mean. I can't get that close to you. We have too much history together to just be friends."

"That was a long time ago, Brynn. We were just—"

"Kids. I know. We were just stupid kids. And now we're not . . . we're not kids." And here we were. Me: lost, sick, broken, a loner. I had nothing. And Colm? My eyes flitted around the hallway to the sanctuary and foyer, with images of smiling and benevolent and peaceful saints dotting the path, and then settled on his collar. He had so much more. He'd found what I'd never even glimpsed: peace and respect and a place where he truly belonged.

He tensed, folded his arms across his chest, and took a step back.

I'd said something wrong. Yet again. "It's fine. I'm fine. Really. Don't worry about me." Another bout of nausea hit me, rolling through my abdomen like stormy waves. My head pounded and whooshed. I clenched my midsection, pushed past him, and headed for the door.

# CHAPTER 27

After leaving the rectory, I spent the rest of the day at the Highway 2 rest stop, curled under the cold light of one of the stalls. I was puked dry by the time I made it up the mountain that evening. Even Wilco had opted to stay in the back seat, away from my barfy smell. The shakes had set in and my head pounded with every heartbeat. I couldn't go home. Gran would know right away. She didn't need the worry. And my bottle was there, and the pills, too. I'd latch onto them like a suckling baby the instant I got home.

I called Meg and made an excuse, something about the case, and asked her to keep a close eye on Gran. I promised her I'd be back first thing in the morning and begged her to stay one more day.

Sleep. I could sleep this off. Everything would be better in the morning.

I'd picked an isolated spot. A small trailhead parking lot not far off the highway. During warmer months, the trail was popular with day hikers. This time of year, few people came out this way. There was little chance I'd be bothered.

I twisted the top off a bottled water and popped a couple pills. Just ibuprofen. But I'd take anything to dull the pain in my muscles and joints. Not my usual remedy of choice, but it'd have to do. This time tomorrow, it'd all be over. A quick pee, plaster on a smile for an inane session with the shrink, and I'd be on my way. Back to normal. Then I'd take the rest of that day off. Go out and find that gun Doogan had tossed and get rid of it for good. After that? Celebrate with something special. Expensive. Maybe a shot of Old Forester. I'd earned it. No pills, though. I was done with the pills. The booze would have to be enough.

*One more freakin' night.*

As the sun set, I turned off the ignition and climbed into the back of my station wagon. Wilco nestled in with me, back hunched as he turned around a couple times and plopped next to me. I spooned my body against his and pulled a sleeping bag, which I kept in the car, over the top of us.

I don't know how long I'd been staring into the darkness, my body refusing to sleep, when light flooded my vehicle. I bolted up, looked out the back hatch. Someone had their car's headlights trained on me. I ducked down, shielded my eyes. The light was blinding. I was a sitting duck.

I scrambled for the front of the car, banged my knee on the seat, fell forward, and cracked my head on the dash. *Shit!* Wilco became frantic, panting and pacing in the small space. I recovered. Slid into the driver's seat. No keys! The keys . . . Where'd I put the keys?

Wilco pawed at me. I pushed him away, bent down, and ran my hand along the floorboard. *Where are the damn keys?*

The window shattered. Glass shards sprayed my body. Wilco growled and snarled and clamored at my side, trying to get past me and to my assailant.

Another window shattered behind me. The back hatch window. Wilco lunged toward the back seat. Shadows darted around the car. Someone yelled out. A deep, male voice. More voices, all masculine. Scuffling. I scrambled to get out, fumbling, glass everywhere. Footsteps, car doors, and the sound of a car peeling out.

I'd heard something else, too: *"Musker."*

Pavees did this. My own people. I must've been followed.

I stood shaking in the dark. Wilco came to my side, panting. The smell of doggy adrenaline filled the air, sour and musky and hot-smelling. Tiny pricks of heat stung my left cheek. I touched it. My fingers came away bloody. I sat back in the car, flicked on my dome light, and flipped down the visor mirror. Glass slivers. A dozen or more lodged under my skin.

I turned to Wilco and checked him over. He was fine. Slivers caught in his thick fur, but nowhere near his skin. Thank, God. Whoever did this would have no hesitation to hurt an animal. Or . . . I grabbed for my phone, shook off the glass splinters that stuck to my palm, and dialed.

"Meg. Get Gran out of the house. Now."

# CHAPTER 28

Dr. Ryan, Daniel Ryan, wore brown trousers, a navy blue button-down cardigan, and wire-rimmed glasses. Old-man attire, odd for someone in his midthirties, as I guessed him to be. Perhaps he thought the ensemble made him look smarter, or older, or more approachable. I was surprised he didn't sport a mustache for effect as well. It didn't matter. Despite his efforts, I disliked him the moment I shook his wimpy hand.

He indicated for me to take the chair across from his desk. "What happened to your face?"

I traced the bandage on my cheek. I'd spent most of the night in the emergency waiting room, getting cleaned up, stitched up, and a prescription written for the pain. A prescription whose presence I could feel even now, hot in my back pocket, begging to be filled the minute I got out of this office. Not that I would— I'd sworn off pills, knew how one step onto that rocky slope would slide me into a black valley yet again. Didn't want to go there. Still . . . I hadn't tossed the prescription. Not yet. "I cut myself cleaning up a broken window." True enough.

That was the story I'd used at the ER and I'd stick with it. I was sure my attackers were members of my own clan, and we were under enough scrutiny as it was. In time, I'd figure out who they were. Attacking a clan member was unforgivable, especially an elder in the clan, like Gran. Sweet Gran. There were no excuses for what they did.

Dr. Ryan made some sort of notation on the clipboard balanced on his knee.

"It looks worse than it is," I added. Glad he hadn't asked about the thin sheen of sweat on my forehead or the trembling of my hand. Physical symptoms had calmed, replaced by intense cravings; my mind screamed for a pill, sweet and easy relief.

Dr. Ryan looked up from his clipboard and smiled. His teeth shimmered pearly white. He probably flossed every night before bed. Stuck those strip things to his enamels to dazzle his patients with his superiority. No way was this guy going to understand me. I squirmed and rubbed moist palms over the knees of my dress pants, navy blue trousers I'd borrowed from Meg's closet. Appearances mattered, she'd always said. I wondered if the doggy hairs clinging lintlike would count against me. I brushed and picked at a few; seeing that my efforts were futile, I sat back and sighed. They should have allowed me to bring my dog. This would go much better if Wilco were here.

Dr. Ryan spoke in one long exhale. "So tell me what's been going on, Brynn. Is it okay if I call you Brynn?"

*Is it okay if I call you asshole?* "Sure."

He continued to stare at me, blue eyes blinking behind wiry frames.

I blinked back and then realized he was waiting for me to talk. "There was an incident last week with my job. My boss wants me to be evaluated."

He retrieved a manila file from the nearby desk and flipped through the papers inside. Like he didn't know what was inside it. "Yes. An FFD"—a fitness for duty exam—"was ordered. Drug testing and a psych workup. Do you have any questions before we get started?"

"No."

"There's a brief history here in your file. It says you're ex-military, a cop now. There are a couple past minor incidents listed: conflicts with a fellow employee, missed workdays, nothing major." He looked up. "You were medically discharged?"

I pulled my shirt back, exposing my neck. "I was hit by an IED."

"I'm sorry."

He sounded like a robot. Flat. Expressionless. Like "Who cares."

"Must've been painful," he said.

"Still is."

"How do you cope?"

*Whiskey to dull the pain, Vicodin from time to time, all the time, to smooth the rough edges. . . .* "Day by day, I guess."

"Flashbacks, nightmares?"

"Both."

"Must've been difficult to be a female Marine."

"Marine."

"Pardon?"

"I was a Marine, period. And, yeah, it's a hard job, but the best job ever. A privilege."

"You miss it?"

"Yes. Absolutely. Most of it, anyway."

"What do you miss?"

"My buddies. Yeah, my buddies. People were real, you know. Something about knowing you could die at any time puts a different spin on things. Friends were friends. Real friends."

"Do you have any 'real friends' now? Here?"

"My dog. Wilco."

He smiled. An oh-that's-so-sweet smile that most people reserved for five-year-olds. "Of course. But I meant human friends."

I thought of Pusser. Grabowski. Parks. *Friends?* I wasn't sure. "My family is here. We're close."

He paused, set his clipboard and file aside, and clasped his hands together. "The aftereffects of war can be difficult for some veterans to deal with, and alcohol or other drugs can become an easy crutch."

I chuckled. "I never would have guessed that, Doc."

"Do you abuse alcohol?"

"I wouldn't say I 'abuse' it."

"What would you say?"

"I have a drink here and there. Just to unwind. Most people do."

"'Unwind'? Do you have anxiety?"

"What do you think?"

"I'm asking you."

"War's not easy."

"I understand."

"Do you?"

He frowned. "Do I what?"

"Understand."

He leaned back. I had his full attention now.

"Ever been in a war, Doc?"

"No."

"Ever been shot at? Killed someone? Handled a bloated, rotting, maggot-infested body? Smelled your own flesh burning?" He was shaking his head. No, of course not. Mr. Creased Pants wouldn't last two seconds in the sandbox without wetting himself.

He shifted. "Tell me about it."

"There's not enough time to go into all that."

"Just one small thing. Something that stands out in your memory."

*One thing?* Every second of the damned war was seared into my memory, branded for eternity in my thoughts. I reached for a tissue, dabbed at my face, blew my nose, tossed it in the can, and shifted my attention back to Mr. Headshrinker. "The heat," I said. "It's always hot. A half hour into a twelve-hour mission and you're dripping sweat. Your mouth feels like cotton. There's never enough water. Sand is everywhere. It works its way under your uniform and into every orifice of your body. You itch, your nose is dried out, your eyes swollen. You can't see shit. And it's loud. Crazy loud. Rounds going out, rounds coming in, grenades and rockets, people yelling. You have no idea who the enemy is, what weapons they have, when they might burst out of hiding and take a shot at you. Adrenaline is constantly pumping through your veins. You're amped up, on edge, ready to die at any moment. That's what it's like, day in and day out. That's what war was like for me, Doc. At least part of the time."

"What was the rest of your time like?"

"Boring as hell. Stretches of mind-dulling boredom where nothing happens. You sit and wait. And wait. Then, out of the blue, a call comes. You're needed. You go. You don't ask questions. You just go. You don't even know where. The only thing you know for sure is that you could die. It hangs over your head constantly. War is a series of relentless extremes. Boredom to certain death. No between. Anxiety becomes a part of who you are. You never turn it off. You do, and you're not on your game, not able to save your own thankless hide, let alone your buddies."

"So you drink to help."

I frowned. "Never on the job. Just at night to help me sleep. There's nothing wrong with that."

"That's probably true."

"So, what's the problem?"

His eyes darted from my sweaty face and shaking hands, to my bouncing legs, before coming back to my face again. "You tell me."

I sat back and glared. "There's no problem. I'm fine. This is a waste of time."

He picked up the file again and shuffled through the papers. "Seems this evaluation was prompted by a particular incident."

"This evaluation was prompted by our jackass of a mayor who thinks his position allows him the right to screw around with people's lives. His son's a suspect in a homicide investigation. I asked too many questions, looked too closely at his spoiled brat, and he doesn't like it. That's all this is."

"Tell me what happened at the cemetery."

I sighed.

He read from the report. "It says here that you acted impaired during the investigation and that resulted in contamination of evidence."

"I was fine."

"Several witnesses confirmed the report."

I sat forward. "Like who? Harris? He's a jerk. I'd love to see the psych eval on that ego of his. He'd say anything to get me fired."

*Who else? Parks? No, she wouldn't. She's on my side. Isn't she?*

"Had you been drinking before arriving on the scene?"

"I worked late the night before. Had a few drinks to unwind before I went to sleep. I didn't know I was going to get called in the middle of the night. It was a mistake. Something like that could happen to anyone."

"But it happened to you. And you're a cop. You carry a gun."

"It was a one-time deal. It won't happen again. I won't let it."

"Only once?" He paged back through my file. "Let me read this to you. 'Officer Callahan has been late to shift three times this month. She has seemed, on several occasions, to be in physical distress and to suffer from extreme fatigue. She is often distracted and absentminded. She's incurred two citizen complaints of misconduct since being inducted into the department last year.'"

I sat back, grinned. "Every cop gets those. People don't like it when you arrest them. They're funny that way. So, what do you expect happens? It's not like they're going to write a thank-you note."

He ignored me and continued: "'These incidents reflect a deterioration from her initial evaluation and demonstrate a pattern of substandard performance—'"

*"Substandard performance?"* My blood boiled. "What the hell does that mean? I'm out there every frickin' day busting my butt for the department. Me and my dog. They're damn lucky to have us. Ask my boss."

"Sheriff Frank Pusser?"

"Yeah."

"He wrote this."

I sprang from my chair. "This is stupid. I'm leaving."

"I wouldn't advise that. This is a mandatory FFD. I think you like your job, Officer. Termination could be the result if you fail to submit."

*Submit.* Like allowing my soul to be raped by this mind-numbing redo of every eval I'd had, and by an anemic paper pusher. I gritted my teeth. But what choice did I have? This was the only job that had mattered to me since the Marines. I sat back down.

"I believe you want to be a good cop. You suffer from a disorder—"

"Enough. Enough. Enough! I'm sick of that label. I don't have a *disorder.* I served this country. I did my job and all people like you can do is label me *disordered.* You attribute every emotion and every angry outburst and every misstep to my wartime trauma, as if I have some sort of mental sickness. Would you do that to a vet with an amputated leg? Would you label him *disordered* because he misses having two good legs? Or because he'll never walk the same? No. Because he has an obvious injury. It's the same for me. I was *injured*." I pulled back my shirt again, and pointed to my scars. "Here. Look at it!" He did. I moved my finger upward and pointed to my head. "And here. My head, my soul, my whole being. Scarred beyond recognition. Even to me."

"That may be, but we still need to address any . . . uh . . . lingering issues that may hinder your job performance."

I threw up my hand. "You know what? This thing at the cemetery was just a fluke. I'm fine. Everything's under control." I stood. "I need to get back to work."

"Okay then." He closed the folder. "We should have the results from your drug test soon. As soon as I have it, I'll write up my recommendation."

# CHAPTER 29

The trailer was dark and empty and lonely. Scummy dishes were piled in the sink, cardboard duct-taped over the broken window, a pair of Meg's jeans strung over the back of the sofa. The smell of last night's cabbage and pork shanks still hung in the air, along with a faint scent of Gran's bath soaps. I closed my eyes and inhaled. Sweet yet sour in a way that speaks of home, of real lives, of sweat and sorrow.

A warm pressure pushed against my legs. I opened my eyes and looked down at my dog. His bright eyes coaxed a smile. I gave him a thumping "good boy" pat and he headed back to the door. So easy for a dog—a thump, a smile, and they were good to go. In this case, literally he was ready to go. I shook my head. Only Wilco could so quickly help me shake off the residual anger from my meeting with Dr. Ryan. I let him out and turned to start my own business of gathering equipment for what I planned to do after work—head up the mountain to find the gun Doogan had tossed. I needed to get Wilco's tactical bag, a water bottle, some snacks. But first, what I really needed.

Meg called as I made my way to my bedroom. "Gran is all settled. She's doing fine. I wanted you to know." A tinge of caustic emotion mixed with a heavy dose of tired. About how I felt as well.

"Good. How's Aunt Tinnie?" I opened the closet door.

"Busy fussing over Gran. I'm going to stay another day or two before coming back. I need to get Gran in to see a doctor."

"Can I talk to her?" I ran my hand along the top shelf until I hit on it. I pulled down the rolled sock with the small Baggie of pills and took out a few.

"Sure, hold on." I heard the sound of muffled voices on the other end. Meg came back on the line. "She says she'll call you later."

"She doesn't want to talk to me?"

"It's not that. She's tired, that's all." Less caustic now. More apologetic or likely pity. I preferred caustic.

"Sure. I understand." I kept one pill out, rolling it between my thumb and forefinger, and pocketed the rest. Not many. Not like before. I'd seen the error in my ways. I'd never go back to taking that many pills again.

"Any more news on Maura's case?"

*Yeah. Let's see . . . another dead body, this one submerged and probably all connected to Maura.* I didn't say any of that, though. "We're still looking into leads." It was premature to tell her about the newest find. Better to backtrack, find that connection. "You said you'd never seen Addy at the diner."

"That's right."

"Any other kids that Maura seemed to be friends with?"

"Nevan, of course. And Winnie, and—"

"Settled kids."

"Isn't Nevan in jail for Maura's murder? Are you letting him out?"

"Please, Meg. Just answer me."

"Mostly just the mayor's boy. A few others, I guess."

"Ever see a dark-haired guy. Short and skinny? Really skinny."

"Yeah, I've seen a kid like that. Once he came in and sat in the back booth. He was working on math. Maura took a break and helped him out. Although he mostly just sat there and drew pictures in his notebook, while she did the actual problems. Nice-enough kid, though. I don't know his name."

"When was the last time you saw him there?"

"I don't remember. A while ago."

I heard a scraping sound at the door. Wilco must've finished his business. I hung up with Meg and went to let him inside. Only Wilco wasn't there. Again I heard the sound. This time from the back of the trailer; not the door, I realized, but the back window. I headed that way, caught a flash of color through the glass.

I darted through the back door. Five men stood in my yard, just a few feet from my window. I recognized one as Pete Riley, Riana's husband. The guys with him wore sweatshirts with the hoods pulled over their heads, a couple with bloodstained sports wraps on their hands. Boxers. Bare-knuckle fighters. Some might call it barbaric, but to us, it was a tradition, a source of honor and pride. I'd seen most of them before. They hung out in car lots around McCreary, behind the pubs mostly, picking fights for cash. Intimidating as hell. Yet, I figured if they'd wanted to hurt me, they would've done so last night. A woman alone, in a deserted location . . . an easy target. So hurting me wasn't part of their agenda. They were just trying to scare me. Flex their intimidation muscles. Get me to leave Bone Gap, just like I'd had to send Gran scurrying away.

*They underestimate me.*

"You looking for me?"

"Maybe so," one of them said.

"What do you want?"

"Just paying you a visit."

"Like you did last night?"

A smirk, and then, "I have no idea what you're talking about."

*Like hell.* "You have something to say to me, Pete?"

"Maura's killin' is clan business. We want you coppers to stay out of it."

"She was murdered. There are laws, things that have to be done—"

"Bullshit. These things have always been handled inside the clan. That's how we do things. Seems like you've forgotten that." At his cohorts' nods, he puffed himself up an inch taller. That's the trouble with bullies. They need reinforcements, support from . . . Suddenly my nerves tingled. *Where's Wilco?* I dared a quick glance. *No Wilco.*

I held my voice steady as my heart pounded. "Times are changing, Pete."

"Because of Pavees like you." He sneered, glanced at

his posse. His look empowered these ringside bullies, each stepped closer, eyes like hungry hyenas. Backed by his cronies, his voice rose. "We want you out of here. You and that grandmother of yours."

The puckered skin on my neck started throbbing. He moved closer. Too close. A whiff of sour sweat and stale beer hit my face. The other guys spread out, a couple of them moving to the left of me. I held his gaze and backed up. "That brick barely missed my grandmother. You could have killed her."

"*Brick?* Someone threw a brick at your grandmother. Ahh. That's too bad." The guys chuckled. Pete reeked of the musky testosterone that surged through him now. "She was smart to leave then. Maybe you should do the same."

"I'm not going anywhere, Pete."

"We'll see." He snorted. His buddies laughed. Pete made a *woof, woof* sound that pierced through me, and another round of raucous laughter broke out. Then like vipers slipping back into the grasslands of an African savanna, the five of them backed off, leaving me shaken and panicked as fear rose like bile in my gut.

*Wilco?* I looked around. No sign of him. I darted to the front of the trailer. Nothing.

*If he's done something to my dog, I'll kill him.*

I rushed down the street, looking under cars, by trash cans, all the usual spots, with Pete's laughter echoing in my mind.

I started knocking on trailer doors. Only Rosie Black answered, her comically round breasts bulging from her scoop-necked T-shirt, hot rollers in her hair, the television blaring behind her. "What's wrong with you? Somethin' on fire?"

"My dog. Have you seen him?"

She rolled her eyes. "No." The door slammed shut.

I scanned the edge of the woods, decided against it, and turned back toward Gran's place. I'd had trouble with him wandering in the past, but he'd been so good about it lately. Maybe he's back.

But he wasn't.

I gripped my hair; my head pounded in rhythm with my heart. Over the *whooshing* in my ears, I heard the faint sound of a dog barking. Wilco's barking.

*Wilco!*

I followed the noise. It took me four trailers down to an old shed in the back of an abandoned trailer. I ripped away a shovel wedged under the handle and threw open the door. Wilco rushed to me, knocking me back, alive and frantic, his wet tongue slobbering my face. I wrapped my arms around his neck and pulled him close.

# CHAPTER 30

Pusser yanked the toothpick from between his lips and pitched it toward the garbage can in the corner of his office. It missed. Wilco scurried over and gave it a sniff. I watched his eager nostrils flare to catch a whiff of this cast-off, his eyes pinpointing the slender object, even his fur standing at alert to the new toy tossed for what he would always consider his personal benefit. Every muscle twitch was clear and ready and vigilant. Thank God, Wilco was fine. I caught a whiff of something sour, hoped it wasn't me, and noticed Wilco sniffing around the trash can. Probably used coffee grounds or a rotting banana peel. His nose never quit. He never quit. Another lesson I needed to keep in mind. Had Pete lured him into that shed with some sort of scent? Or food? Either was possible. I'd been lapsing, too lenient, letting other people feed him treats. I knew better. *My fault, my fault.* The words ran through my mind like a mantra. I'd failed my dog. Put him at risk. And the threat was clear: *Leave the clan, or my dog would . . .*

"Your face," Pusser said. "What happened to your face?"

I pulled my attention from my dog.

"It's nothing." I'd missed the morning status meeting, said nothing about Pete's visit, and was trying to get up-to-date on the case. Pusser and I huddled in front at the stat room's white board. I told him about Jacob Fisher visiting Maura at the diner; then we looked over some photos that'd been added to our lineup, a few snapshots of the Barton girl. She'd been pretty, had dark hair, round brown eyes, a cleft in her chin. "Did they find her body yet?"

"The divers are out. No news yet. The parents are on their way. Grabowski is at the scene waiting on them."

"The only connection we have between Addy and Maura is the credit card charge at the diner, right? Or did something else come up?"

"No. But the drugs in the Barton girl's purse were Rohypnol pills."

"Roofies?"

"Yeah, date-rape pills." Pusser gritted his teeth. "I'm trying to push through the tox workup on Maura. If she had the same thing in her system . . ."

I patted my pocket, glad for the pill I'd taken earlier, my first necessary layer of defense against the day's onslaught. More buffer might be needed later. But not yet. I needed to cut back a bit. The last few days had taught me that. From here on out, I'd be more in control.

"What really happened to you, Callahan?"

"I cut myself on some glass." A half-truth, but it didn't matter. I pretty much knew Pete Riley was responsible for last night's ordeal, and it had nothing to do with the case. Or everything, maybe, but not in the way Pusser would think. Pete had gotten one thing right. Some things needed to be taken care of within the clan. That's why I couldn't tell Pusser anything. Even though I wanted to tell him everything.

Pusser moved across the room and wedged himself into one of the chairs, the type with the small desk attached, almost big enough, but not quite, for a notebook. Wilco followed, curling himself at Pusser's feet.

Pusser bent to give him a pet and let out a little moan, his buttons straining on his shirt. "He did great out there yesterday." He pointed to the seat next to him. "Sit down, Callahan."

I did and waited. Pusser and I often discussed work alone, face-to-face. But not like this. His chin lowered, his neck muscles tensed, it unnerved me. His beady eyes scrutinized me through the folds of his pockmarked cheeks. *My test results. That's what this is about. I failed the urine test.* I shifted and tugged my collar up higher on my neck and steeled myself for the news. A small part of me welcomed it, like a child about to be scolded for something she knew she deserved. Boundaries had never been my thing, neither by heritage nor nature. The Marines had rules and orders, but boundaries were defined in other ways as well. Pusser had established rules, sure; yet with him, it was different, more personal, like . . .

"Are you clean?"

"Yeah." I lied. "Why?"

"I may not be able to hold the mayor off much longer. He wants you out."

"Because his kid's a screwup?"

"Pretty much."

"He's threatened your job, too, hasn't he?"

Pusser grunted.

"Can he do that?" I asked. "His kid is under investigation. It's obvious what he's trying to do."

"He's got the authority to do whatever he wants."

"You want me to walk?"

"No."

"What do you want then?"

"Tell me your urine test is going to come back clean."

"Yes." My answer came fast, too fast. My sweaty palm squeaked on the hard surface of the desk. Pusser raised a brow. Neither one of us said anything. What could I say? Was I clean? Hell no, not now. But I'd done everything to be certain my piss in the cup would pass muster. Would it work? I had no idea.

# CHAPTER 31

It was "double-up" night at the McCreary Pub, two beers for the price of one. I was already on my second double-up. Yeah, I was drinking in public. Not the smartest thing, considering, but Wilco and I were celebrating, or lamenting, take your pick.

Wilco's nose had once again proved successful. At three-thirty this afternoon, despite murky-water conditions, a female body was pulled from the bottom of the river. And for that, I was grateful. It meant a family saved from the lifetime sentence of ambiguity of "presumed dead." No more searching, hoping, waiting, and contemplating the "what-ifs." I thought of Pusser always wondering what happened to his daughter. The Bartons, at least, had a body, and, some might say, a semblance of closure. Although, I'd seen this type of thing before and knew that wasn't true. When a loved one dies, especially a child, the casket may close, but each shovel of dirt that covers it clouds the air with a dust that never settles over a lifetime of grief. There would be no closure for the Bartons.

Blurry-eyed, I leaned on my elbows and stared into my glass as if the frothy amber alcohol held life's answers. It didn't. Two girls dead and I couldn't get a handle on anything. Maura and Nevan, Maura and Hatch, and how did Addy fit into the picture? I picked up my phone and scrolled through the journal entries again, focusing on the early entries, the ones where Maura had talked about her relationship with Nevan.

*January 12*
*Nevan and I can never find any privacy. No one ever leaves us alone. I think his sister suspects that we're doing something.*

*January 13*
*Nevan and me got in a huge fight over something stupid. He thinks I like another guy. I don't. I only love him. I wish I could make him believe me. He hates me now. I saw him in the hallway at school and he wouldn't even look at me. My heart aches. I can't live without him.*

*January 15*
*Good and bad news. Nevan and me made up today. It'd been so long since we'd been together, so we snuck back to his bedroom while his mother was sleeping. Then Riana came in and caught us. She was so mad.*

*January 16*
*Nevan and me can't see each other anymore.*

> *I think I'm going to die of a broken heart.*
> *I've got to see him.*

> *January 17*
> *Something horrible happened and it's all*
> *my fault. I'll never forgive myself.*

Normal teen angst. At least by Traveller standards. Riana caught the kids in the act, they got in trouble, the consequence being that they couldn't see each other anymore. That made sense. And the "something horrible" was when she realized she was one month pregnant—by Hatch. I scrolled back to the end of her first entry at Christmas:

> *I can't believe only a couple weeks ago I*
> *had doubts about Nevan and me being to-*
> *gether. I was so stupid. I never should have*
> *doubted us—I love him so much.*

So in early to mid-December, she'd had doubts about her and Nevan. And the "stupid" could have referred to sleeping with Hatch.

I scrolled forward, found the line in that February 2 entry:

> *Nevan found out today that it's Hatch's*
> *baby. So stupid!*

Again I wondered: Maura and Nevan. Maura and Hatch. But . . . no mention of Addy Barton.

I looked up again when the barmaid pointed her

lacquered nail my way. "Ohmigodohmigodohmigod! That's her!" Then her digit shot toward the television above the bar.

A couple fellows at the bar turned, looked my way and then to the television. An image of Wilco and me in the patrol boat flashed across the screen. The discovery of Addy's body had made the evening news. *Great.* I went back to my beer.

"How's it going?" One of the guys suddenly leaned over me, beer in hand, grin on his face. He was a dark-haircd guy with lots of stubble on his face and eyes like pestering flies that darted from my face to my breasts and lingered. "Can I join you?"

"No."

The grin faded. He glanced at his buddy, who was still at the bar. They exchanged some sort of knowing look before he turned and zeroed back in on me. "You're that cop on television."

"Uh-huh." Wilco was curled at my feet. I nudged him awake. He lumbered out from under the table and yawned.

Another glance at his buddy. A nod. An encouraging smile. He turned back to me. "We heard that the girl pulled from the lake was all chopped up."

*He'd heard wrong.* "I can't comment on the case."

"That other girl . . . guess she was carved up, too."

Wrong again. Wonder where this guy got his information.

"Thing is, my buddy and I might know something."

"And what's that?"

"There's this gypsy guy who comes in here Friday nights with his buddies. A big guy. A real jerk. He buys beers for a couple of the locals, chums them up and then challenges them to a friendly fight. Bare-handed boxing."

"For cash?"

He took my interest as an invitation, pulled out the chair next to me, and plunked down. Wilco went back to his nap. "You didn't hear this from me, okay? But last Friday night, there was a lot of them here."

"'Them'?"

"Gypsies. Pikies. Whatever you want to call them. Bone Gap people. Anyway, must've been a dozen or more. A bunch of kids from the high school were here, too. Some big fight was going down between 'em. Money was changing hands like crazy." He grinned. "And not a cop in sight."

Over his shoulder, I saw Grabowski come in the back door. He caught my eye and veered toward the bar.

The barmaid suddenly appeared at our table, smiling down at us with crimson lips and eyelashes that looked like fuzzy spider legs. "Another round for you two?" I shrugged. Why not? He puffed up like he'd won some trophy. *Yeah, jerk, enjoy paying for my beer.*

"What's your name?" I asked.

"John." His lips curled upward. His voice dropped an octave. His eyes wandered back to my breasts. "What's yours?"

"Something happen at that fight, John?"

"Nothing at first. My buddy and me, we watched a few of the fights. They were bloody, but legit. The pikies usually win. Them gypos know how to fight. Never seen anything like it. Anyways, one of the high-school kids wanted to get in on the action, take a turn with the winning knacker. The big gypsy who runs things—Pete, I think they called him—said no, but the kid flashed around a wad of cash. Probably a few hundred bucks or more. Must've been too much to resist."

Two more beers came. John drained his old one and started on the new.

"So, they fought?"

"Not really. The kid didn't make it for two seconds. Took a punch to the face right away and went down. He weren't too happy about it, neither. Like I said, there was a bunch of high-school kids there. They were laughing and shit. The blond kid didn't like that too much."

"Blond?"

"Blond, good-looking kid. Drove one of them big SUVs."

"A black SUV?"

"Yup. Anyways, the gyps started to divvy up his cash and the kid sort of went crazy. Called that gypsy who'd clobbered him a fag."

That got my attention. Gypsy, pikey, gypos—the ugly words never stopped. But out of all the words leveled at any Pavee man, that one would boil blood. Ironic, really, that a culture that faces so much prejudice would in turn project the same hatred toward other marginalized people. But Pavees, especially the elders of my clan, condemned homosexuals. Gay Travellers were ostracized as if their very existence was a contagion that could threaten the clan's idolization of manhood, family, and clan obedience, the holy trinity of our patriarchal society. Questioning a Pavee man's sexuality was akin to the highest form of insult.

"That gypsy didn't like that none. He went nuts. Went back after the kid. Got him a few times in the face. That's when the kid pulled a blade."

"A knife?"

"I'd say. A frickin' big knife. One of those with a button on the handle that makes it pop out. The sucker was huge, though. Big enough to carve up a deer."

*Or a person.*

John gulped down some beer and swiped his lips with the back of his sleeve. "Them gypsies backed off right away."

"I bet. What'd the kid do?"

"He was still pissed off. I'm thinking he was half high, the way he waved that knife around, making threats. Said the gyps cheated him. Hit him before he was ready, or some crap like that. Sore loser if you ask me. Full of hate. Kept saying that there are only two ways he liked pikies."

"Oh yeah? What's that?"

"Legs spread or dead."


"You okay? You look upset." John had gone back to his buddy, and Grabowski took his place. He had a beer in one hand and his reading glasses in the other. *Reading glasses? Really? In a bar?* My eyes weren't about to focus again anytime soon. I shook my head.

"How'd you find me?"

"You are, if anything, predictable. The body has been officially identified. It is Addy Barton. Autopsy is still in progress, but there were multiple stab wounds to the chest cavity." He slid a piece of paper my way. It was a copy of a newspaper clipping. "And there's another connection."

I glanced over it. A human-interest article on a young Addy Barton. She'd won a blue ribbon at the state fair. Poultry division. "Chickens? You think that's the tie-in?"

He took a drink and shook his head over the rim of his glass. "I can't be sure. According to her parents, Rick and Gayle, their daughter raised a very specialized breed of bird. That's what Addy was doing down here. She brought birds down on a regular basis to sell to another breeder." He cocked an eyebrow. "That's what the parents said, anyway."

"Really? Denial?"

"Ignorance, more likely. Apparently, earlier she struggled in school, social issues, some experimenting with drugs and alcohol, typical teen stuff, according to Gayle. Then Addy got involved with a local 4-H chapter. A wholesome pastime, or so the parents thought." He took another drink and then continued. "Rick is a professor at UT in Knoxville. He sold the downtown condo and relocated the family out to the countryside a couple years back, so their little darling could do the rural thing."

"What's Gayle do?"

"She's a social worker at a counseling firm in Knoxville. They specialize in troubled teens."

"Figures."

Grabowski smirked. "Glad I never had kids." He spoke with conviction, but I noted a tinge of regret in his eyes.

I mulled over this new information about Addy. Or

tried to. I wished I hadn't had so many beers. My thoughts wouldn't stick. I couldn't think of the right questions to ask. I stretched my legs under the table to where Wilco was still sprawled and ran my foot along his back. I hit on one of his sweet spots and he rolled onto his side, lifting his legs, begging for a belly rub. I pulled back. Belly rubs were for training and work only.

Grabowski picked up the thread again. "I know there's some sort of connection to this cockfighting thing, but I can't connect it to Maura's death. And the way she was killed."

"The satanic ritual?"

He nodded slowly. His mind was working on another track. "The profiles don't match."

"What do you mean?"

"I worked up a profile on Maura's killer, based on the death scene. No face trauma, shaving of the hair, or any effort to depersonalize the body. We see that with serial killings, some sort of deep-seated hate for women, usually due to an abusive mother/son relationship, serves as a catalyst for murder in which the killer seeks to degrade and punish his female victims."

I drained my beer.

Grabowski went on: "Other than being tied down, there was no other evidence of torture. A single stab wound, targeted, quick, efficient. No sexual penetration, or any evidence of sexual contact from the killer. In fact, her body was well covered, positioned almost . . . virtuously."

"Chastity was important to the killer?"

"Yes. Or he is totally inept with women. In-experienced. Unpracticed."

"That could point to Nevan." I recalled that too-clean Ken-doll look about him. His reaction when Grabowski accused him of not being man enough. The diary indicated they were having sex when his sister caught them, but it may have been a one-time thing or rare at least. Hatch, however, had a reputation for being more experienced with women.

"Yes. And the crime had several staging elements, which also make me lean toward someone who knew the victim well. Again, most likely Nevan."

He hesitated, his brows furrowing.

"What is it?" I asked.

"I've worked a lot of occult killings. Especially back in the eighties, when I was first in the Bureau. Occult stuff was big back then. People blamed everything on devil worshipers. Satanic Panic they called it. Wear black, you're a Satanist. Tattoo? Satanist. Every adolescent in America was suspected of practicing the occult. In reality, most killings weren't by actual Satanists, but wannabes. Or copycat crimes. Often imitating something from pop culture. Kids obsessed with heavy metal, really into violent video games or slasher movies."

"Is that what we're looking at here? Kids acting out?"

"That's the thing. With an established Satanist, or even with kids mimicking what they've seen in the movies, there's usually something consistent with the symbolism or method of murder at the scene. All we have is a makeshift altar, and several random symbols that don't quite make sense."

I frowned. "How much clearer can you get than a pentagram?"

"Pentagrams are the most obvious symbol associated

with satanic worshiping, although they're used by other groups, too. Not always as a symbol of evil."

"But it *can* be evil."

"Yes. But the other symbols, especially the ones painted in Maura's blood. They're unusual. Random. Untraceable."

"What are you saying? That someone just made them up? What does that matter? Murder is murder. It's evil."

"All I know is that I've never seen these symbols. I've run them through databases, and by colleagues. Nothing. As far as I can tell, this type of symbolism hasn't been used in any similar crimes, nor do they match anything that's been out there in pop culture for the last twenty years. That strikes me as odd."

I agreed. I'd already told the team what Colm said as well, that the Latin verses on the note left with the body were poorly written, inaccurate Scripture at best. "And Addy's murder wasn't staged. Maybe there's no connection."

"Addy's killer was trying to hide the body. He wanted to cover the crime. The autopsy report isn't back. I assume it'll take longer than normal. The body was in bad shape after being submerged so long. But the initial examination showed several puncture wounds. Not methodical, like the way Maura was stabbed. More random, angry."

"So a different killer."

Grabowski shook his head. "Not necessarily. Here's the kicker. The ME says that Addy's wounds are similar to the wound in Maura's chest. Probably incurred by a double-bladed knife. If it turns out to be the same knife, but a different method, it could indicate two or more killers."

"Or one single killer with two very different motives." I told him what John had relayed to me about the knife and the threats. "A blond, pretty-boy type, driving a black SUV. I'm thinking Hatch Anderson."

Grabowski looked at the bar. "Which guy told you all this?"

"The tall one with dark hair. Wearing a flannel shirt."

He stood and pulled out his cell. "I'll find a picture online. If he verifies it was Hatch that night, I'll work on the warrant. By the way, I'm going down to Jefferson County first thing in the morning to have a look around the Bartons' place."

"I'll go with you."

He looked down at the two empty beer glasses on the table, lined up like spent soldiers, and shook his head. "Only if you're sober by then."

"Two beers?" I scoffed. "Give me a break." The fact that it was my second set of double-ups wasn't any of his damned business.

# CHAPTER 32

I stood to the side, huddled in the blue and red siren strobes, not daring to get too close to the scene, but fixated nonetheless. I'd wanted to be there. I'd begged to be there. I'd fantasized about this for a couple weeks and now I was like the voyeur getting a fix.

This was the most fun I'd had in a long time, thanks to Grabowski. Within five hours, he'd set up and executed a plan to get inside Hatch's vehicle. It was a little after midnight and we had Hatch and some buddies pulled over on south Briggs, two blocks down from the Cash & Carry. Hatch had a taillight out, imagine that. Grounds for a traffic stop. The K9 officer just happened to be in the neighborhood at the time. And I'd been invited to the party. Wilco wanted to play, too, but I kept him in the back of my car while the K9 officer worked his dog around Hatch's vehicle.

Another uniformed cop was positioned at the driver's window, taking Hatch's license and registration. "You been drinking tonight, boy?" the officer asked. We already knew he was. Surveillance had picked him up after the high-school basketball game and tracked his every move. A couple stops off at friends' houses and a trip into the convenience store, emerging with what looked like a case of beer. We weren't after booze, though, or pot, but little white pills. Pills that would tie him to Addy Barton's murder and eventually Maura's death.

Hatch didn't say a word, but kept his eye on his side mirror, watching the dog as he sniffed the perimeters of the car. Halfway down the driver's side, the dog hit on something. The K9 officer looked our way. Grabowski nodded.

Hatch was pulled from the car, cuffed, and his joyriding friends, two guys and one girl, relegated to the curb. Not looking too joyful. A search of the vehicle turned up several illegal items, one of them being a small Baggie of white pills. The whole thing was so damn exciting . . .

Until Gina Anderson showed up.

She screeched to a halt in her powder blue Mercedes two-door behind my rust-riddled, busted-window four-door. I swear its shiny propeller logo lifted its nose at having to slum it like that. Gina, too, had her nose lofty and flared as she stomped her way toward us. One of the officers tried to block her way, only to end up in a silly side shuffle like a crossing guard trying to stop a Macy's Thanksgiving Day float.

Grabowski looked disgusted. "Looks like Mommy's here."

Hatch bucked against the cuffs. "Go home. I don't need you here."

Gina splayed a manicured hand across her cashmere jacket as she took a step back at his display of rejection, nearing toppling the hapless cop who had instinctively reached out to prevent her from falling. "Don't say that, baby. I'm here to help you."

"I don't need your help. Just tell Dad to send our attorney."

"He's already on it. Don't you say a word, baby. Not a word. We'll get you out of this."

Laid out on the hood of the car were nine spent beer cans and a tiny bag of pills. Only enough for a possession charge, he'd finagled out of that before, but the pills were the clincher. We'd gotten what we were looking for. Grabowski leaned in closer to the kid. "If those pills are what I think they are, then there ain't going to be no one who can help you, boy."

Hatch looked Grabowski directly in the eye and grinned. Cocky little wuss still thought he was above it all. He was overconfident. Depending on whether or not we could connect all the dots, the bag of pills might be enough to put him away for a lifetime. Grabowski was right. Mommy and Daddy weren't going to be able to fix this one. I smiled to myself.

My smile faded when Gina appeared in front of my face. "You've been out to get my boy from the start. You set this up."

Her moist lips glistened a glossy pink in the reflected streetlight. "That's not true. An officer was patrolling the area and noticed your son's vehicle had a faulty tail—"

"You liar. It's a setup. The entire thing. This is your way of getting back at my husband for making you go through drug testing, isn't it?"

The other officers looked my way, a too-eager audience. The curtain had risen, and they were waiting for the show. The dopey sideshow freak called out by the master of ceremonies to perform. I fought not to react, yet shame and anger bubbled up inside me. I moved closer, in her face now. I didn't give a flying flip who she was; she didn't intimidate me. "Look, lady, your son is a loser. Nothing more than a drug dealer—"

Grabowski stepped in. "Shut up, Callahan."

Gina went rigid, but a glare of triumph edged her eyes. "You're the one with a problem. You're drugged up half the time, screwing up evidence and losing control of that dog of yours. I can't believe they even let one of you gypsies wear a uniform."

Her audience—my uneasy colleagues—fastened their full attention on me and it took everything I had not to call the bitch out. Fact was, there was truth behind some of her words. I swallowed that back, focused on other truths: the reality behind her pointless life and worthless son, with the proof of it that lay spread out for everyone to see. "You can't put this off on me, Gina." I pointed to the hood of Hatch's car. "All that came from your son's car. He's going down for this, one way or another. I'm going to—"

"That's enough." Grabowski jerked me by the arm. "We're taking the boy in. You go home. Get a couple hours of sleep. We have an early morning."

# CHAPTER 33

By noon, we were in the Bartons' backyard, sidestepping chicken crap as we made our way through a field of gamecocks, each tethered around the ankle and tied to small buckets that served as shelters. Wilco was next to me, on a tight lead.

"This is insane," Grabowski said. "What type of kid does this as a hobby?"

"She'd probably made enough money to offset her first year of college."

"She was barely eighteen." He looked my way. "What's a Pavee girl do at eighteen for extra money? Fast food, babysitting?"

Other girls maybe. At eighteen, I was beaten, broken, and homeless. Living on the streets waiting for a recruiter to call to let me know if I'd passed my MEPs and enlistment physical. Hoping I wasn't pregnant with a rape baby. I wanted to believe that I would have loved the child. But maybe I would have left it behind, like my mother had left me. Thankfully, I never had to figure that out. One small blessing. "I never worked fast food," I said. "Or babysat. Kids were never my thing." Still weren't.

He pulled the barn door handle. "Were you close to your own mother?"

"Not especially." Hard to be close to someone you'd never met. I didn't explain any of that to Grabowski, though.

"Was she abusive?"

My muscles tensed. *Regina.* But we all called her Queenie. One of my few friends from childhood. She was stick-legged, all knees and elbows, with a crooked smile and freckles that stretched across her nose when she smiled. Which was rare. She lived three trailers down from us. Her dad was a big, burly fellow, drunk and loud; her mother mousy and somewhat withdrawn. She'd stayed over one night. During a midnight game of Truth or Dare, she'd told me a truth—when she was bad, her mommy burned her legs with a cigarette. She lifted her dress then. A dozen red circles burned bright against her pale thighs. I stared at the freshly charred skin and felt no pity. Nothing but jealousy. Queenie was lucky. I would have done anything for a mother, even let her hurt me.

"No, my mother wasn't abusive." *She wasn't anything.* "You're getting a little personal, aren't you, Grabowski?" I didn't need any more psychoanalysis crap this week. I'd had enough of that from Dr. Ryan.

"Fair enough. I'll stick to the case for now."

*For now. Thanks. Like I get to look forward to you probing my head later.* I wanted to tell him to lay off, but knew that, too, would feed his appetite for getting into my head. And under my skin.

We stepped inside the barn. Moldy hay and the sharp

ammonia smell of bird piss stung my nostrils. Along the
back wall, metal crates caged hens, stacked one on top of
another with white and green excrement dripping between
them. The birds on the bottom were coated in a crusty
layer.

Wilco pulled at his leash. I gave him free rein,
watching as he ran anxiously from one end of the barn
to the other, snorting the smells like a deprived addict
set loose in a pharmacy.

Grabowski looked around. "Quite the little enterprise
Addy had here."

"Why'd the parents let this go on?"

"My guess is they didn't know."

"How could they not?"

He laughed. "Do Gayle and Rick seem like the
country type to you? My guess is they've never ventured
out here." He looked around. "No. This is all their little
darling's doing."

We'd talked to Rick and Gayle back at the house.
Their mantel was covered with their daughter's
awards: 4-H ribbons, Young Farmer of the Year award,
photos of Addy with her chickens, on and on. Eventually
she'd turned her 4-H projects into a small business, Rick
explained. Specialty show birds. "Addy was clever
that way."

*Yes. She was clever.* I wondered how something so
wholesome had turned so sick. And how the parents
hadn't noticed.

Grabowski called me over to where several straw
bales were arranged in a small ring. "A pit." He pointed
to a pool of blood in the middle. "She trained them here.
Maybe demonstrated her bloodline to prospective
clients." There was a pile of cock combs on the ground,

dry and shriveled, like a stack of severed tongues. "She dubbed their combs. It makes them less vulnerable in the ring," he explained. "If they're not removed, the opponent can grab ahold of the comb and use it for leverage."

Grabowski must've been reading up on the subject. Interesting, but not what I was looking for. I knew the girl was raising and selling birds for cockfights. I wanted to know who she was selling them to in McCreary.

As I looked around, Grabowski opened his cell to call in the situation. How long had Addy been dead? What was this place like usually? Addy had apparently been shrewd and enterprising—she would have taken good care of her chickens, not for humane reasons, but just to safeguard her investment.

My Marine lieutenant once said, "Don't count the bodies, just retrieve 'em. We'll sort 'em out later." His perversion of "Don't count your chickens before they hatch." I avoided looking toward the caged chickens, instead noting the barrels of feed nearby, each clearly labeled, a shelf of shiny clean tools, a neatly stacked pile of gloves. And a bloodied white apron on a peg. These creatures might have been well cared for when Addy lived, but all in preparation for the bloodthirsty deaths they would endure. How had this young girl justified her little enterprise? *Don't abuse your chickens before you profit on their abuse.* One new saying to fulfill mankind's blind need to manufacture some rhetorical logic to cover our shameful activities.

I pulled out latex gloves, slipped them on, as much to protect my skin from this filthy scene as to avoid contaminating it.

I found a workstation, a 1950s pink-and-gold-flecked Formica-topped kitchen table, as out of place as a prim grandmother at a sewer plant. It was crammed in the corner of one of the horse stalls. It was littered with papers, manuals, syringes, and vials of poultry antibiotics. Records and . . . bingo! A ledger.

Obvious sales records, income and expenses. Addy had quite the small business going. Smart kid. Sales assets were listed, too. Along with clients' initials. I scrolled through the dates, found the night Maura was murdered. Addy made a delivery that night. The initials next to the entry were *N.M.* Nevan Meath.


Nevan sat slumped in a chair across from me. Parks stood off to the side, arms crossed, lips pressed tight. Department rules: two officers present for an interrogation. So I'd asked Parks to join me and to keep her mouth shut. I'd get more out of Nevan, Pavee to Pavee.

"You need to start talking, Nevan."

He stared at me with bloodshot eyes. "I don't have nothing to say to you."

He seemed out of it, lethargic, half asleep still. "Your arraignment is tomorrow. They have enough evidence to try you for Maura's murder."

I changed tactics. "How do you like being locked up? A Traveller confined. Not easy. Goes against our nature."

He stared at the table again.

"But at least here, people leave you alone. Not so at the pen. And if you don't put a stop to this, that's where you'll be heading."

"The state pen?"

"Yup. You'll be thrown in with a bunch of guys

going cold turkey and eyeing you as their next plaything."

The air filled with sour-smelling fear. Nevan was duly freaked out. Good. I raised my brows and pressed him. "Believe me, the pen will make this place look like kindergarten. You'll wish you could come back here. But by then, it'll be too late."

Sweat broke out in tiny drops around his hairline. He stared blankly ahead, his Adam's apple sliding up and down his throat.

"Tell me about Addy Barton."

His jaw tightened. "She's just a friend."

"She wasn't from around here. How'd you meet?"

He shrugged.

"I was out at her place yesterday. She's in the chicken business. Fighting cocks."

"So?"

"She kept records. A ledger of sorts. Your initials were in it. You buy from her?"

"That has nothing to do with Maura's murder."

"She's dead."

He sat up straighter, then slumped back. "Dead? Addy's dead?" More sweating. He looked sick.

"Yes. Stabbed. Multiple times. Why would someone want her dead?"

He doubled over, clutching his stomach. I leaned in and spoke quietly into his ear. *"Nijesh swibli, geturl."* *Don't be afraid, boy.*

His back stiffened.

I stared at his clamped lips, frustration and anger swirling through my mind. *Maura, Addy, Nevan . . . what is the connection?* I needed to know the connection. "Nothing to say, Nevan?" My hand balled into a fist.

Parks inched closer. "Two girls are dead. Maura was one of *us*. Your *fiancée*. And you have nothing to say?"

His cheeks flushed. "I'd . . . I'd like to talk to my mother."

"Talk to your . . . you pathetic little sissy. Grow up, Nevan." I shot out of my chair, grabbed him by the collar, pulled his body up until his face was inches from mine. "This isn't a game. And you're not going to talk to your—"

"Easy, Callahan." Parks clamped down on my shoulder.

I exhaled and let go of his shirt, pushed him back hard in his chair. "What did you have going on with Addy? What type of scam?"

Sweat broke out on his brow. "Nothing."

"She planned to meet with you that night to give you the birds. Did you see her? Whatever you're into doesn't compare to being prosecuted for murder. The sheriff is building a case against you this very minute. Do you want to go to prison for murder?"

"I didn't do it." His voice came out like a whiny young boy's, thin and high.

I laughed and sat down across from him. "It doesn't matter if you killed her or not. Don't you get that? You're a Pavee. They're building a case against you, and you're sure as hell not going to get the benefit of the doubt."

He considered this, his tongue licking his lips like tasting a bitter truth. I softened my tone. "Tell me about the cockfights. How do they fit into all this?"

"It's just a cash business we got going. You know, something to help us in the winter. We got bills to pay."

"Who's 'we'?"

He shrugged. "Eddie and me, a few others."

"Like the mayor's boy, Hatch?"

Nevan sneered. "Are you serious? Like he needs money."

"Jacob Fisher?"

"He wanted in, but we said no."

"Why?"

"I don't trust the guy."

"Was Maura in on it?"

"Yeah. She helped us with the front money."

"Cash from the diner."

He nodded. "She takes a cut, Winnie too."

*Maura, Winnie, Eddie, and Nevan all in Addy's business. Why not Jacob?*

"Why don't you trust Jacob?"

"I did at first. We'd all go out to his place and party, you know. Then . . . he's . . . Something's not right with him. He's . . . I don't know. Weird."

"Why do you say that?"

Nevan leveled a gloating glare at me, like a terrorist I once saw tracked into a corner who turned to open his shirt, revealing the bombs rigged to his chest. "You need to take a look in his barn. There's this room in there where they used to kill the pigs. There's a grate in the floor. Look under it."

I sat back. "Why? What am I going to find? Occult stuff?"

Nevan's face froze over. Whether with fear or hate, I couldn't tell which. "A body."

# CHAPTER 34

The week of my First Holy Communion, I saw a hog slaughtered.

I'd hidden in the thicket by the clearing, eager and anxious. I wasn't supposed to be there. It was forbidden, which is why I was so curious. But nothing could have prepared me for what I saw that day.

The animal's squeals, like nails on a chalkboard, made my ears curl and my skin shiver. He excreted twice as they forced him from the back of Uncle Bart's trailer. The smell of putrid shit reached my nose and coated the back of my throat, thick and dark and foul-tasting. A fire was started under a barrel of water and a crosslike brace crudely fashioned from fallen tree limbs. Preparations for the slaughter.

I knew it, and so did the pig.

His cries became louder, more intense. To my child's ears, the squeals turned to pleas of mercy. *Don't kill me. Don't kill me.* But no one else seemed to hear.

*The menu is set. The pig must die.*

They forced him to the ground, two men holding him down, while Gramps rammed an ice pick into his jugular. Blood and liquid spurted from the hole like a fountain and formed a foamy puddle around his body. He twisted and turned, his legs frantically treading the air as his fatty back made suction-like sounds against the pooling blood. I wanted to turn away, run, but I didn't. I stood rooted in shock. I said nothing and felt less human for doing so.

"Are you just going to stand there, Callahan?" Harris's voice cut through my memories. He'd pulled back the heavy grate over the drain room and was staring into a large pit. Three heavy hooks swung overhead. A table of crude killing devices hung on a nearby wall.

I turned to him. "This is a slaughterhouse."

"Uh . . . right. They killed pigs here. You eat bacon, don't ya?"

An ugly feeling swirled in my stomach. "Not since I was eight."

Harris scrunched his face and shook his head. *This chick's so weird.* He gave me a nudge. "Come on, Callahan. We don't have all day."

Others stood off at a distance, techs, scene photographers, other officers, all keeping a respectful distance to avoid contaminating the scene. We knew there was something down there. As soon as I arrived on the scene, Wilco bolted for the barn, not stopping, not dipping his nose, until he got to the old wood structure where he alerted immediately. I realized that he'd probably gotten a whiff of decay in our first visit to the farm, which is why he'd behaved so badly at the time.

Harris shifted impatiently and pointed into the drain pit. "Ladies first."

*Jackasses second.*

I flipped on my flashlight, turned, and descended a rusted metal rung ladder. The pit was nothing more than a cold concrete hole in the ground that smelled of must and old blood, sharp and metallic. The walls were stained, a dark, linear mark about a third of the way up, a bloody tideline.

A low table, covered with a quilt, was crammed against the back wall. "There." I pointed my flashlight beam.

Harris jerked back, then started forward. "What the . . . ?"

We approached, kicking up tiny balls of fuzzy material that littered the ground around the table. Nesting material. Mice had ravished holes in the quilt.

Harris breathed hard.

I pinched a corner of material and lifted it to reveal just one edge: strings of gray/blond hair, pink chiffon and lace on bony protrusions, dried skin shriveled over maybe a forearm, a clump of brown flowers. A child's teddy bear tucked in the crook of an arm. "I think it's the mother."

I slept late the next morning, lingering in my sweat-soaked sheets. Remnants of a nightmare hovered in my mind: Maura, naked, her blood-drenched hair falling in long strings against her breasts, blue veins stretched thinly over a baby-swollen belly. She reached out for me, pale lips quivering. "Jezebel," she whispered.

I squeezed my eyes shut, wiped the moisture from my upper lip, and tried to shake the image. It remained.

Wilco's incessant pawing finally drew me from bed. I padded from my room, straight to the back door, opened it, and watched as he hobbled down the steps for a quick pee. A chill swept up my bare legs and swirled under my damp T-shirt. I huddled, and waited for Wilco to finish his business. I was barely going to have enough time to shower and eat before I needed to be back into work. We had all three of the Fisher boys in holding. Besides the dead mother, Wilco's nose had found a piece of damning evidence linking Jacob Fisher to Maura's murder—the picking knife. Or at least one that matched Maura's wound types. It was found hanging with other tools in the slaughterhouse. Wiped clean and hung back in plain sight. But once blood leaves the body, it starts to decompose, making it trackable by Wilco's nose. Closer inspection of the knife showed traces of blood at the base of the handle. Initial testing showed it was human blood and a type match to Maura's blood. We were waiting for the rest of the report, but as far as Pusser was concerned, we had Jacob Fisher nailed for first-degree murder. His interview was first thing this morning. I looked forward to it. My work as a military cop didn't require much interrogating—the dead don't talk much—so suspect interrogations, to me, were like a fun game of cat and mouse: calculated pursuit, near captures, repeated escapes, and then . . . the final pounce.

But as it turned out, I didn't get invited to the game that morning.

I was in the break room waiting for coffee to drip into my mug when Harris intercepted me, all smuglike and gloating. "Sheriff wants to see you," he said, and ushered me down the hall and into our extremely blah interrogation room, with a dented metal table and snot-green walls. I knew what was coming. I sat in a chair bolted to the floor and pondered my future. And my past. Neither gave me much consolation.

Wilco, sensing my mood, never strayed more than a foot from me, his eyes, warm and mellow, watching my every move. I bent down, ran my hand over his back in long, smooth strokes. "It's going to be okay, boy. I promise." It didn't matter that he couldn't hear me; I spoke the words, anyway. I needed to hear them.

Twenty minutes later, Pusser came in, followed by the mayor and another uniformed cop. An official IPRA—Independent Police Review Authority—report was read. I'd failed my drug test. I handed in my gun, filled out a couple forms, and was sent on my way. That was it.

I left the department, drove straight to the McCreary Diner, and slunk into the corner booth, Wilco settling at my feet. I felt angry and stupid and unable to decide if I was wrong, or if I'd been wronged. The only thing I knew for sure was that my job meant more to me than I realized.

Coffee came and the waitress took my order, red-lipstick clogged lines stretching outward from her mouth as she chomped on a wad of gum. "Darlin'" this and "Darlin'" that. Did I want my grits buttered or smothered? The moment she left, I couldn't remember how I'd answered.

In a couple hours, the diner would be packed with folks coming from as far as Johnson City for the fried-catfish lunch special. I was there for a quick bite before heading into the backwoods. I didn't know how long my search would take, but I wanted to start with a full stomach. I also needed time to absorb what had happened this morning. *Temporary suspension without pay pending drug counseling and a cleared drug test.*

*Suspended, not exactly fired,* I told myself. *Well, just not quite fired yet. Counseling? A cleared test? Like either of those is going to happen.*

I shifted, rubbed my neck muscles, stiff vinyl crackled under my weight. The *clanking* of dishes, the low murmur of voices, the *clink, clink* of silverware, it all seemed so distant, like I was watching and listening through a thick, hazy windowpane. A table of local ladies glanced my way, eyed my dog, bent their heads to speak in hushed tones. Harshly whispered words floating on air: *another girl, body, gypsy cop, murder, murder, murder . . .*

A thin-haired man, with a hawkish nose, stared at me over the rim of his mug, his eyes sliding out to my station wagon with its dented panels and duct-taped cardboard windows waving in the breeze. *White trash,* he thought. *White gypsy trash.* I'd been called that all my life. Now I fulfilled the stereotype. Soon to add "unemployed" to the list of damning adjectives.

I shifted in my seat, pulled out my phone, and busied myself scrolling through my most recent text thread with Parks. I remembered Gran once saying that

I could never let a question go unanswered. Questions had haunted my childhood: my birth, my mother and father, my abandonment, did my mother love me? A continuous litany, some of which I'd been able to answer since returning to Bone Gap. Some still lingered, just out of reach, unresolved. A constant pecking away at my sanity.

I couldn't stand to be locked out of this case. Not now. The Fisher boys were being questioned. I wanted to be a part of that, be able to help put in the final pieces of the puzzle.

I sent a text off to Parks: **Were you in on Fisher kid's interrogation?**

Her response came right away: **Yes. But I can't give you any information. Pusser would can me.**

**Pretty please?**

**Sorry . . .**

*Crap. When did Parks get to be such a rule follower?*

I thought of something else and sent another text: **Autopsy on body found in the slaughterhouse?**

There was a long pause. Finally: **Mother. Died as a result of cancerous tumor.**

**Nothing suspicious?**

**You mean like she was left to rot in a slaughterhouse drain room?**

Parks had a point. I clicked off, and a chill ran through me, something was off. When Nevan told us about the barn and a body, when we arrived and Wilco strained to the edge of that pit to alert, and when we found the decayed remains, it all seemed clear. But now . . .

His mother died, apparently of natural causes, leaving him and his brothers subject to the state. Without any other family to step up, they might have been split up between foster homes. Jacob had to hide his mother's body to keep her death a secret. So the flowers, the teddy bear, the careful treatment of her body—that drain room in the slaughterhouse wasn't a cover-up for some heinous crime, but a shrine to a beloved mother. Jacob was doing everything in his power to take care of his brothers and keep the family together.

That didn't sound like a killer to me.

# CHAPTER 35

On the way out of town, I stopped by Southside Package, picked up a bottle, and tucked it into my pack for later. In another fifteen minutes, I was parked on the trailhead above the cave where Doogan had dumped Dublin Costello's body.

HRD dogs sniff out more than just whole bodies. They detect multiple levels of bodily decomposition, which means that they can find body parts, bones, tissue, and blood. The gun Gran used to kill Dublin Costello was likely splattered with minuscule droplets of blood and body tissue, since Gran was in such close range when she pulled the trigger to defend herself. If so, it would be easily detected by Wilco's trained nose.

Wilco and I would start at the cave and spread outward. Doogan had estimated that he'd travelled a mile from the site before tossing the gun by a tree trunk that had been split by lightning. Not such an exact description, but I was hopeful that Wilco's nose would find the gun. So we headed downhill, Wilco off lead and sniffing at random. I walked a good twenty yards behind him, keeping a watchful eye, but not interfering. The cold spell had finally broken, the sun was out and the sky a crisp cerulean, with cotton candy clouds. I lifted my face upward, took a deep breath, and let the sun warm my cheeks. My tension melted away. Out here, in nature, with my dog, doing what we loved most, I felt content. Happy, even.

But Pusser's words crept back into my mind. *Addiction counseling. What a bunch of bullcrap.* I wasn't an addict. I could quit at any time. I'd proved that this week. Almost four days without booze or my meds.

I shifted my pack to relieve my shoulder. The bottle clinked.

I'd have to go back to work at the Sleep Sleazy. I couldn't do that. Didn't want to do that. At least Gran would be happy to hear I'd lost my job. No more shame or embarrassment over her granddaughter the cop. To her mind it was cleaner to scrub vomit from toilets than help *muskers* catch criminals.

I kept moving, focusing on my dog and willing away the dark mood that'd crept over me. Thirty minutes later, I spotted a tree with a large limb, about twenty feet up, hanging precariously. One strong wind would bring it crashing down. Anyone standing under it would be instantly crushed. The widow-maker Doogan told me about it. I waved to get Wilco's attention and led him to that area.

He ran his nose along the forest floor, scooping up scents as he went. Ears pricked, nose twitching, tail high and bushy. Then suddenly he switched back on himself, then back again, and his tail went rigid, almost parallel to the ground.

He was onto a scent.

I waited patiently while he worked, back and forth, his nose pressed to the ground. A snort, then a sneezing fit to clear his snowpacked nostrils, and back to sniffing. I stood stock-still, taking in his every move, feeling every twitch, every ripple of his muscles. We were close. I could feel it.

I waited. And watched. On and on, he went, showing an interest, but no alert. I went to the area and searched the ground. No gun. I kicked around at the ground. Nothing, but a flash of green caught my eye. I bent down for a closer look, wiped away a couple layers of snow, revealed a corner of fabric, scraped some more, and unearthed a green silk scarf. My fingers flew to my neck, my mind zooming in on an image of Katie Doogan standing in the doorway of her home.

It was her scarf.

# CHAPTER 36

I went home and started drinking.

Wilco curled by my legs with his head resting on my lap, both of us on the sofa, watching the cardboard over the front window flap in the wind. The green silk scarf was crumpled on the coffee table. Gran leaving, my job, and now this. I stared at my cell phone, disappointment and betrayal burned inside me. How could Doogan do this to me? And why? He knew how much I wanted that gun. And he'd gone back out to the woods and taken it. I pushed his number.

Katie answered Doogan's phone. Her voice was high and brittle, as if she'd crack and break at any moment. "I knew you'd call. You won't leave him alone, will you?"

*Does Doogan know she has his phone?* "That's not why I'm calling. Is he there?"

"You can't talk to him."

"It's important."

"I don't know what he saw in you."

"Your husband has something of mine."

A thin and haughty tone now: "Did you find my scarf? The green one? It's my prettiest scarf. I left it for you. A gift."

*"A gift?"*

"You need it more than me."

I rubbed a finger over the rough ridges on my neck. "*You* have the gun?"

"Yes. And I know who it killed."

"Katie, I don't think you understand everything—"

"Shut up! I know what happened. He told me. He told me everything. He was upset over his sister's death. Away from me. I wasn't there to comfort him, and you took advantage of that."

"That's not what happened."

"He said touching you was like touching charred meat. But you kept throwing yourself at him."

*Charred meat.* My scar sprang to life, the nerves awakening under the surface like a thousand hot, needling pins.

"He didn't want to be with you. He was just lonely and upset. He thinks you're ugly, repulsive."

*Repulsive.* I squeezed my eyes shut. *Get a grip.* "Do you still have the gun, Katie?"

"Oh yeah. I have the gun. The gun your grandmother used to kill Dublin Costello."

My heart raced. "I need it."

"I've hidden it somewhere safe."

"What do you want? Money?"

"Money?" She chuckled. "No. I don't want money."

"What then?"

"Retribution." She hung up.

\* \* \*

A shot of anger ripped through me, a sharp pang in the depths of numbness. It would never be over. The fear, the worry . . . I'd never find peace.

*Peace.* I'd heard Colm talk about peace many times. But I knew only one type of peace. . . . I retrieved another bottle from the kitchen and went to my room, undressing in front of the dresser mirror, peeling away my jeans and my T-shirt, then my socks, leaving just my bra and panties. The loops of our shag carpet snagged my toes as I turned to study my body. Wilco lay on the floor next to my feet, hovering near me, his head cocked and brown eyes worrying.

I took a long drag on the bottle, put it back on the dresser, and stepped back until my whole body filled the mirror. I lowered my panties next and ran my hands over the skin of my thighs, up past the black triangle between my legs and over my hip bones. I focused there, on the smooth skin, soft and pink like a summer peach. Unmarred skin. Not hideous. Then I worked my hands up my waist, over my rib cage, to my back and the clasp of my bra. I undid it, watched it fall to the floor, then raised my eyes. *Charred meat.* Red, raw steak thrown on the grill. The sound still resonated in my mind: a hissing high-pitched sizzle of my searing skin. The sickening, sweet smell of burning flesh coating the hairs of my nostrils where it lingered. Even now, if I took a deep sniff, I could smell it.

I moved my hands to my breasts, cupping them, one round and soft and sensitive, the other flat with skin of sandpaper. I kneaded and prodded the nipples, my good nipple rose and tightened into a tiny bead. The other remained limp. I slid my hands up my neck and lifted my hair, tilting my head and exposing the full length of my ridged neck. They'd used skin recovered from fresh corpses to graft me, laying the flimsy flesh over me and stapling it to my body like a patchwork quilt. Some of it my body rejected immediately, and it was ripped up, and replaced with new layers of necro-sheets, holding the raw, oozing flesh inside. Like the skin on a hot dog. That's what I looked like. An overcooked hot dog that'd expanded and burst through its casing, juices spurting out, leaving the meat inside dried and shriveled. *Charred meat. Repulsive. Hideous.*

I gulped down more booze, leaving the mirror and my grotesque image, and made my way across the room to my bed. I lifted my mattress and pulled out a Baggie of pills, another hiding place Meg didn't find when she cleared out my stuff after my "episode."

I climbed onto my bed, wedged the bottle between my thighs, and tossed back a couple of the pills. A calmness overcame me, a feeling of control, just knowing that I'd soon be asleep. All I wanted was to sleep and forget. . . . I emptied two more onto my hand, then tossed them into my mouth, washing them down with the whiskey.

I drank some more, couldn't remember how many pills I'd taken, and took another couple for good measure. A weightlessness overcame me, my fingers tingled. I hovered between consciousness and deep sleep. I was floating or falling, and it felt good. So good.

And then sleep. Deep, dark sleep.

"Brynn. Brynn!" Someone was shaking me. "Brynn!"

I knew the voice. It was Colm. *Colm? What is he doing here? In my bedroom? I'm naked. Exposed. Don't look at me! Cover me. . . . Cover me.*

"What have you done, Brynn?"

Another voice. Maybe two more. I couldn't open my eyes. *Others seeing me. Someone, please cover me. Or leave me. I'm tired. So tired.* The comforting blanket of darkness took over again. . . .

My eyes opened. The sky struck my eyes as a painful blue, the clouds too close, and cold air stung my skin. Straps cut across my arms and torso, tight, cinched too tight. I couldn't move.

"One, two, three . . . lift."

I floated upward, closer to the sky, closer and closer, then down with a thud. More voices. Male voices and Colm's voice. He was praying, touching my forehead, my palms. A loud siren and then darkness.

My eyes opened again. A blinding light filled my view. *It's heaven. And it's beautiful. I can't believe . . . I thought I wouldn't make it. . . . There must be a mistake. . . . People like me don't go. . . .* A face appeared and blocked the light. Blue scrubs, a mask, fat eyebrows. *Move, asshole. Move. I want to see the light.* Fingers touched and prodded me. A rhythmic *beep, beep, beep* . . . voices, a lot of voices. Someone forced my mouth open. They jammed something down my throat; it burned. . . . *Stop, stop! I can't swallow. I'm choking. Help me. . . . help* . . . Darkness.

I couldn't open my eyes, but I heard the voices. Gran and Meg and others: " '*Graaltcha Mary, tawn a noos, Swuda's gyay duilsha . . .*' " Rosary beads clicking and women crying . . . *Don't cry, Gran. It's okay. I'm tired. I just want to sleep.* More darkness.

That smell. I knew that smell. It was my dog. *It's Wilco. I love you, Wilco. I love you.* A weight on my chest, a wet nudge. *Good boy. You want a belly rub?*

*What's wrong with my arms? I can't move my arms. I love you, Wilco. I love you. . . .* Again darkness.

I drift and drift. I'm cold. So cold. Water is dripping. No, not water, blood. *Drip, drip, drip . . .* Maura's body on the cold stone: black hair, white skin, eyes blue and glazed over . . . *drip, drip, drip . . .* pale lips move, a whisper of breath: *"Help me. Help me. . . ."* I want to help her, save her, but I can't move. I'm so tired.

Darkness.

My eyes open again. It's night and I'm in the hospital and the lights are dimmed. I am awake. A single monitor beeps with my vitals. A shadow moves in the corner, an outline at first; then I see that it's Pusser. He steps into view, rubbing a hand over his unshaven jawline as he looks down at me. "You're back."

"How long?" My lips cracked with dryness.

"A couple days. You've pretty much been out of it since we found you yesterday. Your neighbor called it in. The dog was going crazy inside your trailer, she got worried and checked and . . . I beat the first responders. So did the priest. We'd all thought . . ."

Wilco appeared, his claws scrabbling at the bedsheets as he worked up on his haunch to get closer to me. I reached over, touched his face, tried to whisper his name, but my tongue felt like sandpaper.

Pusser said something about pulling strings to get Wilco in here. He rambled on as if he were afraid that if he stopped, I'd slip away again. He was right. The darkness was inviting, a peaceful respite. My eyelids felt heavy. I forced them open and looked around the room.

"Meg just took your grandmother home to get some rest. They both got here as soon as they could. And the padre. He's been here, praying. There are so many people who care for you. Don't you know that? Why'd you do it, Callahan?" I focused on his face again. "I came down too damn hard on you. I know that now. I thought in the long run . . . Hell, I don't know. I thought it would help you get straightened out. I didn't think you'd do something so stupid."

*Stupid. Always doing something stupid. But I didn't mean to . . . it was an accident. . . .*

"Don't worry about the case. It's done. Over. Harris and Parks got a confession from the Fisher kid. The pressure of losing his mother, taking care of his brothers . . . he cracked. It happens. Anyway, we got him. The press broke the story yesterday."

*Jacob Fisher? The slaughterhouse, the body so carefully arranged, the flowers . . .*

"His arraignment is today. The confession pretty much seals the deal. And you should be extra happy. Nevan's been released. He's back home. You were right, it wasn't one of your clan."

I licked my lips and tried to talk to Pusser.

"You need to rest, Callahan. We can talk later. Don't worry about anything, okay?"

*But something's not right. . . .*

Pusser patted my hand. "It's all good. Just rest."

# CHAPTER 37

A hospital-appointed psychiatrist ruled that I was at no immediate risk to myself, recommended outpatient therapy, and signed my discharge papers the next day. Meg came to take me home late that afternoon. Except for a few attempts at small talk, the ride was mostly silent, with Meg casting nervous glances my way. Poor Meg. Our sick grandmother, and now me—the crazy, druggie, suicidal cousin. What burdens she bore.

I played nice with Meg, listened to her lectures about booze and pills, and agreed to be a good girl. As soon as I got a second alone, I plopped myself at the kitchen table, opened my phone, and turned back to the journal and the last entry. Who had Maura confided in? I'd assumed it was her school counselor, or a priest. Any of those seemed reasonable. Older, wiser men in positions of authority. Like the men in my life that I would turn to if . . . *No, I'd talk to Gran.* A woman. I nodded. Sure, it made more sense that she'd confide in a woman. Someone close to her. Probably not her mother, but I'd have to start with her.

* * *

The door to Ona Keene's camper dangled on a single hinge. I looked around. No one. No cars parked outside, nothing. As I stepped inside, everything seemed in order, yet selectively sparse—not emptied so much as just vacated. *Ona and Eddie are gone, like gypsies in the night,* I thought, shaking my head.

I poked around. Looked in cabinets, under mattresses, and then my eye caught on a backpack. I dumped the contents on one of the beds. Pretty much empty except for a biology book and a couple notebooks. I leafed through the notebooks: nicely organized notes, neat handwriting. Eddie was a good student.

I set the notebooks aside, then picked them up again. Something niggled at my mind, working its way back and forth from my subconscious to my conscious thoughts. . . .

My cell rang. I looked down, half expecting it to be Meg, checking up on me. It wasn't. "What's up, Parks?" I hoped my curt question curtailed any sentimentality or sympathy over my recent suspension; it wouldn't suit Parks, and I sure as hell didn't want it.

It worked. She got right to the point. "I shouldn't be telling you this, but a strange call came in this afternoon from a female caller."

My heart kicked up a notch. "Yeah."

"Said she had information regarding Dublin Costello's murder, but she wouldn't tell me anything. She said you should be the one to get the information. It was strange, the way she put it."

"Did you get a name?"

"She wouldn't say. Harris tried to track it, but it looks like the call came from a burner phone."

"Harris?" He already suspected something was up with Dublin's murder. Now this stuff with Katie. "Was she going to call back?"

"She said you'd know how to get in contact with her." She paused, suspicion creeping into her tone: "You been working that case on the side?"

"No. I haven't been working any case. I'm suspended, remember?"

"You don't have any idea who she is?"

"None." Accusatory silence on the other end. "I swear, Parks. I don't have any frickin' idea. Is there anything else?"

"No. Guess not."

I hung up. *Crap. What type of game is Katie Doogan playing with me?* Things were falling apart.

A gust of gray cold wind slapped my face as I walked from my car to the front door of the Meaths' trailer. Wilco sniffed the air and looked pleadingly my way. I gave him the signal to go ahead. He bolted straight for the nearest shrub to lift his stub, leaving his calling card.

A tense pause ensued after my knock, then the sound of footsteps. Riana opened the door, wearing a chenille sweater and full makeup.

"I didn't expect you to be here. Where's your mother?"

"Her back's out. She's in bed. I'm fixing her some supper."

I pushed past her and went inside. A frying pan crackled and popped on the burner. The place smelled hot and greasy. Cigarette smoke billowed from an ashtray next to the stove. A lipstick-stained glass of wine rested next to it.

She walked to the stove, turned a piece of chicken, and took a long drag on the cig. "What is it you want, Brynn?"

"I'm looking for Ona. I was just at her place. No one's there. Not Eddie, either. The place looks vacant. I thought maybe you might know—"

"Why would I know anything about where they've gone?"

"Eddie and Nevan are friends. I thought Eddie might have told Nevan—"

"Nevan's not here. I don't know when he'll be back." The same cold-shoulder dismissal I'd gotten from people all along. No one knew anything they'd tell this turncoat *musker*.

"I'm trying to figure something out. Maybe you know." I put my phone on the counter, a page of the journal displayed on the screen. "Maura kept a journal. This is the last entry and it's about how she confided in someone. Was it you, Riana?"

She turned her head, took another long drag on the cig, and scrutinized the journal through the corner of her eye. "No. Why would she talk to me?"

No reason I could think of that anyone would confide in this haughty witch. But Maura had talked to someone. And every tense muscle in Riana's frame told me she knew something. I showed her a couple more entries. "You've known her for a long time. Look here. She talks about you in this entry. Says you caught her and Nevan together—"

"Kids. Certainly, you must remember how it felt to be that age and in love." She narrowed her eyes at me.

"She was pregnant, with nowhere to turn. She was scared. . . ."

She exhaled a long stream of smoke, tipped back her chin, and made a throaty sound. "Poor thing. Guess she shouldn't have gotten herself knocked up."

"There are more entries, where she talks about trying to earn enough money so she and Nevan can go away."

"Sounds like every lovesick teenage girl. Remember back when we were that age? You and Dublin."

Everything in Riana's world—or conversations—came back to her life, her hurt, her needs. "I wasn't lovesick over Dublin Costello. You were."

"Yes. But you were the one who got him."

*Yeah, I got him, alright.*

She sucked on her cig again and blew the smoke my way. "Only he wasn't good enough for you."

I stifled a cough. "Forget all that, would ya, Riana? It was a lifetime ago."

"Yeah. And Dub's dead. Wonder if you cops will ever figure that one out." She half smiled.

I said nothing.

Riana flicked the ash off the end of her cigarette. "Look, Brynn. This is stupid. They already know who killed Maura. That settled boy."

"Jacob Fisher."

"Yeah. He was into all that devil stuff, right?"

"We don't really have proof of that. It may not matter, anyway. I'm not sure he did it."

"You're *not sure*? I heard he confessed."

"He's scared." I shook my head. I didn't read him as a killer. Mixed-up, yeah. Into some weird stuff, but the way he treated his mother's body. The way he cared for his siblings. It didn't fit for me. Then there was the note. The Latin. The Bible verse in that big, loopy scrawl. Was it from Jacob's hand? If I could see a sample of his handwriting, like I'd seen Eddie's in his notebook, then I could . . .

The handwriting . . . there had been something that bothered me about the notebooks, bothered me enough to hold on to it. I looked at the journal entry on my phone. It was the same tight script with that telltale left-handed slant. The writing in Eddie's notebooks matched the handwriting in the journal.

I stared at my phone screen, a slow realization seeping into my mind:

> *No one will understand . . . this doesn't happen to Pavees. . . . I wish I were normal. . . . I can't even trust leaving my journal around here. . . . I told Mother.*

*Mother.*

This wasn't Maura's journal. It was Eddie's. Eddie hand wrote the journal. Maura's only connection was hiding it for him at the diner. That meant . . . "Riana, are Eddie and Nevan . . . ?"

"Are they what?" Riana stabbed her half-smoked cig in the ashtray, and turned her focus back to the chicken, turning and turning the pieces of meat.

"Are they lovers?"

She wheeled and shook the tongs at me. "Shut up. Nevan isn't like that."

Yes, they were, and according to the journal, Riana knew it. Caught them. The realization stunned me.

The room fell silent, the only noise was the chicken

on the stove, popping and sizzling, grease hitting the burners and giving off little puffs of acrid smoke. The sound bothered me. *Sizzle, sizzle . . .* like skin burning. Like my skin burning.

All this time, I'd been looking at the case wrong. My anxiety kicked up, my mind whirred: Nevan and Eddie's relationship. Was that what this was about? Someone had tried to hide their relationship. But Maura had the journal. She knew. Is that why she was killed? But who would kill to keep something like that a secret? I knew who, and I raised my eyes just in time to catch a flash of metal. Hot grease splattered my face. . . .

Blackness.

# CHAPTER 38

"You damn bitch," Riana spat. I was being dragged, my head bouncing along the vinyl floor of Riana's kitchen. *Whoosh . . . thunk . . . whoosh . . . thunk.* Hot pain shot through my right temple, where the pan had connected. My eyes rolled back in my skull. I forced them forward again, opened my lids, saw a blur of the ceiling moving overhead. The effort was too much. I let them roll back again.

"I need your frickin' help, that's what. Now get over here." Riana's voice again. The back of my head was wet, with snow or maybe blood, my arms pinned to my side. A blanket. She'd wrapped me in a blanket and dragged me outside to the dark yard.

"No. She's dead . . . because she knew too much. . . . No, Mama didn't see nothing. She took two of them pills for her back pain, you know how they do her. . . ." Dogs barked in the background. They grew louder and louder. One bark stood out. Wilco's. Wilco was still here.

Footsteps sounded by my head, back and forth, back and forth. Riana was agitated. "Get over here and help me!"

Then her hand slid under my back. I felt my body being lifted up, up, and then I slipped. Powerless to brace myself, I hit the ground hard. A noise escaped my throat.

"What—" Riana said. "You're alive!"

I thrashed, side to side, got one arm loose. More barking. A weight straddled me, so heavy on my chest; one arm was still pinned, it ached, my fingers tingled. The blanket came down, cool air hit my face, the smell of sweat and stale cigarette smoke. I opened my eyes, a strange shadow played across Riana's face like a mask, twisting her features. I shook my head. *No, no, please no. . . .* Her fingers on my neck, thumbs pressed against my throat, my pulse *thumping, thumping. . . .* I thrashed, fought, snot and tears dripped down my temples. I strained against her weight. The stench of her breath hot on my cheeks. "Stop fighting me. . . ."

The blow came hard, straight in the jaw. The blackness started from the edges and closed in on my vision. Then the fingers were back, closing in around my windpipe. I didn't care. I was slipping into the darkness. . . . *I'm going to die. This is it. Finally I'm going to die. . . . I've wanted to die for a long time.*

I spiraled down through the darkness, surrendering myself, welcoming the final escape.

At the last second, I heard something that clouded me with regret and shrouded me in loss—*Wilco's distant bark.*

\* \* \*

For the second time that week, I woke up in a hospital room. This time, it was Pusser standing over me. "Your grandmother's outside, waiting to come in, but I need to talk to you first. Can you talk?" He pushed the button on the bed rail until I was semiupright.

"Yes." Pain scraped my throat as I squeaked out a barely audible reply.

"You're lucky. Riana Meath tried to squeeze the life out of you."

"But how? . . . I should be dead."

"That dog of yours." Pusser swiped at his face. "She claims he went crazy. He tore her up, half her face is gone. A neighbor heard her screams and called 911. She's a couple rooms down. Alive still. But pretty messed up."

*Wilco?* I searched the room.

"He's not here. They've impounded him."

"What!" I started to get up. Pusser pushed me back down. "Take it easy. Had he actually killed her, we'd be in trouble. As it is, it was an act of self-defense. I'm doing everything I can. I promise."

"But impound—"

"Parks is seeing to him. Don't worry."

I tried to swallow, felt the cutting of raw edges in my throat. Finally got out, "Jacob didn't kill Maura."

Pusser frowned, confused. "He confessed. Harris picked him up at the farm, made the arrest. The kid confessed to the murder before Harris even got him in for booking."

"I think Harris coerced the confession."

Pusser shook his head. "I don't know, Callahan. That's a big accusation."

Not really. Harris loved credit for anything—especially solving a case, regardless of whether he was right or not. But I let it drop. I didn't have the energy to argue.

"Doesn't matter," Pusser said. "The confession is just icing on the cake. We found the murder weapon in his barn and some devil stuff in the house."

"Like what?"

"Video games mostly. He played some sick video games."

"A lot of kids do."

We looked up as Grabowski stepped inside. He regarded me with concerned eyes, then spoke to Pusser. "The grandmother's out there and she's spitting mad. Wants in here now."

*Gran?* "Let her in. Oh, wait. Eddie and Nevan?"

Pusser shrugged. "We don't know where they are, but it doesn't look like anyone was there but Riana and her sleeping mother. We found Ona. She's in Nashville." Pusser pulled up a chair. "I need to get a statement from you."

So I told him everything, the best I could. The words spurted out slowly through my raw throat. I struggled to swallow, and spit kept pooling at the corners of my mouth. Pusser dabbed at it with a tissue. Gently. Caringly. I kept talking, and he nodded, encouraging me to continue. I explained about the journal, the handwriting, Eddie, Riana . . . and ended with, "They're lovers. Eddie and Nevan are lovers."

Pusser and Grabowski exchanged a look. Grabowski shrugged. "So? I get what that has to do with Maura, she was Nevan's beard, his cover. But what's it have to do with Addy Barton?"

"I don't know."

# CHAPTER 39

The walls of the McCreary County Detention Center loomed dark against the gray sky. A spike in the temperature had melted off the remaining snow, leaving dirty puddles in the asphalt parking lot. I stepped in one and water seeped through my sneakers and into my wool socks, making my toes stick together.

The jail captain met us at the employees' back entrance and escorted us to a private interrogation room. I was still suspended, but Grabowski got permission to bring me along. He thought Riana might open up to another Pavee. We still hadn't been able to locate Eddie and Nevan to substantiate the case against Jacob and fill in the blanks about the illegal husbandry for fighting cocks. So no more progress had been made on the case.

Grabowski sat next to me, nervously adjusting his tie, a black string bolo with a turquoise-claw centerpiece. Up and down it slid, over and over, until Riana appeared, pasty pale in her orange jumpsuit.

Riana ignored Grabowski, locking eyes with me instead. A jagged gash ran from her eyebrow down to the base of her jawline, puffy pink and red raw with dark, slanted stitches. "Look what your dog did to my face. I'm going to make sure he's put down for this."

My fingers traced the puckered edges of my own scar and around to the front of my neck, still swollen and tender where her fingers had gripped my throat. She deserved what she'd gotten. No doubt about it. But I didn't go there. Instead, I took the discussion in another direction. "We compared the handwriting in the journal to Eddie's handwriting. It's a match. Eddie wrote the journal. He and your brother are lovers."

"Don't believe nothing that lying faggot writes."

The hatred in her voice unsettled me.

Grabowski shifted uncomfortably.

I switched tactics. "The kids must've gotten pretty tight after the accident that took both their fathers. Maura and Nevan, two kids, the same age with dead fathers. If I remember, they became engaged around that time. Arranged by their mothers?"

She didn't respond.

I continued talking. "Were they chaperoned when they dated?" Pavees were protective over their young girl's chastity. Couples didn't date without supervision.

"Of course."

"By you?"

"Sometimes. But I was busy with my own family. Eddie chaperoned. . . ." She pressed her lips together, her gaze turning cold.

*That's when the two boys fell for each other.* Both adolescents. It must have been torturous for them to realize their feelings. Especially as Pavees. "Did you know Maura was pregnant?"

"Yes. A settled boy's baby. If I'd known she'd turn

out to be such a whore, I never would have agreed to their engagement. At least he found out before he actually went through with the marriage."

"Yes. And how convenient that she turned up dead. He didn't even have to break off the engagement." Which would have been another strike against our culture—arranged marriages were sacrosanct.

"Nevan had nothing to do with Maura's death. Neither did I. It was that Fisher kid. That weirdo. He's into some pretty sick stuff, I hear."

"A lot of Pavees, maybe even you, his family, might say that what Eddie and Nevan are into is sick." I needed to get under her skin, say whatever it took to open her up.

Her eyes blazed with anger. "Shut up, Brynn. You don't know what you're saying!"

My heart went out to those two boys. "Did Nevan know as a boy, or maybe he didn't realize it until he met Eddie? Is that how it happened? Did Eddie influence him? Seduce him?"

She shook her head.

"How long did it take Maura to figure it out?"

"There was nothing to figure out. Nevan was in love with her. He wanted to marry her. At least until he found out that she'd been cheating on him."

An arranged marriage can be bad enough for any man and woman. But it must have felt like torture to Nevan, being forced to marry any woman, to live a lifestyle unnatural to him. "I doubt it. I think he probably told her how he felt. She must have been devastated. A young Pavee girl, matched to a gay man. No wonder she fled to Hatch Anderson's arms."

I'd struck a nerve. Riana became unglued. "Shutup-shutupshutup . . ."

"How embarrassing for your family. What was it your mother said to me the other day? Something about our strict code of conduct. Being gay doesn't quite fit into the Pavee code, does it?"

She slammed her hand on the table, her voice venomous. "You Callahans are a piece of work. Who are you to come over here and point fingers at us? We're a good family. Respected. My husband's—"

"Your husband's a wimp-ass bully. Smashing car windows, throwing bricks at night, threatening old women . . . You must be so proud."

"Screw you."

I sat back, about worn down. I had no idea how to get to Riana.

Grabowski took up the slack. "We have you for attempted murder, Riana. Cooperate with us and we'll work to get you a deal. Maybe time off your sentence."

Riana looked bored.

I tried again. "Babies are expensive. That's why Maura got involved in the cockfights, isn't it? She saw the writing on the wall. Hatch wasn't going to be there for her, the clan would shun her, and Nevan was too in love with Eddie to be bothered with her and the baby."

Nothing.

"It's in the journal," I added. "Eddie named all the participants. We have a ledger from the Barton girl's barn to back it up."

Something flashed on Riana's face. Panic? Hatred? She was a difficult one to read.

"And then there's the Barton girl. Addy Barton. You

killed her, too. Why? Was she a witness? Did she know too much?"

"I'm done with this." She walked over and banged on the door. "Guard, guard! Get over here. I want to go back to my cell."

*Get over here.* Her words jarred something in my mind.

Out in the parking lot, I turned to Grabowski. "You need to check Riana's cell phone records. Right before she choked me, she made a call. We need to know who she called."

# CHAPTER 40

The next day, I was in Pusser's office. I'd stopped in, hoping to talk to Pusser in private about getting back to work full-time, but Grabowski was there. They were discussing the case. Pusser invited me to sit with them, and I did. The scent of cinnamon wafted among us, along with thick apprehension. Would I ever earn back Pusser's trust? The photograph of his daughter was turned slightly my way. I remembered Pusser dabbing at my mouth in the hospital, the look of concern in his eyes and the gentleness of his touch. I imagined what he must have been like as a young father, loving and doting and caring.

"I got Riana Meath's phone records," he said. "The call she made was to her husband, Pete."

The case file was open on Pusser's desk with pictures of Maura and Addy from the autopsies.

I tore my eyes from the report, but they landed on another document: the murder note from the scene of Maura's death. I stared hard at it. The words blurred in and out, like an out-of-focus picture. There was a dark stain that showed black in the photocopy—blood, I knew. Maura's blood, dripping from her wound, dripping from the symbols on the wall, dripping onto the ground and mixing with the dirt floor of the cave. *The ground, be so careful; don't destroy the evidence; don't disturb the footprints.* "Footprints." I spoke my thought out loud. "There was more than one set of footprints. They were both there, both Riana and Pete killed Maura." No wonder Pete had come after me, telling me that he and his boys didn't want us coppers to handle the case.

"Looks like it. We brought him in yesterday. We struck a deal with the husband, a shortened sentence and a chance to see his kids grow up if he talked. He did." Pusser turned my way. "Harris may have worked the Fisher kid too hard for a confession. Or maybe the Fisher kid just wanted three squares a day, so he confessed. He and his brothers live in squalor out there at that farm. Must be hard on the boy. Anyway, he's got an appointed advocate working to get him out."

Too late. The brothers will end up as wards of the state. The family separated. I thought of his mother, so carefully and tenderly laid out in the slaughterhouse. Everything Jacob had worked for . . .

"Anyway," Pusser said, "Pete claimed his wife killed Addy, not him, but he helped her dispose of the body."

"Addy and Maura?"

Pusser frowned. "Just Addy, so far. But we'll get him to confess to Maura's murder. Eventually. He's got a high-priced lawyer doing most of his talking. You know how it is. Pete's famous—he's got sponsors and everything. There's a lot of money at stake here. He's being portrayed as an accomplice in Addy's murder.

His people will spin it as he simply got caught up in his wife's rampage, pretty much an innocent participant. You know, like the getaway driver for an armed robbery. People might be willing to forgive that. But two killings? And both young girls. That makes him look like a psychopath."

"The female shoe prints in the cave . . ."

"Size seven. Same size as Riana's."

"Treads?"

"We're still searching for the actual shoes. She must have gotten rid of them." Pusser tossed his toothpick and reached for another. "Frustrating as hell. Those shoe treads are about all we got from that scene. No fingerprints, not much on DNA, actually we don't have jack. Nothing's ever easy, you know."

"So . . . you said Pete confessed. But just to Addy's murder. Why Addy? What was their motive?"

"It's complicated," Pusser said. "Apparently, Riana and Pete discovered Eddie and Nevan together one day. They feared Nevan would come out, once he'd broken the arranged-marriage plan. It's hard to tell which one of them was more disgusted by Nevan's sexual orientation, Riana or Pete. Pete decided that all the boy needed was a little toughing up."

"He beat him."

"Regularly. Here's the sick part. Riana encouraged it. She thought it was for Nevan's own good."

Grabowski spoke up, his voice low and strained. "I don't understand you people. You claim that you're marginalized, prejudiced against because you chose to live differently, yet you persecute people like Eddie and Nevan."

I didn't respond. What could I say?

Pusser ended the silence. "Anyway, that night, Addy delivered a couple birds to Nevan's place. Riana overheard Addy talking to Nevan about getting her mother, the social worker, to help him. We can only guess that either Nevan himself or Eddie or maybe Maura told Addy how Nevan was being treated. Riana knew that she and Pete would be investigated for child abuse. She couldn't afford to have that happen. So Riana caught up to Addy and confronted her. It got heated. They mixed it up, the fight got out of hand, and Addy ended up dead. Then Riana called in Pete to help her dispose of the body."

"I can see why Pete would cop to that," I said. "No premeditation, no direct involvement with the killing, the whole story makes it sound like it was all just one big misunderstanding."

Grabowski shook his head. "Doubt that he'll do much time. Juries always go easy on guys like him."

"But they'll make an argument for premeditation, right? Addy was stabbed, and Riana can't explain away the fact that she had a knife when she confronted Addy. And think about it. Riana couldn't afford to be reported. She'd lose her kids. Not to mention the money she'd give up. Her husband was negotiating a big boxing deal. So killing Addy became the only option. She confronted her with the intent to kill. For all we know, Pete was in on it from the beginning."

Pusser's eyes fell to his daughter's photo and glazed over with sadness. "We can probably make a criminal-intent case against Riana, but doubt we'll be able to prove it for Pete. Maybe once we pin Maura's death on them. There's no getting around the fact that her murder was planned. But we'll have to let the courts decide on the rest. All I know is that both these girls, Addy and Maura, were nothing more than a couple mixed-up teens, making stupid choices, like most teens do, but they didn't deserve to die. They had so much life ahead of them. It's all such a waste."

# CHAPTER 41

The racket of a couple dozen dogs barking shouldn't have hit me so hard. It was an animal shelter, right? Caged animals bark. Still, I cringed to think of my dog there. Concrete, metal pens, utilitarian food bowls, nothing cushy or comfortable—some of our perps had it better than this in the county lockup. And most of them didn't deserve better than my dog.

The receptionist's pack-a-day voice greeted me from behind the counter. This was my third visit since Wilco's impoundment. Mel was her name and we'd become fast friends. "Moved him to a new cage."

"Why?"

"Bigger pen. Better location. I arranged it. Dog's a damn hero protecting you that way. As far as I'm concerned, he's one of us."

Wilco had worked his charm on Mel. Good. I thanked her and headed for the back room. Wilco sensed me immediately, letting out a soulful bale as I worked my way down the kennel past several penned dogs: a cream-colored lab, whining and whimpering, his tongue slopping over his snout; a yappy little mutt-like pooch, head bouncing like a bobble doll; and an unidentifiable mix, charging and snapping, ramming his snout through the metal cage. I knelt down by Wilco and reached between the bars. "Hey, boy, how's the doggy slammer treating you?"

Wilco rubbed his cheek against my hand, his eyes never leaving my face. My heart melted; then a wall, built of logic and caution, sprang up. I wouldn't be here now if it weren't for my dog, but I'd been surprised by the fierceness of Wilco's attack on Riana. I'd be lying if I didn't say it concerned me. I'd seen him defend me before by growling and snapping, but never an actual bite, let alone practically shredding someone's face. Wilco had acted out of his own will. To most people—Mel, my colleagues at work, Pusser even—Wilco had acted heroically. I knew better. I was Wilco's master, head of the pack. His only obedience should be to me. By acting on his own accord, even though it was to protect me, he bypassed the chain of command. He took the dominant role in our relationship. Left unchecked, he could eventually become a safety hazard, biting anyone he perceived to be a threat to me. Eventually he may have to be put down. I'd never forgive myself if that happened. As soon as he got sprung, we'd work on training and reestablishing our relationship roles, his and mine—with me as alpha.

*Alpha dog.* Humans are no different than dogs when it comes to pack mentality. Except for people, it's all about status and exclusivity. I'd learned that lesson early on in high school. I was part of a pack: Riana, Leena, Shannon, and me. Riana was the alpha dog back then. And she'd dominated us like the true alpha bitch she was. And when I dissented, she and the others held me down and shaved my head. Cruel, yes. But simplified, it could be seen as nothing more than a means to reestablish role dominance. A pecking order was reinstated, Riana on top, me—the half-breed Pavee—on bottom.

Status and position were esteem needs to all humans, regardless of our economic or social position. Riana was nothing more than a Pavee, outcast by normal society, yet the head of her own social group. A big fish in a small pond. We all need to feel like we're a bit better than those around us. Some people establish their status through money, brand-named clothing, expensive cars. . . . Others, like Riana, perhaps because financial means are so limited among us Travellers, do so by manipulating and bullying others. She'd done so through grade school, high school, young adulthood, and now she'd arrived on top. By Bone Gap standards, she had it all. Married, five boys, a double-wide trailer, and a famous husband. Nevan's sexual orientation threatened all that. It threatened her pack position.

She tried first to manipulate Nevan by threatening him, beating it out of him. But it didn't work. Then Addy became a direct threat. A settled girl, coming around and threatening her—Addy needed to be put in her place. Or eliminated. Or maybe Pusser was right: Things simply got out of control and Addy ended up dead. And then there was Pete, another pack member under Riana's rule: covering for Addy's murder, threatening my family . . . all of it carefully orchestrated by Riana.

I'd seen this type of thing on other occasions, too.

Years ago, in Iraq, New Year's Eve; a party on base, music, liquor . . . and Emily. Lance Corporal Emily, from somewhere in the middle of nowhere, Kansas. A pretty farm girl. Tough, resilient, and, unfortunately that night, drunk. Bleary-eyed and stumbling, she was cornered by a pack of guys who blocked her way and surrounded her like hungry wolves, groping her, running their hands up her skirt. None of them would have violated her on their own, but together, as a rowdy, horny pack, they became animals of a different nature—predators. It took a half-dozen of us ladies to rescue her from their single-minded pursuit. But even then, the damage had been done. Maybe not physically, but psychologically. Victimized by her own.

Pack mentality. Collectively, humans can do so much good, but with a bad leader, that same collection of people so often descends to its lowest common denominator. It's our animalistic nature.

And Nevan. What type of psychological trauma had he suffered at the hands of his own family? Hopefully, he and Eddie had escaped far, far away from all this ugliness.


I woke at three the next morning, my mouth dry, my body soaked with sweat. The craving for a pill already thick on my tongue. I walked through the darkened trailer to the kitchen. Out the window, there was nothing but stillness. The blackness of night had settled heavy on Bone Gap. And on me. Yesterday had been a difficult day and I'd taken more pills than normal, but today would be better. I was going to cut down on my dosage again.

Water spurted from the tap. I cupped my hands and raised palmfuls to my mouth. I lapped and slurped like a dog. *My dog.* That was the problem. I couldn't sleep without my dog. My bed felt empty and lonely without his warm body curled around mine, our breathing in sync, rhythmic and comforting. I was alone. He was alone. Was he having nightmares, too? Did he think I'd abandoned him?

I went back to my room, tried to sleep for a couple hours, but couldn't. At six, I phoned Pusser at home. He'd lived in the same home for almost forty years, a one-story ranch on Depot Street. He loved to tell the story of how he scrimped for the down payment on an officer's salary to buy the place for his new bride. Many wonderful years they'd spent in that little house. It was a happy little story that Pusser told over and over, but never finished. I only recently learned the ending of the story. Mrs. Pusser was a fastidious house-cleaner. She held firm to the adage: "A place for every-thing, and everything in its place." That's why she'd shot herself in the bathtub. She couldn't bear the thought of all that blood and brain splatter mussing up the house.

Pusser finally answered, his voice graveled and abrupt. "What is it, Callahan? It's six in the morning."

"I know. And I can't sleep because my dog's not here. When are you going to get him out of the doggy slammer and get us back to work?"

"It's just a matter of timing. I'm working through this crap with the mayor's boy, trying to get—"

"What is there to work through? We got him for drug dealing, right?"

He grumbled over the line. "Winnie Joyce recanted

her testimony. She says Golden Boy didn't bring anything to them that night except a little beer."

"The mayor got to her. That's what's going on here.
You know that, right?"

"Yeah, I know it. What do you want me to do about
it? Maura and Addy were the only other two who
could testify against him."

"So he gets off scot-free again?" I swallowed down
the anger rising in me. Hatch Anderson was nothing
more than a scumbag drug dealer. And once again,
Daddy was going to get him out of trouble.

"Listen, Callahan. I want you back. And your dog. I
hate the idea of him being locked up the way he is. Just
trust me. I'm working on it."

I took him at his word and hung up. But it bugged
the crap out of me that the Anderson kid was going to
get nothing more than a slap on the hand.

Outside, lights were just starting to break through
the darkness: a pinpoint of a porch light here and there,
headlight beams from early-morning commuters, and
the soft glow of kitchen lights. Morning was dawning
over Bone Gap. Winnie Joyce would be getting ready
for school. I threw on my parka and headed out the
door. She had some explaining to do.

# CHAPTER 42

They stood next to the car in a knitted huddle of bright hoodies and legging-clad stick legs, long strapped purses bumping against their butts as they shuffled their feet to keep warm.

They shifted in even tighter as I approached. "Good morning, girls."

Furtive glances, but no takers. Heads bowed closer together, whispered words rising in the air along with thin ribbons of cigarette smoke. The trailer door slammed, and Winnie appeared, car keys dangling in her hand. She traipsed over, tugged at the faux-fur collar of her coat, and peered at me through darkened lashes. "What do you want?"

"The truth." I eyed the cherry-red Mustang parked nearby, sales sticker plastered on the passenger window.

She glanced at the girls. "I'm busy right now." She pushed past me and was immediately engulfed in her circle of friends. Someone passed her a cigarette. A ruby ring glowed from her finger as she inhaled. More giggles, more glances my way. *You can see us, but you can't be us.* The story of my life. The fringer, always somewhere that I don't belong.

They turned their backs . . . and *poof!* I'd gone invisible. Chitter, chatter, chitter, chatter . . . talk of boys and movies, nails and makeup, boys and boys and . . . "He's so cute." . . . "Did you see that slut come on to him at lunch?" . . . "He looked at me in gym class." . . . "No freakin' way!" . . . I watched and listened. I was surprised to see Winnie at the hub, orchestrating from the middle, her friends the spokes that made the wheel turn: the dark-haired, doe-eyed girl, rounded shoulders and soft-spoken, still waters; the bold blonde with boy-teasing cleavage, sexy even under the folds of her hoodie; and the go-ahead-and-walk-all-over-me girl, the bottom-feeder, probably put there because of the birthmark on her cheek. (No matter what we say, beauty *isn't* more than skin deep.) They all played a role in their group, their dynamics, reflecting my own high-school clique. Maybe all social groups were the same, with certain positions to be filled, and each of us choosing and filling those roles.

I hadn't seen Winnie as a "queen bee" type before. More of an underling, Maura's sidekick, playing second fiddle. Which made sense now that I thought of it—who better than the second fiddle to fill a vacancy in the lead seat? Now she seemed confident, powerful, the concertmaster even. I cleared my throat. "New car, Winnie?" Mouths quieted, brows raised. No one wanted to turn, to admit that I did still exist, that I was visible, like an inflamed pimple on prom night. Cover it up; ignore it; maybe it will go away. "Where'd you get it?"

Winnie's eyes were two dark pits of tar.

Blondie straightened her shoulders. "You don't have to answer her, Winnie." The gatekeeper protecting her queen.

Winnie's lip twitched. "She doesn't intimidate me."

Quiet One folded her arms across her chest, eyes darting from me to Winnie. *Oh no! Oh no! Conflict.*

I ran my fingertips along the Mustang's hood. "I'm just wondering where you got it, that's all. It's beautiful."

Bottom-Feeder placed her hand on Winnie's shoulder. "Why shouldn't she have something nice? Everything she's been through. Her best friend's death, police questions, Hatch's—"

"Shut up!" Winnie shook off the girl's hand.

"I'm sorry."

Winnie glared her down until she shrank back into the circle, back to her proper underling position, then turned on me. "What is it you want?"

*To get you alone and scratch your eyes out for taking hush money from the stupid mayor and his drug-dealing kid.* "Maybe I want a ride in your new car."

"Don't do it, Winnie." Blondie again.

Winnie faltered a bit, a tiny crack in her façade, then recovered with an icy stare. "No time. We've got to get to school." She pointed the key fob. Two sharp beeps pierced the air.

"Just a short ride. Down the road and back again." I smiled. "Unless you'd find that intimidating."

Quiet One darted glances between us. *Oh no, a challenge!*

Winnie raised her chin, her eyes glimmering. She

tossed her school notebook on the front seat and ordered, "Get in!"

Five minutes later, she was doing about seventy down
Highway 2. She had one hand on the steering wheel, the
other fiddling with the radio. I clutched the door as we
crossed the centerline, not once, but twice. "Easy, Winnie, you don't want to wreck your new car."

"You scared?" she sneered.

"Yeah. Damn right I am."

She laughed. We swerved again.

"Maybe you should keep both hands on the wheel."

"I'm a good driver." As if to prove the point, she
went faster. We were up to almost eighty. "Can that
piece of crap you drive go this fast?"

She had a point. My car hardly ran these days. Especially after Pete and friends got done with it. I ran my
hand along the Mustang's buttery upholstery, car envy
rising from somewhere deep inside me. How ironic.
Almost thirty, I've worked hard my whole life, served
and sacrificed, and what do I have to show for it? A
piece-of-crap car, while little Miss Priss here drove a
brand-new Mustang. "Where'd you get the car, Winnie?"

"I bought it."

*Yeah, with hush money.* The mayor paid her to pull
her testimony on his son. "I noticed the new ring. A
gift?"

A smile tugged at her lips.

"Let me guess. From Hatch?"

"So? He likes me."

"He's using you."

Her jaw tightened. "Maybe I don't mind being used."

"He's a drug dealer. And Maura would still be alive if it weren't for the drugs he gave her that night. She would have been able to fight off her assailant." I rubbed my neck, thinking of Riana's grip, Pete's muscular body. Truth was, Maura wouldn't have stood a chance against those two, drugged up or not.

"You're not going to put that on me."

"You're the witness that links Hatch to those drugs. All you have to do is testify that he gave them to you and Maura that night."

"You're jealous of my new car. That's what this is."

"This has nothing to do with cars." Truth was, Pavees loved their vehicles: cars, trucks, motorcycles, RVs, anything with wheels. Took pride in whatever they owned, even if they couldn't afford an I'm-so-vain blue Mercedes or a red-hot Mustang. Which was why it was an ultimate Traveller insult to bash in even a clunker like mine. I thought of Maura's smashed headlights. Nevan denied vandalizing it. And why would he? It just didn't fit. Not considering . . .

I looked over at Winnie. "You called Nevan that night because Maura was making out with Hatch, right?"

Her smile faded. "I don't want to talk about that right now. Leave it to you to try to spoil my fun." She cranked up the radio.

I turned it down again. "I'm just trying to figure out how things happened that night. For Maura's sake. She was your friend, right?"

"Yeah. My *best* friend. That's why I called Nevan. She was making a fool of herself." She tossed her head, as if flipping loose hair aside or dislodging thoughts. "Besides, I thought he should know. I felt so bad for him. They were engaged."

Only they weren't. They'd broken up. Nevan had no interest in Maura besides friendship and she'd moved on. And she'd cared enough for him to keep his sexual orientation a secret. Even from her best friend. So, why would he bother going up to Stoners' Draw that night?

"Was Nevan upset to hear that his fiancée was with another man?"

She hesitated. "Yeah. Pretty much."

"Not as much as you would have expected, though, right?"

She shot a glance at me. "He was furious, of course. What man wouldn't be?"

*A man in love with another man.* Nevan had no reason to attack her car. He claimed he didn't do it and that the car was intact when he left there. So if the car was fine when Winnie left them, and when Nevan left, maybe Riana or Pete did it when they went up there to kill Maura? Then later, when word blazed through the clan that Nevan was a suspect, Riana planted the bat? Maybe. But that still didn't answer the real question: When was Riana there, and why did she kill Maura at all?

"Did you see Riana that night up at Stoners' Draw?"

"No. I told you. It was just me and Hatch and Maura, and then I left."

"And you went to Jacob's house?"

She took a fast turn, swerving as she rolled her eyes in answer.

"So you and Jacob were pretty good friends, huh?"

She shrugged. "Yeah. I guess."

"You'd been to his place before?"

"A few times."

"Are you and Jacob . . . ?" I let the question hang.

She laughed. "No way. Jacob's nice to me"—that roll of eyes again, like who wouldn't be nice to Miss Priss—"but he's, you know, kind of weird. All we do is hang out and play video games."

*Weird.* I had to agree there. Like having his mother's body holed up in a stinking pig pit. Yet . . . he was respectful in his own way, too. Mrs. Fisher, the flowers, pretty dress, teddy bear . . . respected and treated right.

My mind zoomed in on the image of Maura's body in that blood-splattered cave. Yes, she was stabbed, but the way she was laid out, her skirt adjusted just so, tucked around her legs, prim and proper. Maura's body was given some respect. Could it be that Jacob's confession wasn't coerced by Harris? He'd really been there? But what was Jacob's connection to Riana? My eyes slid toward Winnie.

"Did Jacob know Riana?"

"I don't think so. Maybe a little. He knew Nevan. Maybe he'd met Riana at some point." She looked my way. "Why do you care? Thought you cops had Riana pinned for killing both Addy and Maura."

"Addy, yes. But Maura . . ." I cocked my head at her and she faced forward, refusing to make eye contact now. "You don't mind lying about Hatch's drugs to enjoy a few pretty perks. Are you protecting Jacob, too? Because he's a friend?"

Winnie tensed. "That's stupid! I've gotta get back to

my girls." She swung the wheel over, the car careened into a U-turn, her notebook slid to the floor at my feet as I was thrown against the side door.

I grabbed my head where it hit the side window. *Ouch!* But I knew I'd hit a nerve with Winnie, too, and I persisted. "Jacob's video games, occult stuff, right? He had a thing about death, didn't he? Did he tell you what happened later that night?" I saw her jaw clamp and she stepped on the accelerator. We would be back any minute now and I didn't know what button to push. But I could smell that I was close.

She sped through a stop sign, twisted around a corner, knocking me to the side again, my feet tangling in her now-opened and upside-down notebook on the floor. I reached down to the floorboard, picked it up, and as I turned it over to set it back on the seat, my eyes fell on a paper she'd written for a class. Big, loopy script. The same as the bold and bloody handwriting desecrating the cave where Maura had been dragged and killed . . . Suddenly my blood boiled.

Winnie wasn't protecting Jacob at all. I'd underestimated her. We all had. Especially Maura. Winnie wanted to be the queen of the clique all along. Motivated by desire for Hatch, envy over Maura's relationship with him, and her own sick need for status, she'd wanted to eliminate Maura. She used Jacob, the weird boy, and his obsession with satanic video games, to help her carry out her scheme. No, Winnie wasn't protecting Jacob—she was protecting herself.

The only connection between Addy's murder and Maura's murder was the fact that both were orchestrated by manipulative bitches. "What did you offer Jacob, Winnie?"

Winnie's head snapped my way. A curve was coming up. She was going too fast. "Winnie, keep your eye on—"

A tire dropped at the road edge, the car jerked and swerved, we spun out of control. . . . Winnie screamed and slammed on the brakes . . . screeching tires, burned rubber. I braced myself. We hit the ditch hard, glass shattering, metal popping, then silence. . . .

My head spun. Then a noise drew my attention: Winnie was out the door and running.

I pushed at my own door, but it wouldn't open. I climbed across the seat, snagged my foot on the steering wheel getting through the driver's door, fell, and hit the cold, squishy ground. I recovered and went after her.

I closed the distance as her new designer boots slipped on the moldy layers of wet leaves. Just inside the woods, I leapt and tackled her. We hit the ground with a thud. She kicked and twisted, threw a punch meant for my face, but it hit my chest. *And damn it hurt!* I punched back. Only, I didn't miss.

She went out cold.

"Hey, Parks." I stood over Winnie's limp body, holding my sore chest with my right arm, my knuckles throbbing, and made the call. "It's Brynn. I need assistance."

# CHAPTER 43

My cell phone woke me. I ignored it and pulled Wilco closer. Eventually it stopped. I sighed. My dog was back, and as far as I was concerned, everything was right in the world.

All I needed was a little sleep. The past week had been grueling, hours and hours of testimony had to be sorted through to piece together the events of Maura's murder.

Winnie had orchestrated the entire thing, including manipulating Jacob Fisher into helping her.

It'd started a few weeks earlier when she learned that Maura was pregnant with Hatch's baby. She'd had a crush on Hatch and felt betrayed by her best friend. That night, out on Stoners' Draw, she and Maura got in a fight over Hatch. Hatch thought it was funny. Two girls in love with him. He kept passing out more pills, telling Maura that they wouldn't hurt the baby, trying to get both girls stoned. Only, Maura passed out right away. Winnie had thought that was her opportunity to have Hatch to herself, but he wasn't interested. Winnie became enraged and took the bat to Maura's car and then ran.

She'd been to Jacob's house many times before. No parents, no rules, it was the perfect place for a young Pavee girl to let loose and party. In the past, she'd played Jacob for the loser she perceived him to be, leading him on, doing just enough to get him to buy more booze, or whatever else she needed. He was easy to manipulate. He'd do anything she wanted.

And that night, she wanted Maura dead. Sort of.

A simple statement—"I wish she was dead"—turned into something more. The booze, the video games, it was all so surreal. The idea kept percolating, heating up, until finally it seemed like it was the answer to all her problems.

It'd be easy, she told Jacob.

She got the occult idea from the video games they were playing. It seemed like the perfect way to mislead the cops. And the note was her special touch. She knew the press would eventually get ahold of it and Maura would be exposed as the Jezebel she was.

It was like a fire burning out of control. Before she knew it, they'd grabbed some rope and used one of the old knives from out in the barn and went up to the Stoners' Draw to find Maura. She was still there, passed out, just like Winnie had left her. They bound her and took her to the cave. She never even woke up. If she'd woke up, neither one of them would have had the nerve. But she already looked dead. Just lying there, looking dead . . . All Winnie had to do was stick the knife into her. It'd be so easy. . . .

Jacob freaked out and ran. He left her there with the knife and Maura asleep on the rock. And she did it. God help her, she did it.

It was easy.

Until it wasn't.

Jacob came back. He was distraught; he kept fussing over Maura. Fixing her skirt, making her just so; all the while, he babbled on and on about his mother.

But she convinced him that she hadn't meant it. It was the booze, the pills, whatever . . . but she didn't mean it. Not really.

Jacob believed her. He loved her. He'd do anything for her.

Such a stupid boy.

They drew the evil symbols with Maura's blood. And left her there. The next day, nervous, they desecrated the cemetery, hoping to keep the sham going. Only, things got complicated. The cops didn't quite buy the occult angle, so Winnie decided to frame Nevan. He had motive. His fiancée was pregnant with another man's baby. That's when she decided to toss the bat at Nevan's place. At the time, she didn't know about Eddie and Nevan.

Then there was Hatch. He knew what had really happened that night. Most of it, anyway. The rest he'd pieced together. But she had something on him, too. The drugs. His silence was easy to guarantee.

But when Nevan pointed in the direction of Jacob, and the cops found a dead body in his barn, she saw the perfect opportunity to frame Jacob. Besides, the loser was so in love with her—he'd do anything for her, even go to prison.

Riana and Winnie. They had so much in common: Both were in love with losers, Dublin and Hatch. Both lost that love to another woman; both settled for another man, whom they could manipulate to get what they wanted. But in the end, neither woman succeeded. Both were going to prison.

Wilco snuggled in closer, made little whimpering sounds, his three paws twitching. "That's right, boy. Sweet dreams. We've done good and it's time to rest." Although, even as I nodded off, Katie Doogan's name popped into my mind. I pushed it aside. There'd be time to deal with her later.

My cell rang again. I reluctantly rolled over, pushed Wilco aside, and answered. It was Nevan.

"Do you believe in Heaven?"

His voice was so shallow, like he had no air left. "Nevan? Where are you? What's going on? How did you get my . . . ?"

"I asked you if you believe in Heaven."

"Yes. Yes, Nevan. I do."

"And people who are good. They go there, right?"

I was up, sliding on my pants, looking for my car keys. "Where are you?"

"Please answer me. I need to know."

"Yes. If you're good, you get to go there."

"I've been good, Brynn. Both Eddie and I have been good. We haven't done anything wrong. All we've done is love each other. That's not wrong, is it?"

I sat on the edge of my bed. My heart slammed against my chest. "Listen to me, you need to tell me where you are. I want to help—"

"Eddie's gone to Heaven and I'm going to go, too. So we can be together."

"What? No, Nevan. No. You just mentioned love. Think about all the people who love you."

He kind of choked or laughed, I couldn't tell. "Who?"

"Your mother . . ."

"She's embarrassed by me."

"No, that's not true. Listen, I almost died a week ago, because I thought no one would care, no one at all, but I was wrong, Nevan. And you're wrong. People do love you. Your mother loves you, Nevan. She loves you very much." I was up, pacing. "Don't do this. Please."

"I'm leaving now, Brynn. Eddie and me, we left something here for you. Make sure you look for it."

"No. Listen—"

"Room number six."

The line went dead.

# CHAPTER 44

They were spooned together, back to front, entwined like pale pretzels. A mixed jumble of body parts: skinny shoulders, an impish chin, a jutting elbow here, knobby knee there, an awkward angled foot, dark swatch of hair . . . so tightly embraced that it was impossible to tell where one began and the other ended. They'd achieved in death what they never attained in life. They were together.

Red and blue lights strobed through the room. Wilco's high-pitched whines reached my ears. Despite being confined to a cruiser out in the lot, his sensitive nose had detected the scent of fresh decay.

Grabowski handed me a plastic bag. Zipped inside was a piece of lined paper torn from a notebook. "It's dated today. It's written as the final journal entry."

My hands trembled as I took the bag and walked toward the nightstand lamp. Eddie's handwriting, easily recognizable now.

*March 1*
*This is my last journal page. I am writing it for you, Mom. Nevan and me can't take it anymore. We have been beaten and spit on and called names, like faggots, losers, and fairies. The kids at school hate us because we're Pavees. Our own people hate us because we love each other. Nevan's family told him that if he wants to be queer, he'll have to leave the clan forever. They don't want a faggot in their family. I didn't want to be this way. I tried not to be and I tried to make things right for Nevan and me, but everything kept getting messed up more. It's not your fault that you have me for a son. You and Maura are the only ones who really loved me for who I am. But now Maura is dead. I miss her. I know you do, too, Mom. I'm sorry you will be alone, but life will be easier for you when I'm gone. I don't want you to be hated the way I am hated. I don't want people to call you names and put you down all the time. I just want you to laugh and smile like you used to when we were all together as a normal family. Please don't be sad, Mom. Nevan and me will be happy in Heaven. I know we will. I'll see you there. I'll be with Dad and Maura and Nevan. We will be waiting for you.*

*It's time for me to go. I am feeling happier now. I want you to know that it's ending and*

*I am feeling really good now. I'm not crying. I'm not scared, Mom. I will be so happy in Heaven because I won't be a fag, just a person, and I will be loved.*

# CHAPTER 45

After one of the longest cold spells in eastern Tennessee history, spring finally showed itself, arriving on and off in spurts and finally settling in early April after a cold snap that locals called the Redbud Winter, a couple of below-freezing days that occur every year when the redbuds bloom. Wilco and I used the warm weather to get in extra training time. I needed to keep my skills, and his nose, sharp. We both needed to reestablish the order of our relationship.

I'd cleared my drug test and would soon be reinstated at work.

Three weeks had passed without further contact from Katie Doogan, but I knew it was just a matter of time before she'd make her next move. I was on borrowed time. And so was Gran. But I'd been seeing Dr. Ryan for a month and had managed to stay sober for part of that time. There were days still when the anxiety was so vicious and demanding that I needed a little something to take the edge off. But I was getting better. Dr. Ryan showed me that I'd spent the last few years of my life living from crisis to crisis, skimming the surface, numbing myself from the pains of life. It was time to feel the pain and learn to cope with it. That's what I planned to do with the next crisis. When the time comes to face Katie Doogan, I'd do it sober and strong.

The news of what really happened to Maura Keene and Addy Barton rocked our clan. Most didn't believe that Riana Meath was capable of such a heinous crime and chalked it up as another settled law conspiracy against our people. Riana went down as a martyr for the people; Addy's death, a settled girl, just a misunderstanding.

Winnie was written off by the clan, left to rot in a settled prison. Pavees simply didn't kill each other. It was as if Winnie had never existed. And Maura? A sad death that would never be spoken of other than with sad shakes of heads and signs of the cross.

I delivered the death notices for Eddie and Nevan.

Kitty Meath took the news standing straight and rigid while anger and hateful disdain flashed through her eyes like lightning through pitch-blackness. No tears, no cries of anguish, simply silence. Then she shut the door. I haven't seen her since. Not even at Nevan's funeral.

When we told Ona that her Eddie had died, her pain exploded, dark and raw, forceful, sucking in everything around it, churning and churning, making me queasy and weak. So much death, her husband and now both her children. So much loss. Ona Keene was only a shell of the woman she was before. She told us that she planned to move on to Kentucky and live with her sister. She no longer felt like she belonged in Bone Gap.

The deaths of Eddie and Nevan set something in motion for me. I began wrestling with the realities of my Pavee culture, rules that guided our lives and defined our heritage, kept us strong and united, but yet alienated so many. We called non-Pavees outsiders. And we meant it. We kept our boundaries tight and adhered to a strict moral code, but somewhere along the line, we'd forgotten to allow for humanness.

Rules and rigidness had replaced love and mercy.

And four young people had died because of it.

Eddie's final journal entry haunted me. I'd walked along the same edge, teetering between suffering and possible relief. Waking up every day with a gnawing feeling, hoping it'd get better, trying to push it away, realizing that it was only getting worse. All this time, I've struggled to find acceptance, in the Pavee world and in the settled world, even as a female in the Marines, not quite fitting in anywhere. That feeling of not belonging, of no identity, helplessness, isolation . . . I'd been there so many times, reached the point of exhaustion, where I simply couldn't fight it anymore . . . and I'd tried, so many times, to escape the despair of this world. What I'd learned, what I knew for sure, was that those last few seconds, right before that final step to death, were the most unspeakably lonely times of my life. My prayer for Eddie and Nevan was that they made it through that dark sea of loneliness and found peace on the other side.

# Acknowledgments

I'd like to thank the following people for their contribution to this book. First and foremost, my hardworking agent, Jessica Faust, and her team at BookEnds Literary Agency. My editor, Michaela Hamilton; my publicist, Lulu Martinez; and all the people working behind the scenes at Kensington Publishing. Thank you also to freelance editor Sandra Haven. I'm always grateful for your expertise.

For those of you familiar with the symptoms of PTS and substance abuse withdrawals, you may notice differences between the facts of these subjects and the way I've portrayed them in this novel. These are not research mistakes, but choices I've made to fit the story's timeline and increase drama. I'd like to thank the following people who have taken time to provide me with the research information to write this story: John Burley, MD; William Novak, MD, FACC; Amanda Bourg, PhD, psychologist; Sergeant Leanna Miller-Ferguson, USMC disabled veteran; Indiana K9 Search and Recovery; Kathy Chiodo Holbert, owner of Chiodo Kennels and former civilian HRD canine handler, Iraq and Afghanistan; and Staff Sergeant Vern Smart, U.S. Army veteran, RSO and firearms expert; Elizabeth Roderick, sensitivity reader.

A special thank you to my husband for covering dinners, dishes, and homework duty on the late nights leading up to my deadline. And always, thank you to our children for cheering me on and encouraging me to do my best.

Don't miss Susan Furlong's next compelling
Bone Gap Travellers Novel

SHATTERED JUSTICE

Coming soon from Kensington Publishing Corp.

Keep reading to enjoy a sample excerpt . . .

The next morning's sun broke hot and angry through the cracks in my pink lace curtains. I slept in my childhood room, in the only home I've ever known—my grandmother's thirty-year-old mobile home. Larger than most of our neighbors' trailers and campers, and still movable—something that was important in our nomadic culture—yet aesthetically rooted in the late 1980s. Gran never was one for change.

I pulled Wilco close, his muscles rippling against my body, pulsating and twitching, and accompanied by little whimpers. A dream. A good one, I hoped. Like me, my sixty-pound former combat partner, and once the best damn HRD (human remains detection) dog in the entire Middle Eastern conflict, suffered from flashbacks and reoccurring nightmares. Getting blown up by an IED tends to do that to a girl. And her dog.

I sat up and brushed the back of my hand against his dark snout. He was a Belgian Malinois, and so his coat was darker than a German shepherd's, his face sleeker, and eyes more alert. Though smaller than the shep-

herds, which were so often used in military and law enforcement work, the Malinois were more aggressive,
more energetic, and faster, too. Not fast enough to
avoid an IED, however. No one was.

A twitch of a whisker, a slight curl of his lip, and a
cock of his ears. His ears, two black triangles, erect and
ready, yet useless. The explosion had robbed Wilco of
his hearing, and more. So much more. I moved my
hand along the ridge of his spine, from neck to withers,
then down to the rounded nub of his back leg. It was
gone, too. Bone and bloody flesh alike, blown off his
body in one searing instant, practically disintegrating
midair. Gone forever. I knew the feeling. I ran my hand
under my sweat-soaked T-shirt. My breasts, two
mounds, but one soft and plump, alive; the other a hard
bulge, dead and useless, like my dog's nubby leg.
Wilco and I were alike in that way. We'd both lost part
of ourselves out there in the desert.

But we had each other. It had been a struggle to get
the Marines to turn him over to me, but maybe that was
the one blessing from the injuries we shared: Neither
of us was deemed fit for further service. So we were
released as a team. Always would be.

My cell rang. It was my boss, Sheriff Frank Pusser.

"You home?" he asked.

"Yeah."

"Sober?"

*Every damn time I talk to him . . .* "It's six o'clock in
the morning. What do you think?"

"I've seen you high out of your mind this early in
the morning. Have you forgotten?"

"No."

"Good. Don't. We need you at McCreary Elementary. A piece of a body was found."

My fingertips fell from my breast to my bare leg. "Which part?"

"Come see for yourself. And bring the dog."

My throat constricted with anxiety as I drove by a line of cop cars blocking off access to the playground area. *Not a kid. Please, God, not a kid.* I continued two blocks down and slipped my crappy station wagon between two economy-sized cars and headed the rest of the way on foot, keeping a tight grip on Wilco's lead. About fifty yards out, the scent hit his nose, his over two hundred olfactory cells kicking into action. He pulled against my hold, tail rigid, ears twitching, his head bobbing as he scooped up scents, anxious to move us toward the decay. Displaying clear signs of his alert, trained into him as his singular task, was something he still did well, even deaf and three legged.

"Good boy, good boy." I yanked him to a stop, and followed this with a generous belly rub. He'd detected the partial. No surprise about that, as we knew it was there, but he'd still done his job and earned his reward.

Not wanting him too close to the scene, I secured him to a basketball post and headed solo to where Pusser stood with a group of people—some uniformed city cops; a couple of my colleagues, Deputies Parks and Harris; and a few civilians I didn't recognize. School workers, probably. A perimeter around nearby monkey bars had been cordoned off. A department photographer was already snapping shots, while a group of forensics specialists stood off to the side, ready and waiting. One hell of a turnout for so early in the day.

Pusser spied me and broke from the group. "Come look at this."

I followed him, my feet crunching into the graveled ground, my eyes already trained on the crudely scrawled words spray-painted on the concrete pad in front the jungle gym. I turned to Pusser. "Hear no evil?"

He bit down hard on a toothpick between his teeth and motioned for the photographer to move out of the way. He did. And I saw it. A pair of severed ears hanging from a low bar, blood-stained, blue-tinged flesh, strung up to dry like anemic chili peppers.

The sun glinted off an all too familiar earring piercing one of the lobes—a silver horseshoe stud.

So much for good-luck symbols.